Surrender, Dorothy

a novel

MEG WOLITZER

Scribner

SCRIBNER
1230 Avenue of the Americas
New York, NY 10020

SCRIBNER and design are trademarks of
Simon & Schuster Inc.

Designed by Brooke Zimmer
Set in Granjon
Manufactured in the United States of America

10 9 8 7 6 5 4 3 2

Library of Congress Cataloging-in-Publication Data

Wolitzer, Meg
Surrender, Dorothy: a novel/Meg Wolitzer.
p.   cm.
I. Title.
PS3573.O564S87   1999   98-47007
813'.54—dc21   CIP

ISBN 0-684-84844-9

For Mary Gordon

With many thanks to the National Endowment for the Arts, whose generosity made this book possible.

Surrender, Dorothy

Prologue

I mmortality was the vehicle that transported me, every summer, to the squalid little house we called our own. Immortality was the thing I rode in, barely noticing. I was like a member of the ruling class being held in the spindly arms of a rickshaw, never once looking down at the long bamboo joints, or thinking to observe the nape of the neck of the boy who bent to hold the conveyance aloft.

I was content merely to stay aloft, imagining that the ride would go on and on like one of the lengthy dinners we used to have in the house. I was held aloft for so many summers that I took the ride for granted. Death was for others: the imperfect, or the far too perfect, whose goldenness would be remarked upon forever by the survivors in fits of wonder and loss. Death was the province of parents, grandparents, and the valiant young men who walked in soldierly groups, the weak supporting the weaker. Death was not for us, certainly not for me.

I bristled with sorrow for those who had died; it lived within me, nestled side by side with the sensation of immortality. I was held aloft and shimmering for years, never knowing that this in itself was an impressive feat, an anomaly, until one day, at age thirty, I landed.

I

Brown-Eyed Girl

What a couple they made, the heterosexual woman and the homosexual man! Not just this particular couple, but all others like them, men and women freed from the netting of sexual love, from the calamities that regularly plagued their more predictably coupled-up friends. They felt sorry for those friends, who always seemed to tangle together in unhappy beds and who fought viciously in the dead of night, the men clattering down flights of stairs, Nikes still unlaced, belts still lolling unbuckled, the women standing at the top in tears, calling out vaguely, "Wait!"

Sex led to crying; this was a universal truth. There were tears in the beginning, when you were young and frightened by desire, and then there were tears at the point of impact, when you realized you had irrevocably begun a life of sex and all its complica-

tions. And much later there were tears after you had grown accus-
tomed to sex and understood that it might someday be taken from
you. People left each other all the time; people who swore they
couldn't live without each other left each other. They managed;
they survived. They ate nuts and berries in the wilderness, lived
among wolves and crouched by streams to wash. They took
classes, adult education workshops in car repair, pottery, perhaps
a Romance language. Some of them fled their echoing apartments, the places where *he* had been and was no longer, cashed in
their frequent-flier mileage, upgraded to business-class, and flew
somewhere madcap, like Italy. They were in the process of frantically forgetting, and could do what they liked.

Once in Italy, they stared at Titians and Tintorettos with a
kind of zeal that would have won them good grades in their college art survey class, although during that class they had mostly
slept, for the room was dark and the chair was soft, and life at age
twenty held other interests, mostly sexual ones. But now they
tried to fall in love with the nonsexual parts of the world, the
details that they had never noticed before. They attempted to
adjust; they called their friends late at night, and the other newly
single ones were grateful for the distraction, taking the cordless
phone across the apartment to grab a spoon and a jar of Nutella
from the kitchen cabinet (for this would be a long, leisurely,
sugar-and-shortening-propelled conversation), while the married
friends were magnanimous, silently signaling to the husbands
beside them, with whom they had probably just been clashing:
Our depressed friend is needy tonight. I'll be quick.

But the heterosexual woman and the homosexual man would
be forever exempt from lovers' woes. No lust snapped in the air
between them, making them behave like odd, shifty teenagers
who have just had sex for the first time and can't believe their
good luck. Nothing could ruin what these two had, because what
they had was built on a simple foundation of allegiance and relief.

When Sara Swerdlow and Adam Langer rode in the car side

by side, they were as contented as twin babies in a double stroller. They listened to tapes and they made themselves right at home. Hanging from the rearview mirror was a little plastic smiling Buddha that Adam had bought for Sara for good luck, and it swung on its silk rope as the car moved. They talked about men, how disappointing they were as a group, agreeing that neither of them liked the floral stink of aftershave, or the puzzlingly popular aesthetic of boxer shorts, which transformed all men into their uncles. They were great friends and had been for many years, during which time his hairline had retreated coastally, and her whippet-thin body had thickened at the hips, as though to ready her for the inevitable task of childbirth.

Everyone who knew Sara and Adam understood that their friendship was something to be envied, something lofty and sacred. They would never fall into a heap in bed, although they had, on occasion, accidentally seen each other naked. He thought she had startling but beautiful breasts; she thought he had the whitest legs in the universe. Friendship was a thing of extraordinary value, ever since it had become clear to both of them that lovers never lasted, and that families were the traps you walked into on major holidays and emerged from the next day, stuffed with carbohydrates and seething. But friendship, at least a friendship such as this, stayed put. It didn't matter whether one person was more successful than the other; what they had seemed outside the arena of mean little jealousies.

Everyone but Sara was jealous of Adam, who had become famous at age twenty-six for his play *Take Us to Your Leader,* a light comedy about a Jewish family on Mars. When the play moved to Broadway, several of the other students in his playwrights' workshop developed unexplained intestinal ailments and sleep disorders, and tacked on extra sessions with their therapists. The huge and wildly positive review in the *Times* opened with the line "What if Neil Simon were gay?" and as a result the play ran and ran. Busloads of theater groups and temple sisterhoods rolled in from the suburbs to see it, leaving matinees clutching scrolled Playbills and muttering favorite lines, still weepy with laughter.

The other workshop members despised Adam's flagrant display of commercialism, yet cursed their own bargain-basement Sam Shepard noodling. They would never have expected this to happen to Adam Langer, of all people; he was the shy, forgettable person hunched in the corner of the classroom, the one with the nails bitten down to tiny smiles. Why hadn't fame tapped someone else among them, such as the thin man whose plays were all set in cruel British reform schools, or the pale, freckle-chested redhead from Keetersville, Georgia, who gave her Southern characters colorful names like Jehovah Biggins and Lady Fandango?

As it turned out, Adam was the perfect receptacle for fame. With his boyish unease and long, studious face, he seemed modest and he photographed surprisingly well. He became a popular and natural interview subject, speaking easily and at length about everything from the changing shape of the American family to the role of the gay person in society, casually referring to Rimbaud and Verlaine and Oscar Wilde as if they had all worked on the high school literary magazine together. Adam represented a certain mainstream brand of gay culture that was bookish and appealing and highly presentable. People were always asking him questions—in print and in person—and Adam Langer loved to answer.

He had been an awkward adolescent, unloved by anyone but his mother and father. Adam's ears were perpetually red-hot, like someone who seems to have just come back from the barbershop, and he was a jiggler; a crossed leg often went flapping like a wing, and if a pencil happened to make its way into his hand, it would soon be put into service tapping out a rhythm that no one in the otherwise silent coffee shop or classroom wanted to hear. But after his play reached Broadway and stayed there, Adam developed an instantaneous and nearly alarming sexual popularity. Suddenly, other men wanted to sleep with him, he who had been turned down often throughout college, managing only a few brief liaisons, including one with a mutely shy exchange student from Nepal. Now he had a handsome boyfriend named Shawn Best, who would be riding out to the beach house this very afternoon on the bus line whose young female attendants gave all passengers little bottles of Squaw Creek spring water when they got on board.

Sara had had a series of disappointing lovers. Most recently, there had been an environmental lawyer named Sloan, who came around a few nights a week, folding his pants over the back of her chair and letting a spill of coins hit the floor; Sloan was affable and shaggy and was, as her mother, Natalie, might have said, "fun in the sack." But then he had gone up to British Columbia for some complex logging legislation, and that had been that, which was just as well, since after several weeks of sleeping with him Sara still hadn't been able to imagine what this overflow of sex might lead to. And besides, there were details about him that she didn't like; he had admitted to her that he had changed his name from something more ordinary—either Steven or John, she couldn't remember which—and Adam pointed out that this was a suspect and pretentious thing to do.

Sara was a graduate student at Columbia, and had made her peace with the fact that she might be in school forever, a program in Japanese history ambling slowly toward a doctoral dissertation that would grow to become biblical in length, with footnotes jamming up the bottom third of each page. She didn't mind the prospect of being an eternal student, although she pretended to; school offered a familiar swaddling, and Sara wasn't really sure if she would ever be good enough at what she did to snag one of the very few academic positions available. A friend of hers from Columbia who had completed the program a year earlier had given up looking for a teaching post and had taken a job translating the instructions for the assembly of Japanese-made toys sold in the States ("Your new Turbo Robot-Pak is easy to play with, and

will delight you and your friends for hours!!!"). Sara was terrified
of winding up with such a job. If she tried to imagine herself
somewhere ten years from now, she was unable to picture herself
doing anything at all. The screen was simply blank and unreveal-
ing. When Sara was deeply immersed in the text of a Japanese
book, she loved the intricacy of the language, the thrill of the chase
as she tracked down the meanings of unusual phrases. But when
she objectified what she was doing, she understood that the world
would not welcome a scholar of Japan with open arms. She would
probably have to translate the folded instructions inside toys
someday, or else marry well.

Sara and Adam continued to take the house in Springs every
August along with Maddy, who was a lawyer, and her husband,
Peter, a teacher in a public high school, even though there were
better deals to be found, bigger houses with wider lawns and
higher ceilings. Even though, after anyone took a shower in the
downstairs bathroom, a few slender, bobbing mushrooms often
pushed their snub noses up between the aqua tiles. They continued to take the house even though Adam, for one, could have certainly afforded his own place by now. The house made them feel
unhurried, dumbly caught in that vague nebula of the late twen-
ties/early thirties, when you don't yet feel frantic to own property
or to breed, when you can lie around smoking cigarettes and eating an alternation of heavily salted snack foods and sweet, spongy
packaged cupcakes, and no one cares.

In previous summers, they had all slept until noon every day of
the vacation, but the shape of this summer would be somewhat
different. Seven months earlier, Maddy had given birth to a baby
named Duncan, who would certainly change the atmosphere this
month. The baby, with its endless, insatiable needs—and with its
own portable infant monitor that its parents toted from room to
room, lest they miss a single coo or explosion of gas—was both an
advertisement for fertility and a deterrent. Sara wasn't remotely
ready to have a baby; she hadn't even started to scale the walls of

awareness of her unreadiness, yet was vaguely worried that an abortion she'd had a few years earlier had rendered her infertile. Although she'd had almost no ambivalence about the abortion at the time, she had still known that an older, more mature and focused version of herself would probably want children someday. But the actual thought of being a mother was still so unpleasant that she held her diaphragm up to the light before sex for an extended moment of squinting inspection. No pinholes, no apertures. She had no idea of what kind of mother she'd be: Would she behave the way her own mother had—overinvolved, frenetic, or would she find her own style? There was no way to know. She couldn't tell if it would be worse having a baby now, like Maddy, or never being able to. At this point in her life, sex was for energetic body-slamming and the kind of yowling, cats-in-an-alley orgasms that made the neighbors long to be young again.

Now Sara stopped the car in front of a lunch stand, and she and Adam ate at a picnic table. "This taste," Adam said as he swallowed the first bite of a crab roll, "is like Proust's *madeleine*. When I'm not young anymore, this taste will bring every sensation back to me."

"No offense, but you're already not young anymore," said Sara. "Young was two summers ago. Last summer was the cusp. This summer it's all over."

"Then I guess I should get on with my life," said Adam, as a clump of crabmeat tumbled down the front of his shirt. "I should start writing about different things. Not set all my plays in my parents' paneled rec room. I should write a play called *Bosnia*. I should write about oppression, or cruelty." They both laughed, because he was no good with such material; it would have been a huge stretch. Instead, he sat here wiping a mess of crab off his shirt, leaving an oblong stain behind. His clothes were full of old, faded stains. "Shawn is cruel," Adam added. "At least, he has a cruel mouth; you'll see what I mean. Do I get extra credit for that?"

Shawn Best had recently pushed his way across a crowded reception in the city to get to Adam at a meet-the-playwrights evening. In a clutch of admirers, Shawn stood out as particularly striking and aggressive, inquiring whether Adam would listen to a cassette tape of songs from *his* play, and then, even though Adam politely declined, sending it to him by messenger the next morning. The tape, as far as Adam could tell—having listened to only a few songs and not particularly liking musicals—wasn't good, but at least it wasn't truly terrible; he remembered that it had to do with the plight of two American spinsters in Rome. There was a passport mix-up in the second act, and one of the spinsters fell into a fountain and sang a long ballad about all the missed opportunities in her life. A few days after he had sent over the tape, Shawn telephoned for Adam's response, and arranged to pick up the cassette in person. Adam, dazed and passive, had let this stranger into his apartment, where he made himself instantly at home, wandering into the kitchen, where he took a peach Snapple out of the refrigerator without asking, popped it open and drank. When he was done, he sat on the couch in the living room, put the bottle down on the coffee table, then suddenly produced a condom from his wallet.

"What are you doing?" Adam asked, slightly frightened.

"Oh, you don't want to?" said Shawn.

"Well, I don't know . . . ," said Adam. "I hadn't thought about it. I don't even know you. This is very confusing." Actually, he *had* thought about it; he'd imagined being wrapped in Shawn's arms, inhaling the vaguely brothy sweat-smell of him. Shawn seemed to know all of this without being told; he took it for granted that other men had these thoughts about him.

Shawn tore the packet open with his teeth, then stood up and led Adam to the bedroom. "Wait. Wait. *No,*" Adam had said on the way, because his knee-jerk reaction to sex was always "No." But now there was no reason for "No." It wasn't as though he was a teenager with an impending curfew, frantically making out with someone in the azaleas beside his house, while nearby his parents lay in bed as innocent as children, lulled by the gentle tedium of *The Tonight Show.* With Shawn, who was a complete stranger, there was the question of safety, of HIV status, but he held a condom in his hand like a peace offering. "Are you, are you . . . *you* know . . . ," Adam whispered a little later in bed, cringing at his own question.

"Am I *what?*"

"Healthy," said Adam. "Clean. Negative."

"Well, to be honest, I don't know," Shawn said.

"You don't know?" said Adam, incredulous—he who had already been tested several times.

"I'm not ready to take the test," said Shawn. "The idea of it freaks me out. The abolute black or white quality. The yes or no." He paused. "But look," he added, "this will be totally safe. I've got this little latex raincoat here." So Adam closed his eyes and let himself fall back against the bed.

That night, seconds after Shawn was gone, Adam had called Sara up and babbled details to her: the line of hair running down Shawn's stomach like an arrow leading the eye to its destination; the way Adam had felt frightened at the idea of having sex in daylight, where his own body and all its pores and imperfections would be on display, but how Shawn had made him feel at ease; and how, after the sex was through and Adam's heart was still beating as fast as a hamster's, the two men had lain on the bed and played Twenty Questions, which Adam had played during every long car ride of his childhood. Lying in bed with a lover after sex was almost like a long car ride. Times stood still; you didn't know how long you would be there, inert bodies stuck together in this small space, limbs bumping, but you didn't really care.

This had all happened only a few weeks earlier, and somehow it had led to Adam inviting Shawn out to the beach house in Springs for the first weekend of August. He would be arriving in a few hours.

Now Adam and Sara finished their lunch and climbed back into her mother's Toyota, which was already hot from sitting in a parking lot in the sun. They drove a few miles more until Sara noticed a stand by the side of the road with a sign that read "PIES." Sara thought they ought to buy one for their landlady, Mrs. Moyles, and so they did. She hopped out and returned with a fresh raspberry pie with a latticework crust. As they drove on toward the house, the pie box slid around on the seat between them, and Adam steadied it with his hand, feeling an intense swell of contentment.

He could have driven with Sara forever; this was so much better than almost everything else in his life, certainly better than the writing that lately seemed to go nowhere. He knew that the follow-up to his first success would be closely watched. Everyone would want to know if he could do it again; could he make those matinee audiences weep with laughter? Oh, he thought, probably not. This summer he would finish his second play, and in the fall he would show it to Melville Wolf, his producer. "Make it funny," Mel had warned. "Make it really, really funny. Make me bite my tongue, it's so funny. Make the inside of my mouth bleed."

Adam constantly dwelled on the burden of his early success, and on the futility of even vaguely approximating the experience again. He had seen a TV talk show recently that featured a panel of ex–child stars; clips of their early work were shown, and in each case it was extremely painful to observe the long-gone purity of skin, silkiness of hair, and open-faced hopefulness of those children, and then have to compare that with the lumpy plainness of their fully formed, adult selves. Adam thought of his own father, a businessman who had enjoyed a big success very early in his career when he invested in an electric fan company called, dully, FanCo, and how, when air-conditioning blew across the parched American landscape, his father had lost all his money.

There was one aspect of Adam's life that was removed from all anxiety. Sara was that aspect, as good and loyal a friend as he had ever known. He thought that women understood the world in a way that men did not. A woman could lead you, could take you by the hand and show you which of your shirts to wear, and which to destroy. His love for her was so great that when they were apart for too long he felt as unbalanced as a newlywed and almost lightheaded. During the year they saw each other at least once a week for a cheap Tandoori meal at an Indian restaurant draped to resemble a caravan, and they usually talked on the phone a few times a day. They even watched television together on the phone late at night—explicit nature documentaries and peeks into celebrity palazzos—lying in their separate beds in separate apartments, laughing softly across miles of telephone wire.

Now August had arrived and they would be living in the same house for a month. Adam wanted to live with Sara forever. His fantasies often placed them both in Europe; he saw them living in the South of France and having children, a boy and a girl who could romp in a vineyard and be effortlessly bilingual. The idea of marrying Sara excited him, then always burned away in the gas of its own foolishness. He didn't want her, and she certainly didn't want him. They would spend August together, the high point of the year, and when Labor Day came they would part, as they always did.

When they pulled into the driveway of the house now, Adam was asleep against her shoulder, his head big and heavy and damp. She woke him up, and they carried their belongings up the weedy path, noticing that each year the small mustard-colored house looked a little worse upon approach, and that one year it would look so awful that they would back away without entering, and never return again. Sara lifted the stiff brass knocker on the front door and let it drop; the sound it made seemed tinny and insignificant, yet from inside they heard immediate footsteps, as though the landlady had been huddling by the door, awaiting their arrival.

Mrs. Moyles looked the same as last year, only a little worse, not unlike her house. She was a pudding-faced woman whom they suspected of alcoholism or dementia, or both, and who had a head of hair that looked as though she cut it herself while blindfolded. There was nothing charming about her house, either, no details that you could point out to guests, such as a secret passageway, or a set of fireplace pokers with handles shaped like mermaids. It was a no-frills house, a place to stay if you wanted to spend a month in the vicinity of a fancy beach resort and didn't mind the presence of linoleum and a hive of tiny, hot rooms.

"So you made it," she said to Sara and Adam, the same words she said every year when they arrived.

"Yes," they invariably said in return, nodding their heads in an attempt at politeness in the face of her indifference. Now Adam held out the pie box, but she didn't make any attempt to lift her hands up and take it. "This is for you," he prompted. "Raspberry."

Mrs. Moyles peered down at the box in his arms and said, "What am I supposed to do with that? I have diabetes!" As though they should have known. But they knew nothing about her, other than the fact that she owned this cheerless little house at 17 Diller Way, which she agreed to rent to them each summer for an uncommonly low price.

So they kept the pie for themselves, and Mrs. Moyles handed Sara the key to the house, muttered a few things about the gas jets on the stove, the sprinkler on the back lawn, and the list of emergency telephone numbers on the refrigerator. And then, to their relief, she was gone, driving south to her sister's house for the rest of the summer in her ancient, boat-sized Chevrolet. Adam and Sara turned to each other, giddy with expectation, and took a look around, observing the warped, upright piano, a Stüttland, an ancient Bavarian brand no one had ever heard of, and the unmatched living room chairs, one with illustrations of Paul Revere and Betsy Ross all over it, and the windows with their ill-fitting screens. Then, accepting their fate with a shrug and a laugh, feeling the filth and gloom of the house steal over them, they went upstairs to unpack in their separate bedrooms.

Adam stood in the small, sloping room that he inhabited every August, opening the drawers of a bureau and putting away his clothing. The room was furnished with a collection of badly painted pieces, now flaking in a paint-chip snowfall to the splintery floor. He slid a drawer closed, or tried to, for it had no runner, and needed to be worked into its slot. Finally he put a palm against it and slammed it the final inch shut.

Across the hall, Sara opened a drawer of her own small bureau to put away her underpants and her red leather notebook that she wrote in exclusively in Japanese, and found inside an old copy of *Heidi,* by Johanna Spyri, and a single, filthy gardening glove. The drawer smelled of earth, and when she looked around the room she saw that the paisley wallpaper was the color of mud, and buckling. How many more years would they take this house? she wondered. How many more years could they tolerate living like teenagers? She sat down on the small bed, feeling it groan even under her delicate weight. This summer would be different from the others, she thought. This summer she would become less flighty, more substantial. She would engage with people her own age, people other than Adam, and she would try to disengage from her mother.

Everyone who knew Sara Swerdlow well also knew her mother, Natalie Swerdlow, a travel agent who lived in suburban New Jersey. Natalie could be a demanding, edgy, overbearing mother, and while Sara sometimes spoke against her to her friends ("She's too nosy," she'd say, or "I wish she'd get a life"), she always felt guilty afterward, and would telephone her mother for a long, purgative session of girl talk. Mother and daughter had been virtually inseparable since Natalie's divorce when Sara was small. The marriage had frayed and Sara's father had shrugged off to Dayton, Ohio. He was an alarmingly passive man who had never been expressive with his daughter, and Sara found that she didn't really miss him as much as she missed the idea of him: *a father*. Someone like all the other girls had, who picked you up after band practice, or who drove a carful of you and your hysterically giggling friends to the mall, sitting up front alone like a poker-faced chauffeur in a pea jacket. A father who spent a lot of time examining his new leaf-blower from Sears, apparently fascinated by the force with which the leaves were sucked into the bag. A father you could not know, because you were a girl and he was a man, and there was a vast, awkward gulf between you. Everything you would do together would be difficult, and it would only grow worse. When Sara's father left home, she consoled herself with the idea that she would be spared the discomfort of spending so much time with a man she could not talk to, and who could not, or would not, talk to her.

She would spend much more time with her mother, she decided, and apparently her mother had the same idea, for in the face of their newfound aloneness, the mother had clung to her only daughter. They looked alike, these two fine-boned Swerdlow women. Natalie still spoke to Sara on the telephone every day. It was she, in fact, who made the first call to the house that summer. Sara and Adam had been inside for less than twenty minutes, when the telephone rang. "Sara!" Adam called. "It's for you!" She knew who it was; who else would think to call her here, so soon after she had arrived?

"Hello?" she said into the telephone.

"Surrender, Dorothy," said her mother.

"Hey, Mom," said Sara. "What took you so long?"

"Oh," said her mother, "I thought I'd give you a little space."

"Yeah, right," said Sara. She rolled her eyes at Adam, as if to signal, *My crazy mother,* but in truth she enjoyed these conversations. Her mother, though an extremely intrusive person, was also a source of comfort. Sara had been a shy girl who drew pictures of small woodland animals and read books about blind or orphaned children. Her mother thought of her as sensitive and tender, which was so different from the way everyone thought of her mother. Natalie Swerdlow had a hard laugh and great good looks, with a body that appeared more elastic than it had reason to at her age. She also had a sense of fun that was often drummed out under the dull, quotidian beats of suburban life. How had Natalie wound up in New Jersey, she used to ask herself, living in a big house and married to a *dentist?* ("A periodontist," Ed would correct, and she would say, "Pardon me.") Her daughter, Sara, was the saving grace, the small, swaying plant that had resulted from this unlikely union. As the marriage to Ed Swerdlow, D.D.S., turned into a festival of bickering at home and in various restaurants, Natalie swiveled her attentions and hopes onto her daughter.

Sara loved receiving such a flood of attention from her overwhelming, wonderful mother, and together mother and daughter developed an alliance: the big and the small, the formed and the unformed. They sang songs, they paged through fashion magazines, they once even bleached their hair with temporary dye, transforming themselves into mother-daughter platinum-blond starlets for one night only. Each received a borrowed burst of voltage from the other, the appropriation of qualities that would otherwise never be available.

Natalie understood early on that her daughter would one day be more beautiful than she herself had ever been; Sara's neck and fingers were longer, her eyes larger, her hair perfectly straight. Sara attracted everyone—men, women, children, pets—through her gentle elegance and hints of melancholy darkness. You wanted to be near her because she smelled woodsily good and had a simple, easy laugh. You knew that Sara would always remember your birthday with an interesting little gift, and that she also had an inner life that you didn't fully comprehend. She was pretty, but not vacant. She wasn't merely one of those uncomplicated girls who invest everything in the boys in their midst, stringing necklaces for them made of shells and attending every dull lacrosse game, sitting on the bleachers in the grassy air, hugging themselves in the cold, while the boys ran with their big, strange, netted sticks. Sara, it was clear, was different.

But so, too, was Natalie, although in other ways. Natalie had been very sexy back in the sixties—slightly brazen in swept-up hairdos and a series of very short dresses the color of Necco wafers. Now Necco wafers didn't exist (or did they—in the back of some dusty candy store?) and those hairstyles and dresses had long been retired, but Natalie had made a graceful transition to the styles of the seventies and then the eighties and the nineties, emerging fully intact: a slim travel agent who looked far younger than she was. She was freer than her daughter, louder and more assertive. She was the mother who appeared at PTA meetings looking so good that the assistant principal hovered solicitously and flirtatiously all evening. She was the jazzy mother who was creative in everything she did. When she made salads for Sara, she arranged the iceberg lettuce leaves, carrots, tomatoes, and olives into the approximate shape of a girl. Natalie threw herself into Sara because this gave her a pleasure greater than any other.

There were actually very few pleasures elsewhere in her life back then. Her marriage was over and for a while she was celibate, uninterested in starting up anything new. Sex with Ed had mostly been pathetic; sometimes, during the marriage, he came home from the office still wearing his papery white dental tunic, looking vaguely futuristic. She thought of his hands, imagined them exploring the intricacies of some stranger's teeth and gums. Why, she wondered, would anyone want to be a dentist?

When she and Ed had first met one summer at a hotel in the Catskills, she had asked him this. It was a challenge, a put-down, she knew, but he did not seem offended. Instead, he seemed to enjoy the chance to explain to her the inner workings of the mouth.

She had sat with him at the bar of the Concord Hotel, while he drew a picture of the upper jaw for her on a cocktail napkin. God, I'm bored, she thought at the time, but it did not stop her from seeing him again. In fact, her boredom with Ed Swerdlow became a constant, pleasurable topic of conversation she could have with her friends. "That man is so boring!" Natalie would say to a girlfriend on the phone after an evening spent with Ed. But in an odd way she liked him—his single-mindedness about becoming a dentist, his straightforwardness, and even the shape of his head.

Ed looked in her mouth on one of their early dates, sitting her under a strong light and tilting her head up. "Not bad," he said, referring to the fillings that other dentists had packed into the hollows over the years. Sitting with her head thrown back like that, she understood that she would never really love him. Her friends spoke of undying love for men, and Natalie pretended to know what they meant, but she was an unabashed narcissist at heart, and her interests did not stray far from herself. Until there was Sara.

Sometimes, in August at the beach house, other members of the house casually eavesdropped on Sara's telephone conversations with Natalie, because the way Sara and her mother spoke to each other was compelling. First came the inevitable "Surrender, Dorothy" salutation, then an odd, colloquial banter laced with affection and tension. The others in the house had by now let their own parents drop away from their lives to a certain extent, becoming entwined with them mostly when there was a cash-flow problem that only a parent could solve, or a family scandal worth discussing, or a holiday arrangement to be made. This summer, the bond between Natalie and Sara was more complicated than usual, because Natalie had lent her daughter her second, slightly rundown car, also a Toyota. The car was a simple loan for August, yet it came with warnings attached. "If you bang it up, I'll kill you," Natalie had said. "And don't let any of your friends take it for a joy ride." *Joy ride.* Her mother saw them as irresponsible teenagers, instead of this crew of careful, faithful friends hurtling in a pack toward the middle of their lives.

Natalie hadn't been to the house in Springs, and Sara wanted to leave this the one place her mother would never see. When she was thirteen, Sara had told her mother everything, because she assumed that was what all girls did. She had told Natalie about how she had cheated on her geography test, and she had told her about stealing a nugget of hashish from Alison Bikel's father's nighttable drawer. And when, during a game of Seven Minutes in Heaven, Neil Grolier had put his hand inside Sara's underpants, the feelings that hand had engendered were so wild and peculiar that she had needed to tell her mother about them, too.

But her mother had simply looked at Sara and said, "Yes, a man's hands can be a wonderful thing." Then she went on to describe for Sara all that awaited her in the combustible universe of sex. It was terrifying and disgusting to hear the details, but somehow still exciting. "When the time comes," Natalie had said, stroking her daughter's head like a dog and gazing off, "you'll know what I mean."

Two years later, she learned what her mother had meant. Because she was a beautiful girl of a certain type (long, shining fair hair parted in the middle, astonishingly clear skin, turquoise beads ringing her slender neck), a certain type of soulful boy liked her. The boys actually resembled Sara; their own hair was shining and parted in the middle, too. One of them wrote out the lyrics to "Stairway to Heaven" for her in painstaking calligraphy on parchment paper. She had sex with him in her white canopy bed while her mother was at her desk at the Seven Seas Travel Agency in the city, arranging a whirlwind Spain-Portugal itinerary for a honeymoon couple. Neither Sara nor this boy knew exactly what they were doing; they both fumbled around on the bed and made a few inadvertent mewing noises, then a reservoir-tip Trojan was produced with much fanfare and there was a great deal of pain and a little blood, and suddenly what had been awkward and joyless became serious, sublime.

Over the years, both mother and daughter became involved

with an assortment of men, and the big house in New Jersey became a place to bring them. Natalie dated amiable, divorced businessmen with middle-aged waistlines and a predilection for no-iron slacks. It amazed Sara that her mother could be attracted to these men, yet Natalie felt the same way about Sara's boyfriends, whose mouths vacantly hung open, and whose hands smelled of all things fried. During Sara's adolescence, sex was an open secret in the house; the teenaged daughter's diaphragm was hidden under a stack of inorganic chemistry homework in her top dresser drawer, and the mother's older, more weatherbeaten version was hidden under an Anne Klein scarf in her bottom dresser drawer.

Off at Wesleyan freshman year, Sara called Natalie at seven in the morning while a boy lay beside her in her narrow dormitory bed. She put the phone up to his sleeping lips. "Listen," she whispered to her mother. "He's breathing."

And her mother held the phone up to the lips of the systems analyst lying in her own bed. "Listen," Natalie whispered back. "He's snoring."

This summer, neither woman had a man in her bed, at least not yet. There was time; August had barely begun.

SHAWN BEST arrived in Springs at six o'clock, his arms and legs freezing from the aggressive air conditioner of the luxury bus. He had brought a bayberry-scented candle as a housegift, in a spun-glass vessel made to resemble a Druid. It looked like a prop from a stage version of *The Hobbit*. Shawn did have a cruel mouth, Sara thought, but his eyes looked too innocent to contain anything that could truly be described as sadistic.

The men were formal around each other, careful not to touch or betray any intimacy. Shawn seemed disappointed in the summer house; he had probably imagined something palatial, even though Adam had warned him the place was nothing special.

"Well," said Sara, "I'm going to take a rest before Maddy and

Peter and the baby get here." She extricated herself, her smile tight.

In the late afternoon, Maddy and Peter arrived in the red Ford pickup that Peter had been driving since college, their baby trapped into a rear-facing car seat between them. There were hurried, excited greetings, and exclamations over the baby, who had a head of spiky hair and questioning, dark eyes. Then everyone found their rooms and began to unpack their bags, working open the old dresser drawers and settling in. They could hear Duncan crying, his sobs rhythmic and cartoonish.

Later, Peter went out and bought lobsters and beer, and another haphazard dinner got under way. Shawn brought out matches and lit his ugly bayberry candle. They all talked about the year, their jobs, the news of the world. They somehow began a discussion of the genital mutilation of girls in Africa, which had Maddy and Sara speaking in quiet, angry voices. Maddy had been independently researching the topic from a legal standpoint and hoped to publish an article about it in a law journal, even though it had nothing to do with her area of expertise, which was torts. But it had all been put on hold after her baby was born and she went on leave from the law firm.

At dinner, the serious discussion about genital mutilation led to some silly talk about Notary Publics. "What *is* a Notary Public, anyway?" Peter asked. "I know everyone has to use them once in a while, and sometimes you can find them in the weirdest places, like the back of a hardware store, just *sitting* there under a display of Phillips head screwdrivers or something, and you pay them to stamp your papers, but who are they? And how did they get to be who they are?"

"I think they have to go to school for it," said Maddy.

"But what do they learn in Notary Public school?" asked Sara. "What's on the final exam?"

"And why," said Peter, "would someone *want* to be a Notary Public? This is the great mystery of the universe; forget about why the dinosaurs disappeared. There are a million jobs to choose from out there, and this is the one they pick." They were laughing now, enjoying the familiar cadences of their conversation.

The group had come together freshman year at Wesleyan, when they had lived together on the third floor of a dormitory. Their humor, and many of their references, were often inaccessible to anyone else. Their entire view of the world was tilted and limited, a fact that they recognized. In earlier years they had considered themselves ageless, their bodies unlined and resilient, their experiences somehow meaningless.

But that was their twenties; now they were thirty. Everything was different at thirty; nothing was taken lightly or carelessly. Now they talked and talked, these thirty-year-olds, in the kitchen they sat in every August. The kitchen chairs were uncomfortable in a 1950s suburban way—coral vinyl bolted down with metal studs—and the tablecloth was shiny oilcloth, but the company (except for Shawn, the unknown presence) was so welcome and comforting, that everyone seemed on the verge of nostalgic tears. This day, after all, served as the letting-go of the held breath of all the months, the release from a year in New York that had been particularly grim, locking them into their fluorescent cubicles at work, and the small apartments they called home. They had barely gone outside all winter; they had ordered movies from the video store, and a rotation of take-out dinners (Chinese, Thai, barbecue), waiting for it to become bearable outdoors, and for the world to once again seem approachable. The newspapers reported that people had frozen on the streets that January in record numbers, the alcohol in their blood quickening death. But then spring arrived, transforming seamlessly into summer. Now here they were again, wearing shorts and gathering to eat the tender meat of local lobsters, and it seemed as though winter had never even taken place.

Later that first evening, after the sun set and they were all sitting on the deck that looked out over the scrubby yard, Adam announced that he wanted to drive to town to buy ice cream to go atop the raspberry pie. Sara agreed to take him in the car. Shawn went inside and planted himself in front of the awful old piano, lightly playing one of the songs from his musical. Adam climbed back into the car with Sara and they headed out to the Fro-Z-Cone on the edge of town. The sky was still pale, and even though you couldn't see the ocean from this road, you knew it was around here somewhere. Your hair felt damp; you thought you smelled salt, although you weren't sure if salt really had a smell.

"You hate him," said Adam, as the car pulled out of the driveway. "Shawn, I mean."

"I don't know what you're talking about."

"It's all right. I hate him a little bit too," said Adam. "He's kind of an opportunist. He's very nervy. But he really likes me. And there's actually something sweet about him."

"I don't know him well enough to hate him," said Sara. "I'm sure he's perfectly fine."

"He's good in bed," Adam said, sheepishly.

"Well, good for you," said Sara.

"You know, you could at least pretend to like him," said Adam. "God knows I've pretended to like some of the losers you've brought to the house over the years."

"Losers? Who?" demanded Sara.

"The gem guy, for one," said Adam.

The gem guy had been a man a few summers earlier who dealt in rare stones and the occasional coin. He was from Bahrain and was quite handsome, yet it turned out that he maintained archaic, obnoxious notions about sex roles, and was uncomfortable around Adam because Adam was, as the gem guy had phrased it, "an unrepentant sodomite."

"The gem guy was a long time ago. And he was about sex, pure and simple," said Sara. "He was a pig, and he insisted on scrubbing his penis with scalding water, a loofah sponge, and Lava soap after he was done. He would have used turpentine if we'd had it in the house."

"You know what I wish?" Adam suddenly said.

"Yes," said Sara, sighing. "What you always wish."

"Well, is that so bad?" said Adam. "Wishing that we loved each other, you and I? That way?"

"You mean," said Sara, "that lovely, intimate, fluid-exchanging way."

"You're such a fucking romantic," said Adam.

"Actually, I am."

"But not with me," said Adam softly. "Oh, well. So it goes." The Fro-Z-Cone came into view, its immense neon ice cream cone icon buzzing and sputtering in the twilight. "Look at that thing," said Adam. "It's so *phallic*. It just looms over everyone, and we all head toward it. We're all making a mecca toward the giant penis in the sky." Sara laughed, and he continued. "Oh help us, giant Fro-Z-Cone," he said. "Help us distinguish right from wrong, and good from evil. Pleasure us, giant Fro-Z-Cone, with your giant frozen . . . cone."

Sara parked the car in the lot beside a BMW that belonged to a bunch of teenagers clustered around the counter of the ice cream stand. "Look," she said. "The bearded woman still works here."

"Poor bearded woman," said Adam. "Why doesn't she at least trim it? It wouldn't be so prominent."

"Maybe it's a political statement," said Sara, and they both laughed meanly. "God, we're terrible," she said. The bearded woman was elderly, with a milky eye and long strands running from her chin like a witch in a fairy tale. She had been here for years and years, "since ice cream had been invented," according to Adam. Now they ordered a tub of vanilla, watching as the woman held a container under the nozzle of the soft-serve machine, the ice cream being extruded in a long turban. In the distance, the teenagers smoked and howled and broke bottles, the glass cracking almost musically against the blacktop of the parking lot, while bugs jumped all around them in the neon light.

Sara and Adam paid for the ice cream and then ducked back into the car. As Sara started the engine, she saw that one of the headlights no longer worked. Adam got out and stepped around to the front. She craned through the open car window. "Busted," he said, shaking his head. "We can take it in tomorrow. There's an auto shop in town."

"How would you know?" asked Sara. "That's like the last thing in the world you would ever know about. Transmissions. Carburetors. It's kind of outside the Adam Langer Sphere of Knowledge."

"Well, ha-ha to you, missy," he said. "I guess I'm full of surprises." He paused, smiling. "Actually," he said, "the only reason I know about it is because there's this guy who works out front, and he never wears a shirt, just a bandanna around his neck. I call him the Hairless Mechanic."

"I thought it was something like that," said Sara.

They saw that the teenagers had scattered; one of them must have casually smashed the light with a bottle. Adam got back inside and they headed off. The single working headlight swung its solo beam onto the half of the road under its watch. How strange it felt to be driving like this; it was like having one eye open. The sky was turning truly dark; back at the house, everyone would already have gone inside, waiting for their plates of pie and ice cream. Sara felt that the house was where she belonged, and yet she knew that as a life it was imperfect, makeshift, good for summers only.

Had she been doing the kinds of things that would eventually lead to a life she wanted to live year-round? Her friends were like bodyguards who kept one another from the perils and disappointments of the larger world, and yet she wondered if she was prepared for her life. She should set her expectations lower, she thought, finding some fairly ordinary job that involved a mastery of the Japanese language, which she had become skilled at but not brilliant.

Adam was brilliant, she thought, in a way that came to him naturally and effortlessly. But Sara continually tried hard and she could almost feel the tug of all that trying. Inevitably, she was someone who *meant well*. In graduate school, she had known students who simply blazed their way through seminars. One woman, Adrian Pomerantz, was so intelligent that the professors always lit up when Adrian spoke; her eloquent, cogent analyses forced them not to be lazy, not to repeat themselves. Adrian was small and dark, with a fine film of hair above her upper lip and a wardrobe made up of odd little dresses that she purchased from an antique store in the Village, but which looked as though they should be worn by Shakers. She was a sturdy little chestnut of a woman who had probably been winning academic prizes her entire life, but somehow, no matter what she did or how much she dazzled, Adrian Pomerantz would only be admired, never loved.

Sara would be loved. Sara Swerdlow would get away with it; she would float through everything she undertook, and no one would mind.

There was a young assistant professor at Columbia named Ron Getman, who had been particularly helpful to Sara when she was trying to decide upon a dissertation topic. He had sat with her in coffee shops on Broadway, and in his gloomy little office, and he had gazed at her steadily as they discussed her thesis, which was to be about propagandistic images of the Japanese people during World War II. He was virtuous and would not kiss her without some sort of sign of encouragement on her part. She considered giving him such a sign but rejected the idea, knowing that it might have been possible to find love with this man who had fair, fading hair and spoke Japanese with a rapidity that amazed her. She didn't deserve Ron Getman; no, she didn't really want him. She didn't know *what* she wanted. Not him, not Sloan the environmental lawyer who had changed his name, and not even Adam, whom she loved so deeply. That was the problem, and it informed almost everything she did. *What did she want?* What could she get out of studying Japanese—a pathetic nowhere job with a toy company? What could she get from men? A litany of orgasms, babies, a mortgage, a future? And then there was the question of her mother; lately she thought she had been deprived of oxygen during all these years they had spent together. It was all too much—Natalie wanting to know everything, and Sara willingly telling her. In some ways, she even hated her mother.

The only arena in which she was secure, and fully herself, was at the beach house every August. She almost felt as though she wanted to hurry back to the house now, and so she stepped more firmly on the gas pedal. The car radio played a song that was riveting in its associations: Van Morrison's "Brown-Eyed Girl," an oldie which had played throughout much of Sara and Adam's adolescence. Boys had sung it to Sara: a sexy, durable summer song, her own brown eyes wide with pleasure. And Adam, she knew, had sung it to himself in his bedroom along with a clock radio, wondering why he wasn't attracted to girls, girls with brown eyes, with blue eyes, with long, constantly shampooed hair, and whether he ever would be.

They were both singing now, when a car backed out of a driveway into the road and right into the driver's side of Sara's car. At first there was a shuddering smack of metal and a feeling that must be like giving birth, or being born—a ripping apart, a disconnection, and a pain that was bigger than you were, so that you slipped right inside it, as if in hiding. There was sound with it, too: the groaning of metal as it gives up and collapses into itself.

Her mother would kill her, Sara thought as the door of her car pushed into her, overtaking her like a tide. The Buddha on the mirror swung back and forth, and Adam's mouth was open as if forming a question, and the carton of ice cream bounded across the seat. For some reason she thought of the bearded woman standing at the Fro-Z-Cone year after year. Nothing really changed, at least not so you could see it. Even aging was done surreptitiously, behind a smeary partition, under unnatural light. Sara Swerdlow cried out once, briefly, and then she died.

2

Girl Talk

Natalie Swerdlow had been having sex all evening, which was a daunting task if you were past your prime and on estrogen and had been at work since eight in the morning. But she had read that one of the first signs of old age was a diminished interest in sex, and was determined to ward off this fate by a regimen of sexual bombardment. Friends said she looked much younger than her age; her body was still tight and boyish and she could even fit into her daughter's jeans, when her daughter happened to leave a pair at home. Natalie was more flamboyant than Sara, but this was only because she knew that quiet simplicity would allow the other person a reflective moment that might accidentally reveal her true age. Better to dazzle and accessorize and cover up. Better to have strenuous sex all evening than not at all.

The man in her bed was a tall, thin, widowed cutlery salesman named Harvey Wise. She had met him through friends, and they easily began a little two-step of flirtation and dating. Sex between a man and woman of fifty bore little resemblance to sex during earlier decades of life. There were no longer any starry fantasies that this lovemaking might lead to an entire life together: a house, a lawn, a few babies down the pike. Harvey Wise was handsome in a gaunt, hangdog way, and after two unmemorable dinners— one in a chophouse, one in a trattoria—she had invited him home. They traveled from the city to Jersey in separate cars; as she pulled up the driveway of her house with the lights of his car eagerly right behind her, she felt her body tense up as it often did in the moments immediately before sex.

Then he was in her bed, and as soon as they were upon each other, the telephone rang. Out of instinct she grabbed it. "Hello?" she said, and she could immediately see the annoyance register on Harvey's face. It was her best friend, Carol, on the line, outraged about something, as always.

"Remember those contractors?" Carol was saying. "The ones I hired after the plumbing exploded and I needed a new ceiling in the den? Well, Natalie, like an idiot I called them again—"

"Carol," said Natalie. "Carol, I can't talk."

"Someone there?"

"Yes," she said. "Someone is."

"Does he have a penis?"

"Actually, I was about to find out."

"Well, good for you, Natalie," said Carol. "I don't mean to interrupt the party. Call me in the morning." And then she clicked off.

Natalie turned to the man beside her, noticing the dark hairiness of his arms against her pale summery sheets. "Sorry about that, Harvey," she said. "I tend to get a lot of calls."

"Maybe we could unplug the phone tonight," he said. "You know, not even hear it ring. Then we could really focus on each other."

This was a novelty; Natalie Swerdlow lived by, and for, the telephone. Every day at the Seven Seas Travel Agency in midtown Manhattan, she took calls from people eager to flee their lives for all points exotic, and in the evening she talked on the phone to her friends and her daughter. To turn off the telephone would be an aberration. But when she looked at Harvey Wise, she was surprised to see just how serious he was. He wanted this time alone in bed with her; he didn't want the telephone to ring. She realized that this was a moment of some importance, which could tip the relationship one way or the other. If she refused to unplug the telephone, he would know that the possibilities with her were limited. No matter what happened between them, she would never belong to him. And she did like him, with his long face and wrinkled suit. So, without blinking, Natalie reached out and unclicked the phone jack from the wall. Harvey Wise smiled at her, and soon brought her to orgasm.

The telephone rang and rang silently all night. Natalie Swerdlow was lying right beside its small corpse, the short cord lying coiled, and there was no sound to disturb her. Her body kept responding and clenching and reaching, while the telephone silently rang. With the bedroom door closed and the air conditioner humming, the other, plugged-in extensions in the house could not be heard. The pleasures that she felt with this man were profound, and she knew that this would make a good story to tell to Carol: *the night I chose between a man and a telephone, and lived to tell the tale.*

In the morning Harvey was still there in her bed, his face creased with sleep. She went into the bathroom and showered, during which time the telephone resumed its silent ringing. By the time she was dressed and downstairs, within earshot of the other extensions, it had stopped ringing altogether. Harvey woke up shortly and didn't bother to shower, but merely came downstairs, hungry and friendly. She cooked him an egg-white omelet and they made brief conversation about their cholesterol and triglyceride levels, and then they sat reading the paper together.

When they were standing in the doorway, ready to head for their Manhattan offices in separate cars, he reached his hand out and touched her collar, saying, "Natalie, I had a really nice time. I'd like to see you again very, very soon." This pleased her; she thought it would carry her through the entire day at work.

Then they got into their cars, he into his Nissan Maxima and she into her Toyota. Natalie felt uncommonly good this morning; apparently it was worth it to make the effort with someone new, worth it not to close off your divorced, estrogen-gobbling self from the carnal world.

As she drove onto the highway, the telephone resumed ringing back in her empty house, and then after a while it gave up and stopped. Some thirty minutes later, when she was just a minute or two from the mouth of the tunnel that led into Manhattan, Natalie Swerdlow's car phone finally rang, and this time she answered it. Almost no one ever called her on the car phone except for Carol or the office manager at Seven Seas, but it was too early for either of them. That meant it was Sara on the phone, Sara who would want to hear all about Natalie's night with Harvey Wise, Sara who would say, "Spare me no detail."

Why did Sara want to know everything? The answer was simple: because Natalie wanted to know everything about Sara. They had struck a bargain when Sara was young, and when Natalie became lonely after Ed left the family and moved to Ohio. They had become a couple, of sorts, watching *The Wizard of Oz,* doing their nails, going to the mall, and they were a couple that told each other everything. So it remained, an unusual arrangement that sometimes aroused jealousy in Natalie's friends, whose own daughters tended to be sullen and uncommunicative.

"She never tells me anything," her friend Carol would say of her daughter Tina, who seemed to have become a lesbian almost overnight, complete with an entirely new set of lesbian friends. What Natalie and Sara had—perhaps it had lost some of its luster over the years, or some of its usefulness—but still it held them together, made them keep picking up the telephone and starting a conversation with, "Surrender, Dorothy."

Now the car telephone was ringing, and Natalie picked up the receiver and said the line, already starting up the old give and take, the familiar girl talk that they did best.

But instead, a man was on the line, with a tortured, stuttering voice. "Mrs. Swerdlow," he said. "Now, Mrs. Swerdlow, you've got to listen to me." It was one of Sara's friends, a boy named Peter, telling her he had something terrible to say. Then he took a ragged breath and said it, and she felt her throat catch and her hands fly to her face. Suddenly, she found herself inside the tunnel; day became night, illuminated a tundra white, tiles shining, and Natalie had the sensation that her life, which she had until this very moment taken for granted, was over.

Natalie stopped holding on to the wheel of the car, and instead passively watched as it left its lane and grazed up against another car packed full of passengers. She felt the smack, the powerful vibration of two cars momentarily meeting. Then there was loud, aggravated honking, and in the next instant her car was slanted in the middle of rush hour, while behind her other cars stopped short against one another, brakes squealing so that the whole tunnel sounded like a slaughterhouse full of panicky animals.

In the shocked moment of silence after Natalie's car came to a halt, she put a hand up and realized her lip was split and bleeding. The policemen took her out of the car tenderly, and she kept talking to them about how her daughter Sara had been killed in a crash. They were confused by her words, thinking her daughter had been killed in *this* crash, and they carefully examined the car, even under the seat, in the place where gum wrappers and supermarket circulars congregate, as though another person could possibly be hiding under there.

"Ma'am, there is no one in this car with you," said an overburdened policeman with a round, red face.

"I know," she said. "I know." Then, in an attempt at explanation, she pointed to the car phone, whose cord was looped around the steering wheel. But of course he couldn't understand, and she couldn't speak anymore in order to tell him, and he simply put his arm around her and she felt the warm skin of his upper arm in his short-sleeved uniform, and smelled his summer cop sweat. Holding her against him like a lover, or like a genial father with his little girl, the officer turned away to speak softly into his walkie-talkie. Soon the ambulance had arrived, threading its way through the stopped-up tunnel. She wondered if she might in fact be dying from some hidden, painless internal injury she'd just received; she felt as though she was about to hallucinate. Every coherent thought became liquid quickly. It had not occurred to her yet that she wasn't really hurt, and that what she felt was only the unfamiliar new sensation of loss.

The mind tended to hallucinate to fight off the truth; it was almost like antibodies being manufactured and sent scattering to counter some profound illness. For some people, she thought, the antibodies came in the form of little angels, emissaries of God who fluttered down into you and reminded you that He has his ways. But if you didn't believe in God, if you were a middle-aged, atheist travel agent from New Jersey with no certainty about anything other than the continued fluctuation of airfares, then you manufactured a limited kind of craziness which sent your mind back into the past, back to bathing the baby or watching *The Wizard of Oz* with your little girl.

Natalie pictured herself with her friend Carol, the two women standing in the stark, treeless light of a playground in the winter of 1968, pushing their daughters on bucket swings. Back then, there were no Sunday fathers lurking awkwardly in the playground; only women ever came out, and of the large group of them, Carol and Natalie had found each other and become fast friends. Their daughters never really grew to like each other; Sara was so sensitive and shyly quick, Tina impulsive and loud. But still the mothers hung on, and over the years both got divorced, both reconfigured their lives. And now Natalie had experienced the worst possible thing a mother could experience, and she knew that Carol would come running.

Carol did, that evening. Held in the hospital for observation, Natalie lay lolling in a bed with rails. Carol arrived and held Natalie's hand and cried with her and told her that all the arrangements would be taken care of: the transportation of Sara's body, the burial, the works. Through the thin webbing of the sedative they had given her, Natalie announced to Carol that she wanted to die. She knew exactly how to do it, too; had read a book about it once, for macabre fun.

"You're not going to die," said Carol. "I won't let you. Listen to me, Natalie: *I won't let you.*"

In the morning a small, crisply appointed Indian physician appeared in the doorway. His name was Dr. Chatterjee, and he was from the Department of Psychiatry. *Lady Chatterjee's Lover,* Natalie thought to herself giddily as he stood over the bed. He announced that he understood Natalie had been in an accident, and that she had just lost her daughter in another accident. He wanted to ask her a few questions, in order to determine whether she was ready to be discharged tomorrow. Clearing his throat, he asked, "Can you tell me who the president is?"

She murmured the president's name, a man she did not trust but whom she had voted for nonetheless. Idly, she wondered if she would ever vote again. She couldn't imagine it ever mattering to her: the voting booth, with its silly curtain, seemed frivolous now, and her single vote ridiculous.

"And how old are you, Mrs. Swerdlow?" Dr. Chatterjee asked, a question that seemed to slap her in the face with its own insolence. She was old, but not too old; she would have a long way to go in life without her daughter.

"None of your business," she said sharply.

He behaved as though he hadn't heard, and blithely continued. "Listen to this expression," he said. " 'None are so blind as those who will not see.' Can you tell me its meaning?"

Natalie did not say anything, so after a moment Carol spoke. "Oh, that's an easy one," she said. "It refers to—"

"I was asking Mrs. Swerdlow," said the doctor, and at that point Natalie began to weep and could not find a way to stop.

"I see," Dr. Chatterjee said, clicking the button on his pen and replacing it in his pocket, and then he was gone from the room.

They kept Natalie in the hospital for one more day, transferring her to the psychiatric unit, where she sat among confused men and women in bathrobes, and skittish anorexic girls who refused to take their medication without first knowing its caloric content. Natalie stayed in a corner on an orange vinyl chair and cried, and although she freely admitted to Dr. Chatterjee that yes, she was probably suicidal, she was released in the morning.

Carol came to pick her up, gently shepherding her across the parking lot. "Look at you, sweetie," Carol said. "You're not ready to be out yet, are you? Well, tell that to your dumbass HMO. *They* think you're ready."

At Natalie's request, Carol drove her directly to the funeral home. She had decided to take a look at her daughter's body in the purplish light of that place, because if she didn't, she knew she would always wonder: Did Sara really die? Was it her on that table, or someone else entirely? Was the whole thing a grotesque mix-up, with Sara actually sneaking off to Japan, living in a house with rice-paper screens and sleeping on a tatami mat beside a devoted and elegant Japanese husband? So she looked, and what she saw was like a vision of Sara viewed through some sort of thick material. Death blurred what was once sharp; a face lost its singularity. Sara had somehow joined that pool of placid bodies who lay flat on tables, in morgues, in police snapshots, in the cradles of open caskets.

Back at home, Natalie sat at the table with her head down all afternoon. She thought of Sara sitting at this same table as a child, drinking juice from the collection of Flintstones jelly jars that Natalie still kept. Children loved juice; they lived on it, they were thirsty all the time. They wanted things to drink, to eat, to wear, to buy. They asked you for money, shaking you down for it, and you always gave. Their thirst never stopped; you marveled at its endurance.

The telephone rang often now and Carol answered it, speaking in a soft, worried voice in another room. Carol made burial arrangements; Natalie was aware of Carol speaking in an authoritative voice to someone at the mortuary. Sara's friends called too, wanting to know when the funeral was. But at Natalie's instruction, Carol told them there would be no formal funeral for Sara— just the body transported back here for a private family burial. Her friends were eager to come, of course, but it would have been too much for Natalie, all those people hovering, and so she said no; there would be a memorial at a later date, and they could all come then. They could play Sara's favorite depressing rock songs, and the movement from Mahler's Fifth that she liked so much. They could read aloud Japanese poems and reminisce about the first day they had met her at college. But Natalie could not tolerate any of that right now.

Ed Swerdlow flew in for the funeral from Dayton, where he practiced periodontics and lived with his dental-assistant second wife and their young children. He sobbed at the cemetery, even though his relationship with his daughter had been tenuous and vague at best. He hadn't been a terrible father—merely, like many men of his generation, a father who was in the dark when it came to the lives of girls. Over the years since the divorce, he had made handsome payments to Natalie and had dutifully come to visit Sara twice a year, bringing gifts that demonstrated his lack of knowledge of anything young and female. When Sara was thirteen, he had brought her a Miss Tussy Cologne and Makeup Kit, even though she and her friends had long been dabbing patchouli and ylang-ylang onto their wrists and getting ankle tattoos and smoking fat, damp joints in the parking lot behind the local Rite-Aid drugstore and hitchhiking home from school. Her father didn't have a clue, but it didn't really matter, for her mother was the primary parent, and her mother knew everything.

After the burial, the small group congregated at the house, eating the cheese Danish and the hard knots of rugelach that Carol had somehow found the time to buy, and speaking in shocked, muted voices. Later, when everyone was gone, Natalie knew that the only things left for her to contend with were infinite space and time; it was August, and most of Natalie's clients were already off on the vacations she had planned for them. Friends called, but no one could speak with any real authority or conviction.

Sara's friends kept phoning from the summer house: Adam, sobbing and apologizing and saying something incomprehensible about a raspberry pie, and Maddy, with a voice as soft and hesitant as a child's. She cried with them on the telephone, then at the end they all hung up, feeling no better. Some of Natalie's friends dropped by to hold her hand and bring fruit, then retreated meekly. Hard, shiny pears, apricots, and grapefruits as big as bowling balls littered her kitchen counters. Even Harvey Wise ambled in, mumbled and held her one last time, then fled. He said he was "no good with death." It frightened him, and he clearly wasn't up to being heroic with this woman he had slept with only once.

A fountain of coffee was continually brewed and served, and the house took on the aroma of one of those new coffee boutiques that had begun to pop up everywhere lately. After the first week of mourning, the volume of visitors diminished. Soon no one wanted coffee; soon it was just two tired women in this large house in a suburb that now seemed far from civilization.

It was Carol who suggested they go for a drive. Natalie hadn't been outside since the trip to the cemetery. She hadn't even gotten dressed, but had simply stayed in her nightgown, padding slowly around the house. But now Carol handed her a set of clothes which she dutifully donned, and combed her hair for her and walked her outside, where the sunlight struck Natalie as both pleasurable and deeply inappropriate. They went to Natalie's dented but intact car; Carol took the wheel.

"Where to, kiddo?" said Carol. "A movie, maybe? There's that thing at the sixplex with Brad Pitt as Disraeli."

But Natalie shook her head. "No," she said.

"Then where?" said Carol. "Come on, I'll take you any-where."

"Anywhere? Really?" asked Natalie.

"Yes. What did you have in mind?"

Natalie paused a moment before answering, and then she said, "The house."

"But the whole point was to get you *out* of the house for a while," said Carol.

"Not my house," said Natalie. "Sara's."

"What?" said Carol. "But why?"

"I don't know," said Natalie. "I just suddenly feel as though I'd like to see where she went every summer. To see the place, finally."

"Shouldn't we call first?" asked Carol.

Natalie shrugged, then quietly said, "I'm her mother."

The drive to the house seemed endless; Natalie felt like an impatient child needing distractions. She itched to change the radio station, even when a song came on that she liked. That was what death had done: It taken away the possibility of complex and sustained thought, leaving her simpleminded, with basic, constantly shifting needs. The only complex topic she could think about was her daughter's death, and that was too awful, so she shut her mind off, let it lie slack. She sometimes thought she could almost feel her mind sloshing around in its own pan of chemicals.

"Let's stop at the grocery store first," Natalie said, as they came to a massive Price Chopper. "You know kids, how they like to eat."

"They're hardly kids," Carol said, but then she knew enough not to say more. Sara, at least, would remain a "kid." She was not fully formed as an adult—the shell hadn't had time to harden. She would be a girl forever, and all of her adult traits would slowly be loosened from her, so that finally Natalie would imagine that she had lost a literal child—a preschooler drowned at a neighbor's pool, or an infant who had succumbed in the night to crib death. Natalie would join that large, unconnected club of mourning parents. They were easy to spot; they were the ones who looked like the living dead, wandering through shopping malls and the carpeted halls of offices where they worked. People gave them a wide berth when they passed to use the water cooler or the copy machine: *Step back—grieving mother coming through.*

Now, inside the supermarket, Natalie walked the wide, ice-cold aisles with a kind of wonder. "Look at this," she said, plucking from the shelves all sorts of junk food that she hadn't even known existed. These were the kinds of items that were always advertised during the Saturday morning cartoons. "Frooty Rollers," she read aloud, picking up a package of some fruit-flavored candy item that contained no actual fruit and appeared to be made of latex. "Now," she read, "in bright blue jazzberry flavor!"

"There is no such thing as a jazzberry," said Carol, disapproving. "And, as you know, this color blue does not exist in nature."

"For God's sake," said Natalie, "I'm not looking for nature here. I'm trying to buy them something they'll like."

She kept on like that, loading the cart with ranch-flavored chips and jumbo bags of red licorice. She realized that she did not know what sorts of things Sara's friends ate, in actuality, but actual food held no appeal to her, so how could it to *them*? This was novelty food; if you ate it, it was better than nothing, better than subsisting on air. From her perch by the register at this unfamiliar supermarket, the checkout woman in her green smock took a cursory look at the items on the belt and said, knowingly, "Houseful of teenagers?"

"Yes," said Natalie quickly. "That's right."

"I can't get mine to eat anything decent either," the woman went on, dragging each item over the price-code light buried under glass. "Kids today, their teeth rot in their heads, they kill themselves with drugs and I don't know what else." She shook her head, and Natalie shook hers too, momentarily enjoying the solidarity, enjoying being able to convey the impression that she, Natalie, still had a child. *Kids today,* she thought.

But she felt sorry for these "kids," these thirty-year-olds to whom she was bringing gifts of near-food. She had refused to let them come to the burial—it was too overwhelming to imagine them all there, standing in the sun and crying, and then she would have had to have them to the house afterward. But they had plagued her with phone calls, telling her of their sorrow, wanting her to know about it, and finally, today, she understood that their sorrow was real. So she would attempt to placate them with Frooty Rollers and other such things. Her arms full of shopping bags, she walked from the cool of the store into the startling heat of the parking lot. The blacktop felt spongy and soft in the heat.

"Natalie, wait up!" Carol said from somewhere behind her. Carol was a faithful friend who was becoming less relevant to this mission, Natalie thought as she loaded the trunk of the car with shopping bags. Carol hurried over to Natalie. "I'm here for you, you know," Carol said, but the comment was something of a non sequitur.

"No," said Natalie simply, "you're not." She closed the car door and let herself in the front passenger side.

"How can you say that?" Carol said, her voice getting shrill as she herself went around and opened the driver's door.

The two women faced each other in the little box of heat. "Because you still have a daughter, and I don't," Natalie said.

"Natalie, I *barely* have a child," Carol said. "I mean, let's face it, Tina is not exactly what I would have chosen."

Natalie stared. "How can *you* say that?" she asked.

Carol's remark reminded her that the world had divided, separating the devastated-by-loss from the untouched-by-loss. Carol had a daughter; her daughter had a heart that still beat inside her chest. It was true that Carol did not approve of Tina, and that while she claimed to love her, the love seemed founded more on ancient history (a Mary Cassatt vision of bathing a pink baby) than on anything that still lasted. For the pink-complected Mary Cassatt baby had turned into a large Doberman of a woman—a lesbian with a particular interest in self-defense issues. Tina ran a dojo near her home in Northampton, Massachusetts. Her hair had been sculpted into a brush cut, giving her the look of a handsome male pilot for a commercial airline. She seemed corporate, strong-jawed, and yet she lived outside the mainstream culture, in a small two-family house with an older woman named Ronnie, who taught feminist film criticism at a local college.

Who knew why children chose the paths they did? Why had Tina become a lesbian, and Sara been attracted to men? But why, too, was Tina in a committed, live-in relationship at thirty—a marriage, of sorts—while Sara, unattached, lived every summer among her college friends?

Carol had vowed to take care of Natalie, living with her during August and continuing to heat the array of international casseroles that the neighbors had delivered. But suddenly Natalie didn't want that sort of aid—she wanted to reject it, bitterly. It seemed unfair to hurt Carol's feelings, she who had done so much for her already. But chance had given them separate paths: the hectic, commuter's pace of the untouched-by-loss, and the slow, Thorazine shuffle of the devastated-by-loss.

Good-bye, Carol, good-bye, Natalie thought as they got back into the car. Suddenly she was in a hurry to get to the house of

Sara's friends. They were a mess, they had said on the telephone, and so was she. They could all be one big, unwieldy mess together.

Natalie buckled herself into the seat, making sure she heard the unambiguous click of the safety belt, and then they drove to the house without stopping.

3

The Friends of Sara Swerdlow

For three days and nights following the accident, Sara's sorrowing friends lived like squatters in the darkness of a tunnel. They fell easily into a pattern of drinking—repetitively lifting and lowering a glass to the mouth, something they had done in college and still knew how to do without much thought. In the rooms of the house they let themselves collectively fall. Down, down, down they went, to a place at the bottom where there was no light, just further thoughts about their friend and housemate Sara and how they would never see her again.

It was on day three that Maddy found herself up on the roof of the house with Adam. In the past, they would bring a boom box and a cooler of beer up here, and cover themselves with either a high-SPF lotion or a slick of melanoma-welcoming oil, then lie on towels spread on the slanting roof for much of the day, looking down on the tips of trees and the street, and the thin strip of ocean in the distance. But now, when staying in the house seemed intolerable, yet going out into the real world seemed even worse, Maddy and Adam—who had both been hit the hardest by the news—opened the hatch that led to the broad slope of shingled roof. Hoisting themselves up, they sat in the early morning light with the unbearable world beneath them. This was the first air they had gotten in three days; death, by nature, was an airless event.

Adam had been largely unhurt in the accident, and so had the young vacationing investment banker who had backed out of the driveway. They had stood in the road together with the police lights spinning and Sara in the car. Adam was sobbing and the banker clumsily tried to comfort him, but he was inconsolable. At the local hospital, a nurse asked if Adam "wanted something," and he swallowed a tiny orange pill gratefully. He cracked his knuckles and paced the small room they had put him in, waiting for the pill to take effect and his friends to arrive.

"Remember her voice," said Adam softly now, not a question. Sara's voice had been unusual, a smoky, laughing voice; she was much smarter than the voice might let you believe. Hers was the voice of a beautiful waitress in cutoffs at a cowboy bar, someone you would always have a good time with.

"And remember the song?" said Maddy. "Her backwards song? She sang it that first night at college, as we lay there in that little room in the dark. It was so weird, and I loved her immediately." Now Maddy began to sing the backwards version of "Tears on My Pillow" that Sara used to sing: "Uoy t'nod rebmemer em / Tub I rebmemer uoy / Ti t'nsaw gnol oga / uoy ekorb ym traeh ni owt . . ."

Adam closed his eyes. The bruises on his arm had already faded from the dark plum color of a fresh accident to a paler, less alarming denim. He had been spared in the accident, "miraculously," people tended to say, although if he had been on the driver's side *she* would have been spared, not him. If he had been driving it would be his voice that would be missed, not that sweet, reedy voice of Sara's, remembered for having sung a backwards song in the middle of the night.

"I know that life will simply *go on* without her," Maddy said, "but I also know that I am going to be different now. I'm not sure how, but it's already happened." She reached into her pocket and took out a crush-proof pack of cigarettes, aware, as she did, that there was a total absence of wind up there on the roof. The morning was calm, utterly still, as if poised on the edge of something. She handed a cigarette to Adam and he took it, even though he had never been known to smoke. It didn't matter; identifying traits were no longer reliable. Anyone could do anything now, and no one would be surprised.

They sat on the roof and smoked for a while. "Why didn't her mother let us come?" said Adam suddenly. "That's the thing I don't understand. I know there'll be a memorial service eventually, but I wanted to go to the cemetery."

"On the phone her friend said it was private, just for family," said Maddy. "Apparently, Sara's mother is having some sort of nervous breakdown, and she didn't want anyone else around to see. I can understand that, can't you?"

Adam shrugged. "She never liked me," he said lightly. "She thought I was preventing Sara from falling madly in love with some straight guy. But that's not what prevented her."

"No," said Maddy. "She just hadn't met that perfect straight man yet."

"I don't even know if she wanted that," said Adam. "Anyway, you're the only woman in North America with the perfect straight man," said Adam. "Other than Peter, it's slim pickings. Look at who she went out with—that record-label lawyer, and that creepy professor, and that guy *Sloan.*" They both sneered slightly at the idea of Sloan, and Maddy became aware that no man would have gotten past their sarcasm and contempt; in their minds, no one was acceptable for Sara. "We were talking about men right before the crash," Adam went on. "How we'd both probably be dissatisfied with them for our entire lives."

"You've got Shawn here with you," said Maddy. "Isn't he at all satisfying?"

"Oh, Shawn," said Adam. "What we have with each other, it's not love. I invited him out here for the weekend, and the whole thing was like a game of musical chairs in which he happened to be here when Sara was killed. So now he's simply *here* in the middle of everything." He shrugged, letting some ash flutter from his cigarette over the side of the house. "He's very handsome," he said. "But I don't want handsome anymore. I don't want anything. Sara and I were laughing, both of us, and listening to the radio. Van Morrison was playing," he continued, "and we were happy because here it was the start of another August." Suddenly Adam tossed his cigarette over the side of the house and stood up, wobbly on the incline.

"Sit down," said Maddy, "you're scaring me."

"Oh, what's the point?" said Adam. "I don't even like anyone else. No offense," he added quickly. "She was my best friend in the world, Maddy. You don't generally get any new best friends after thirty. This is it; it's over now." They looked at each other in the morning light, these two rumpled people who had never felt great affection for each other, these two people whose connective tissue was Sara Swerdlow.

"She was my best friend too," Maddy said. "But I'm not going to break my neck falling off the roof for her. Sit the fuck down, Adam." And obediently, he did.

LATER, BACK inside the house, Duncan fussed in Maddy's arms and opened and closed his mouth like a chick's. It was astonishing to Maddy that even now, the baby still needed food. She took a swig of vodka from a mug, then opened her blouse and let her breast spring out like a jack-in-the-box. While he drank milk, she drank vodka; it was the only way they could get through this terrible time. Her breasts still filled and emptied, even though Sara was dead; this fact was astonishing, but it was also a relief. As she looked down at the top of Duncan's head, the place where the bones didn't quite join, she thought of how fragile he was, and what a mistake it had been to bring him into the world. She was now terrified of something happening to him; when he slept in his Portacrib, she started at the receiver of the infant monitor, hypnotized by watching the red lights rise and fall with his breathing.

She remembered how, the moment Duncan was born, Peter had turned to her, his expression clearly overwhelmed and inconsolable, although he later claimed he had been merely happy. "This is my *son!*" he'd explained, and he'd gone on to insist that apparently all men felt a particular sensation of being overcome when their wives delivered a boy.

Lately Peter hovered over her again, as much a useless appendage as he had been during labor, when he had lurked in the background of the delivery room, a stooping, somewhat useless figure in green scrubs and silly paper clown shoes. He seemed useless right now, too, for although he had been crying and drinking constantly since the crash, he hadn't been terribly close to Sara; she was Maddy's friend, not his, and Peter had never even seemed to like her. But still, Peter was drinking along with everyone and crying and shaking his head in somber, inarticulate shock. So, for that matter, was Shawn, who had had no relationship with Sara at all—having only just met her the night she was killed. It became a house of drunks, the air itself taking on that familiar bad-breath stink of drinking.

The only thing that saved them from falling into total disaster, Maddy thought now, as Duncan tugged rhythmically and gratingly at her left nipple, was the fact that there was a baby in the house. Duncan had his clockwork needs, regardless of anything that was going on around him, and he forced you to turn away from your sorrow and pay attention to him.

"I know people always say this, and it doesn't make any sense," said Maddy as they all lay around the living room, "but the thing I can't get over is that we just saw her. She was right here, sitting beside me on this couch, and we were discussing what we were going to do tomorrow—and then we were talking about other things, like her work. She showed me all these World War Two propaganda cartoons she'd collected, of buck-toothed, slanty-eyed evil Japanese people. She just knew so much about the war, about history, and it reminded me of how little I know about everything."

"You know a lot," Peter said reflexively.

"Oh, right," she said. "Every dull fact they taught me in law school. And all about breastfeeding. Those are my two pathetic areas of expertise. Sara was the one who knew things," she said. "And I just can't believe this has happened to her." And then her voice broke up once again into a new round of sobs.

Peter rubbed Maddy's shoulders and clasped her lightly in his arms. "It's like that joke," he said after a long moment. "Descartes walks into a bar, and the bartender asks him, 'Would you like a drink?' And Descartes says, 'I think not,' and then he disappears." He paused, adding, "She just *disappeared.*"

No one laughed. Finally Maddy said, "I can't believe you're making a joke now."

"I'm sorry," he said. "I don't know what I'm supposed to say."

"Then just say nothing" she said, and the subtext was that Sara had been her close friend, not his, and that he ought to shut up forever. *At least I have Duncan,* Maddy thought. For she could go to her baby and bury her face in his sweet neck; it was a simple and uncomplicated act. Everything was much more complicated with Peter. Maddy had often discussed her husband intimately with Sara; such talk tempered the whole exclusionary experience of marriage, made it feel less lonely.

"You don't know what it's like, living with someone year after year," Maddy had said one summer, as she and Sara went for a walk along the weedy dunes of the local beach. They were smoking and walking, two best friends, one beautiful, the other less so. "He leaves the toilet seat up," Maddy went on. "He plays his old obnoxious CDs early in the morning. He lifts these weights and leaves them laying around where I can trip on them. And he's *male*. And therefore, I don't think he understands women. That's the main thing."

"You know, it's too bad that we're not lesbians," Sara had said, "because then we could be together all the time and be totally devoted."

"Yes," Maddy had agreed, "it's too bad," and as she spoke a man ran past on the sand with a dog. His chest was bare, gleaming and hairless. His legs had a golden summer fur on them, and as he and his dog raced by he glanced over at Sara and smiled.

"You see," said Sara, "we need that around." She included Maddy in the moment of male appreciation, although what the moment was really about was Sara and this man on the beach, who appreciated her right back. When men were interested in you, they made you feel you had something unique and unbearably exciting. Men winced with pleasure at the sight of a woman undressing. Even Maddy, whose body was imperfect, whose breasts had always seemed to her balloonishly large, had caused several men to wince and moan and nearly seem on the verge of having their eyes roll up in their heads. Peter had been that way the first time they slept together and he still was that way, to a lesser extent.

Sara had been very encouraging when Peter first showed an interest in Maddy back at Wesleyan, and after their first unofficial "date" (no one called it that), Maddy rushed to Sara's dorm room to provide a blow-by-blow account. When Maddy and Peter moved into an attic apartment with sloping ceilings off-campus, Sara grew closer to Adam by default, turning to him for the late-night companionship and availability that Maddy could no longer provide. Sara and Adam found they loved being together; what had started out as a consolation-prize friendship quickly transformed into something very satisfying. Now Maddy suddenly didn't know how she could stay married to Peter without having Sara to bounce everything off of. She suddenly didn't know how she could do much of anything without Sara.

All the reading they had done in college, all the Jung and Thomas Merton and Elisabeth Kübler-Ross, all the high holidays spent neatly dressed in synagogues or churches with their families, all the Junior Year Abroad visits to Chartres to see the stained glass and reflect on the passage of time, and all the long, bloated, free-associative conversations they had taken part in over the years about the subjects of death, rebirth, and the nature of the spirit-self—none of it helped now.

No one slept much those first days after the accident; instead, they moved from living room to kitchen, where they sat around the table, opening bottles and pouring drinks. Mrs. Moyles may have been a terrible housekeeper, but she had a cabinet impressively stocked with partially empty scotch and vodka and brandy bottles, the liquids at different levels, like the collection of a musician who taps out tunes on bottles with a spoon. They cried for a long, long time in unbroken, phlegmy sobs, and they muttered and embraced. They cried and drank, except for Shawn, who mostly just drank. Eventually the alcohol seemed to stopper the crying. There were whimpers, and mumbling, and then they actually resumed talking.

"Oh, why did I want ice cream for that raspberry pie?" said Adam at three in the morning, drunk as he hadn't been since his bar mitzvah reception, when his cousins carried him on their shoulders and he sang "Hava Nagila" and "Bridge Over Troubled Water" in off-key abandon. "It would have been perfectly fine without it."

"It's not your fault," everyone chorused.

"I always thought," said Adam after a while, "that Sara and I were going to know each other for a very long time, probably well into our eighties. It seems so ridiculous now, so *optimistic,* but I never even considered the fact that we might not get old together. At least not after I had my HIV test. Before I got tested, I thought maybe it would be *me* who would die when I was young, me who would leave her, all because I once got fucked without a condom by some moron named Warren, some *exercise instructor* who ran a class on the *QE2*. He bored me to death, comparing the *QE2* with the *Princess* line." He paused. "Why am I talking about this?" he said. "There's nothing that's appropriate to talk about; it all seems indecent."

They all agreed that talk was indecent, and then they sat in silence for the next hour, the only sounds coming from the play of ice in their glasses, and Duncan gurgling and chirping in his obliviousness. Sometime in the night, it was decided that they would all leave the house. No one wanted to stay there for the summer, continuing their hellish descent in these dingy little rooms. But, as Peter pointed out, there still remained the inevitable, sheepish question of whether they would get their money back if they left.

"Was that awful of me to mention the money?" Peter asked Maddy when they climbed into bed at dawn. Across the room, the baby now breathed softly in the downy depths of his Portacrib.

"No," said Maddy. "It's not awful. But I don't want to talk about money anymore." She lay against the stiff, camphorous pillow. In other summers, this room had felt both terrible and comfortable, and she had always loved it; being here offered a kind of sameness, a suspension in what was familiar. But without Sara, suddenly everything felt strangely unknown.

The two women had known each other as children, attending the same all-girls summer camp in the Adirondacks, where they sat around a bonfire at night and sang the lyrics to the Camp Ojibway song: "We will always be true to Ojibway / No matter if we're young or old / We will always be true to Ojibway / No matter if we're meek or bold . . ." There, among a sea of cunning, slightly nasty campers who competed to the death during color war, they recognized a similarity, a shared type of intelligence.

"You read all the time," Sara had said to her in the bunk one afternoon, and what had seemed to be an accusation was in fact a compliment. "I do, too," she added.

"Really?" said Maddy.

"Yes," said Sara. Then she said proudly, "Right now, I'm reading Rilke's *Letters to a Young Poet*."

Maddy was suitably impressed; Sara was not only popular, she was smart too, a combination that was unusual. Whenever Sara walked across the lawn at camp, other girls stopped her to discuss their problems. From a distance, you could see another girl looking pinched with unhappiness, and Sara leaning close to her in concern.

Under trees and by the darkening lake at dusk, the two girls talked about the other campers in exhaustive detail, making lists of those they liked and those they despised. "Erica Engels," said Sara, "is fat on the outside, and extremely pathetic at first glance, but I think we should pay special attention to her. I wouldn't be surprised if one day she became a neurosurgeon, or even Secretary of State." Maddy nodded, impressed by Sara's powers of observation.

"And what about Susan Lottman?" she asked Sara. "Evil incarnate, right?"

"Right," said Sara. "Just because she can dive well, and her father practically owns Clinique, she thinks she's so special. But keep an eye on her. I think she's big trouble; I can sense it in my bones. She'll probably end up in prison for grand larceny, or worse." Maddy nodded, contented at the knowing intimacy of these conversations.

Camp Ojibway was filled with rich girls from Manhattan, children of divorce who flounced around the bunk, speaking either in code or in perfect conversational French. Maddy was part of a group of semi-outcasts, a handful of city girls whose families lived in identical high-rise rental apartments with porous walls and low, stippled ceilings. Girls who understood, through the haze of pain native to girlhood, that eventually all this would pass, and that if they waited long enough, the rich, stupid girls would falter and topple, and the brainy, off-kilter girls would inherit the earth. Sara was not in Maddy's social group; she was too pretty for that, but she truly liked Maddy and admired her. The attention was flattering and unnerving. When you were with Sara, boys from Camp Iroquois across the lake stopped and hung around you, angling to engage in pointless, arch conversations. Friendship with Sara gave Maddy great pleasure but also instilled in her a budding feeling of despair. Getting dressed for a swim at camp, she would catch a flash of Sara's smooth, white back that arched as gracefully as a seahorse, and she would think: *I hate myself.*

Over the years, Sara and Maddy attempted to top each other's intimate accounts of self-loathing. There was a requisite, mutual flirtation with bulimia in the late teens, and a period devoted to reading Anne Sexton and Sylvia Plath exclusively. And always, along the way, there were excruciating tales of boys. Later, both of them wound up at Wesleyan, where they met the two men who would become central to their lives: Adam and Peter. It had surprised Maddy when Peter showed a real interest in her; he was better-looking than the men who usually liked her. He was better-looking than she was, a shirtless campus Frisbee player with tanned, hairy legs, someone who flirted easily with women. He was handsome yet slightly lost—almost homeless-seeming, in a way—and so he wasn't intimidating in the way of many good-looking men. Sara had encouraged Maddy, telling her she clearly had an esteem problem and that Peter would be *lucky* to go out with her. So Maddy had been bolder than usual, surprising him by looking him over in a way that was more than playful. He responded by looking back, his eyebrows lifting, setting off something lightly percussive inside her: a quick pulse, a drumbeat signifying some strange and improbable pleasure ahead. Soon they were a campus couple, the whole transaction having taken place as quietly and discreetly as a drug deal. She didn't really know what he saw in her, although Sara said there was much to see. "You're lovely!" Sara had said. "Don't you know that by now?" Actually, Maddy thought of herself as an extremely *decent* person, and pretty in a somewhat dull, wildflower-patterned-dress-wearing way. But she was devoted to Peter, even when he seemed distracted, inattentive, off in a nebula of abstract thoughts that didn't include her. Maddy, Peter, Adam, and Sara hung around a pizza place near campus late at night, and spent hours on the deep, springless couches of the library lounge during the reading period before exams.

After college, Maddy and Peter lived in a terrible railroad apartment in New York City—she starting law school, he teaching ninth grade at a public high school—and Sara began what would be a long chain of unfulfilling relationships with men. The men were of the sort that had usually been unavailable to Maddy—handsome in a sculptural way, or perhaps very powerful.

What was sex with these men like? Maddy knew she would never get the answer from personal experience. She and Peter had settled into a pattern of frequent and mostly ordinary sex; they had their gasping orgasms: first her, then him, each of them skittering across the finishing line, and then someone would wash up or get a glass of water, and then they would lie in bed for a while, perhaps picking up the remote control to see what was on television, perhaps not. It was pleasurable but not thrilling. Somewhere else, Maddy knew, Sara was probably wrapping her long and enveloping legs around a brooding, worldly man, practically bringing him to tears with pleasure. Now Sara would never have a baby, would never even get married, would never experience the natural arc of life that everyone assumed was their birthright.

Maddy and Peter rustled and turned in bed, and across the room, as if in synchrony, so did the baby. Down the hall, Adam and Shawn rustled and turned too. Despite the tragedy, the entire household was moving softly in preparation for sleep; there was no choice. Finally, before morning arrived, everyone slept. The house fell silent for a while until suddenly there was a series of creaks and oddly heavy, stumbling footsteps that seemed close by. Maddy and Peter woke at the same time and lay listening, puzzled and a little scared. Then Peter got up and opened the door, and there in the hall they saw Adam, wandering around in the dark and trying doorknobs. First he opened the bathroom and peered in, then he went into the linen closet. It was as though he was looking for something, but he seemed strange, clumsier than usual.

"Adam?" said Peter. "Are you okay?" But Adam barely heard him. He had pulled open the door of Sara's room and was walking right in. "Adam?" Peter said again, but it was pointless. Behind Peter came Maddy and Shawn, who was naked to the waist, the hair on his head standing up in sleep-clumps.

"What's going on?" Shawn asked nervously. "I woke up and he was gone. Then I heard this weird stomping around."

"He's sleepwalking," said Peter. They all looked at Adam, who was now yawning the open-mouthed yawn of a child, then climbing up onto the bed Sara Swerdlow had slept in every August, his head on her pillow.

4

With Sara

Mrs. Hope Moyles spent every August in Virginia, visiting her sister Verna. Both women had long been widowed, and their children never came around anymore, so once again, as it had been in childhood, they had each other.

That had always been the thing about Hope's house: although it wasn't very nice, she could rent it out in August and make enough money to help her get through the winter. Who would have predicted this, so many years ago when she and her husband had bought the place? The island had always been rigidly stratified: Rich summering families had their mansions on the water, and everyone else—lobstermen, policemen, plumbers—had their small houses and neat quarter-acres of land. The summer people fled on Labor Day, packing up their cars and leaving behind noth-

ing but the occasional abandoned inner tube. Everyone else stayed
on all year, the regular local folk and a few eccentric types, writers
and painters and the like, who decided that the beach was the
place to be all winter. The children all attended the public school
with its unvarying line-up of teachers: Miss Hill, Mrs. Cullen, and
Miss Manzino. For the rest of the year the wind blew hard across
the island, and the sky darkened early. In summer, though, the
children were set free, and they swam and ran and crabbed and
came home with sudden blond, beach-baked heads of hair. One
summer, the island no longer seemed to belong to them; it
belonged to the rich people with their big houses and their own
children, who came to the beach with snorkels and expensive
sound systems and suntan lotions that smelled of coconut and
vanilla. Then other people followed, less rich but still privileged,
renting anything they could grab, and soon all of the Moyles's
friends were letting strangers stay in their unexceptional houses
for shocking sums of money, and taking their own families off to
Jersey until Labor Day, struck dumb by this new good luck. So
Hope and Jack Moyles did the same, and the money was so good
each year that they came to count on it.

When Jack died, Hope continued to rent out the house with
more urgency than ever. As a widow she had taken up the hobby
of drinking, and she liked to spend her money on good vodka and
gin that she purchased at Springs Liquors. Every year the same
group came to the house: odd young people from the city who
paid through the nose for use of her appalling little home. Why
they wanted the house she couldn't imagine; she just hoped they
were decent. Decency was important to her. But money, that was
the main thing.

So when one of them, the girl with the halting voice, called
Hope at her sister's house a few days into the month to tell her a
horrible story about how the other girl in the house had been
killed, and that they were all an emotional wreck, and was there
any way they could have their money back, Hope was stunned.

She had been drinking before the call, and her response was slow and suspicious. She wondered if such a terrible story could really be true. How low would they stoop to get their money back? Had they finally decided that her house was too disgusting, even for them? Maybe the waterbugs were back, with their delicate cilia, appearing out of nowhere against the porcelain of the bathtub, like someone's misplaced false eyelashes. Or maybe it was the septic tank backing up, making the house smell like a bathroom in a bus station; it had to be something bad to make them tell such an outrageous tale.

"It's the waterbugs, am I right?" she asked, her voice rising. "Or maybe you saw a bat. A waterbug won't kill you, neither will a bat. Bats may look ugly as heck with those ears and pointy teeth, but they're perfectly harmless."

"Excuse me, Mrs. Moyles," said the girl. "I don't know what you're talking about."

"You can't have your money back," said Hope. "You just can't. We have an agreement. It's all legal. I can't just rent the house to someone else at this late date. I'm down here with my sister until Labor Day. I'm sorry; I can't give you back your money."

There was silence, and then the girl quietly said good-bye, and Hope returned to her drink. She drank throughout the hot afternoon, and at some point she began wondering uneasily if perhaps it might be true about that car accident after all, but she didn't do anything about it. Those kids had the house until Labor Day, and nothing would change that.

MADDY AND Peter went out to the beach early the following Monday morning, hoping that the sunlight might make them feel partly human again. Maddy sat quietly and rubbed lotion into Peter's back; he never used actual sun block like you were supposed to, just some sweet-smelling, unprotective cream. As a result, he tanned beautifully, and by Labor Day he would always return to the city with dark skin and a head of golden hair, and the female teachers at his school and even some of the students would flirt with him openly.

His wife was moving her hands in concentric circles across his back, and he felt safe with her hands on him. He had always felt safe around a certain kind of woman. When he had first met Maddy at Wesleyan, she lived off-campus in a feminist cooperative often referred to as "Dyke House," and so he assumed she was not interested in men. But then, one night at a party, it seemed to him that she was flirting, being provocative, fingering the sleeve of his shirt and saying she needed to buy a Christmas present for her father, and where had he bought this shirt? The next day he took her to the sad, faded men's store in Middletown where he had bought it. She wasn't a lesbian at all, had never even dabbled with a female friend to the late-night strains of k.d. lang during the stress of final exams. She was a feminist who volunteered at the local rape hotline, and clearly she was interested in men. In *him*. So they went back to Dyke House together later that day, walking past the authentic lesbians who sat playing poker and reading Jacques Derrida in the living room, and they went upstairs to Maddy's room, where she removed her onyx earrings and placed them on a square of cotton in a little box like tiny dolls being put to sleep, then she climbed into bed. The removal of the earrings made Peter think of the ways in which women were so tender, so heartbreaking, and why men needed them so badly. A woman would remove her earrings for you, and she would spread suntan lotion across your back in tiny, feathery circles for the rest of your life.

They had gotten married in a small suburban ceremony when they were twenty-five. They were the first to go, the first to formalize their love. It was a shocking betrayal to their friends, like suddenly becoming Republicans after years of leftist leafleting and vocal contempt for the rich white men who ran the country. They were saying good-bye to the group rituals of nights spent in a bare-bones club in the East Village, and listening to Peter's over-amplified band, Disgruntled Postal Workers, and to the drunken sing-alongs around Adam's piano, and, most of all, to the mix-and-match aspect of sex that gave it spontaneity and surprise.

These days, you could wait as long as you liked to get married, and no one thought you were peculiar; you didn't even have to get married at all. But they wanted to, Maddy and Peter, partially out of love, partially out of a shared terror of the world and all its dangers. The world *was* dangerous, Peter now knew, thinking of Sara. He sat with his wife's hands painting circles on his bare back, and his thoughts turned to Sara, and to their long and complicated friendship. Peter could never understand why a girl as beautiful as Sara would spend so much of her time with a gay man. But a lot of women did; maybe it was safe for them, safer than the despicable charms of so many straight men. Women were always telling stories of how certain men had left them ragged and lifeless; the litany of complaints had the quality of a country-and-western song. Adam Langer had no interest in hurting women, and he truly seemed to sympathize with them. Yet Peter had always secretly felt irritated that Adam was gay and couldn't love Sara sexually, the way she needed to be loved. Peter twisted the circumstances around until he had almost convinced himself that Adam could have been straight if he'd really wanted to. He could have loved Sara if he'd been less selfish, less involved with theater, less in love with his own sensitive childhood, which had taken place in the franchise-studded wilds of Long Island, but which, over years of telling anecdotes about it, he had turned into something out of Truffaut: the misunderstood schoolboy with short pants and a phallic baguette under his arm and a sweet, pouting face.

If Peter could have loved Sara, he would have. Had he been free, had he not met Maddy at such a young age and sealed his fate, he might have pursued Sara strenuously, the way he had pursued very few women in his life. He had never actually needed to *pursue* Maddy at all; early on it became clear how approachable and willing she was. They liked the same kind of books and movies, they enjoyed each other's company; even their parents enjoyed each others' company. So, much to their friends' shock and displeasure, they settled into a facsimile of married life well before they actually got married.

But after they were officially hitched, Peter still thought of Sara from time to time, imagining her as his lover. He never actually cheated on Maddy in these images, but simply cast her as the one who had broken up with *him,* leaving him for another man. In his daydreams he pictured himself as the eternally wronged party, the sad loser who wandered lonely as a cloud for months, until one day Sara consoled him with mulled cider in front of a fire (Whose fire? No one he knew had a fireplace. But this was the nature of fantasies) until they both became so aroused that they reached for each other at the same moment, mouths colliding and clothes unfurling.

The reality, when it actually happened, was very different. He and Maddy had been married for a year, and she went off to London for six weeks as part of an exchange program her law firm ran with a solicitor's office. Maddy's friends took turns asking him to dinner, as though a man left to fend for himself would shrivel up and die of malnutrition.

One night it was Sara's turn to feed and nourish him. She invited him to her gloomy apartment on the periphery of the Columbia campus, where, as in his fantasies, a benign conversation on a couch led right to a kiss, which astonished both of them equally. He thought of Maddy in London; it was the middle of the night across the Atlantic, and she was certainly sleeping, her contact lenses taken out and floating in tiny pools of saline, leaving her pinkly hamster-eyed and almost blind, lying in bed in some dowdy nightshirt, the kind of asexual item she enjoyed wearing when Peter wasn't around: football jerseys or oversized shirts advertising a beer or rock band. Maddy slept with her mouth slightly open, scenting the air with middle-of-the-night breath, the kind of breath only a lover could love. He did love her, but when he thought of her in London, vulnerable in sleep to the perils of dowdiness—she who during waking hours was certainly pretty—he felt indifferent to her sexually, almost cold.

Sara, however, made him almost scream in sexual delight, and when he first kissed her he felt himself becoming twined to her in ropes of excitement and horror. Hands slipped easily under clothes. She reached down and began to open his button-fly jeans, then lowered his shorts and opened and lowered her own pants, pressing him against her. He was poised at the edge, his penis resting inside her. He shifted position, rocking toward and away from her, and he had an orgasm so quickly that it was like adolescence all over again, a time in his life when he couldn't control himself, and when managing sex seemed beyond him, like trying to catch an orb of mercury as it changed shape and slid away. But Sara herself came quickly, with an abbreviated scream. He lay with her full-length on the sofa, and the heat began to come in through the heavy antique radiator near their heads. As the steam pushed into the room, it served as a vapor that made them both unbearably frightened at what they had just done.

"I want you to know that I can't do this again," Sara said, looking up at him. "I'd never be able to live with it. I mean, I *love* Maddy. I'd have to kill myself. I'd have to commit seppuku, like Mishima did."

"I can't do it either," said Peter. He looked away and discreetly slipped out of her. "At least we're in agreement," he added, rearranging himself in his clothes.

"I know this doesn't excuse it, but I've just been so incredibly lonely," said Sara, and suddenly she was in tears. "You have no idea of what it's like, being a graduate student and spending all your nights in a university library trying to read Japanese. The Japanese letters are so tiny," she said. "I'm going blind looking at them, and the librarian *hates* me, she thinks I hog the Xerox machine. And it's not as though the Japanese are exactly a welcoming bunch; I mean, you probably have this image of bonsai trees and beautiful tea ceremonies and haiku, but really, it's usually not like that. Did you know that some of the women in Japan read comic books about how wonderful it is to be raped? I swear, you can see secretaries on the subway totally engrossed in them. They've been oppressed by men for so long that they've eroticized the oppression. There's actually a popular comic book out there called *Penetrate Me with Violence, Stranger!* And another one is called *I Deserve to Be Beaten Like a Mangy Cur.* And the men in Japan, a lot of them are these type-A technocrats and almost nobody cares about literature. I have no future at all." She paused, then added, "I deserve to be beaten like a mangy cur."

"Oh, it can't be that bad, can it?" he asked her, his arm clumsily patting her back.

"Sometimes," said Sara, "when I see you and Maddy together, I actually feel angry, and as though something must be wrong with me. I want to know why I can't have something like you have. Why I have to waste my time with these different men who never make me happy, and never will. But each time I meet one, I act like maybe this time I might feel contented, maybe this time it just might work. But it doesn't, of course—*duh*—and I have to wonder: Is it because I'm too close to Adam, like my mother says I am, and it scares straight men away, or is it maybe because I'm too close to my crazy *mother?*"

"Your mother's not really crazy, is she?" asked Peter. "I thought you two were close."

"Well, we are and we aren't," said Sara. "I've let it drag on, this whole suffocating mother-daughter thing. You know, 'Surrender, Dorothy,' and telling each other every intimate detail from each waking hour. I'm sick of it, actually, and I wish there were a few more boundaries, you know? But it's not so easy. For a long time, it was just the two of us. And now she's all alone." Sara paused, then added, "And I guess I am, too. I can't imagine what it would be like to be married, to have this intense intimacy only with the person you're married to. Right now, half the time it's like I'm married to my mother, and the other half it's like I'm married to Adam."

"Real marriage is extremely complicated," Peter said, attempting to add an extra layer to what he had in his marriage, to spread some darkness between himself and his wife in order to justify the fact that he had been poking around under Sara Swerdlow's clothing, and even, briefly, inside her.

"Complicated how?" asked Sara. "I understand the concept only in an abstract way."

He stalled for a moment. "All marriages take infinite patience and hours of labor," said Peter, winging it. "It's not as though you can just say, 'Okay, we're married, *bingo,*' and have it all be terrific. It takes maintenance, sometimes high maintenance. When you're married, you wonder if the other person is actually right for you, and if maybe, in some other place on the globe—in an igloo in Alaska, maybe—there's not someone who'd make you happier."

"Oh, yeah," said Sara, "you and the Eskimo girls would really have a lot to talk about. You could discuss the three hundred different words for snow. Come on, Peter, admit it. You know you and Maddy are right for each other. You made a good choice, both of you."

And he had to sigh and admit that in fact they were well-matched. Even after this brief moment of adultery, he could not find anything critical to say about his wife. She took care of him and was intelligent and pretty, and she gave him back rubs of infinite duration; she loved him more than any Eskimo girl ever would. He left Sara's apartment soon after; she had spent half the afternoon preparing a Japanese dinner for them, complete with hand-rolled maki and a delicate broth that smelled uncannily like his mother's Obsession perfume, but neither of them wanted to eat. They wanted to be away from each other and to turn this event into something that just hadn't happened. He shuffled out of her apartment with his collar up, his head bent down against the wind, like a married man leaving the house of his lover—which she barely was. Nothing profound had happened today, Peter insisted to himself as he walked south on Broadway; he had dipped into Sara Swerdlow for a moment, and it really didn't count for much.

Still, he continued to experience a persistent reflex of guilt. When Maddy returned from London, Peter behaved strangely at first. He was distant and mumbling with her, and blamed it on the weeks they had been apart, saying something about how they'd have to get used to each other again. He and Sara never spoke of their "incident." A short time later, Sara was planted on their living room couch with her feet up, laughing and drinking seltzer with his wife. He came into the room cautiously. The two women had a friendship that went back so far into the past; it was much more stirring and meaningful than what had happened between Peter and Sara.

So his relationship with Sara became one of cordiality and all-round wariness, and sometimes Maddy complained that he and Sara seemed to dislike each other, a fact that made her unhappy, so he worked on lifting the wariness and taking the weight of it elsewhere. He laughed when he was with Sara, trying to enjoy her graduate school and bad-men anecdotes, her humor, but his response was always forced. And in time, all the images from their moment together began to recede—the heat of her skin under his cool, big hands, his breath coming heavy, her hair smelling of some assertively female shampoo—and once again she became simply his wife's best friend.

And there she stayed, fixed in that safe place until her death. Now, after a long, uninterrupted time of willed amnesia, it all suddenly returned to him with a vengeance, and he wanted Sara back and mourned her in some fierce, possessive way, as though he had loved her all these years.

5

The Visitor

The two women emerged from the car, blinking in the shock of light and heat. They had traveled all the way from New Jersey with the air conditioner on high, and here they were, standing in front of a surprisingly shabby mustard-colored house in the middle of a summer vacation enclave. They made their approach side by side, carrying sacks of junk-food groceries, and heard strains of cacophonous music coming from behind the door with its ill-fitting screen.

"Yoo-hoo!" called Carol.

Maddy came to the door in a sundress, squinting through the screen. "Mrs. *Swerdlow*?" she said, astonished. "Oh my God, come in!" The women hugged in a bony, clumsy way, then both began to cry, as they had done once over the telephone since Sara died, and had continued to do separately since then. Right behind

Maddy appeared Peter, and then Adam, and soon all of them were in an embrace, muttering and crying and attached to one another like some ungainly organism.

"Well, kids," said Natalie finally, pulling back slightly and attempting a trembling, breaking smile, "I was in the neighborhood." She held out one of the bags from the supermarket. "And I brought you a few things."

AT NIGHT, when the beach emptied except for a few people with the same unoriginal childhood memories of twilight campfires and fat potatoes roasted in tinfoil, Adam and Natalie sat on beach chairs at the top of a small dune. He sat peeling the cellophane off a Frooty Roller. The candy was so sweet it hurt his jaw, and although he would never have eaten such an item under any other circumstances, it would have been rude to refuse Natalie's offerings. Besides, the more he ate, the more he felt that, in some peculiar way, he required this influx of sugar; it was like those people who ate handfuls of sand or dirt or paint chips, because their bodies seemed to require the minerals contained obscurely within.

He didn't know what to say to Sara's mother; he had never particularly liked her, and had always understood that she disapproved of his friendship with Sara. Adam and Natalie had always been cordial, but never at ease. And now he and Sara's mother discussed the death scene, blow by blow. At least Sara had been driving and not him, Adam thought, because otherwise Natalie would hate him forever. He had talked to her about the accident on the telephone, his voice halting and breathless, but now, in person, she wanted an unabridged version.

"I just want to hear it again," she said. "From the start."

So he told her again about the Fro-Z-Cone stand, and the car that had obliviously backed out into the road, crashing into the driver's side of their car—Sara's side. Natalie nodded and cried, and the way she cried reminded him of the way Sara used to cry, with a kind of intensity and implicit violence buried under the civilized exterior. He wondered suddenly if Natalie might hit him, the way women sometimes hit men in movies when they were upset, pummeling them with a fusillade of fists, the men passively receiving the blows. He had always been intimidated by Sara's mother; she was formidable, with her tight body and constantly appraising eyes. Or maybe he was just intimidated by overtly sexual women in general. In high school, he had done a perfunctory amount of kissing with a girl in his homeroom named Steffi, but he had barely touched her breasts; instead he had simply grazed them in frozen acknowledgment.

But it wasn't breasts that disturbed him, or even the thought of female genitals, with their complex, blanketing creases, which reminded him of having to fold the flag at school, and how flummoxed he had been with all that soft cloth in his unskilled hands. What would he do with a woman in his hands? Embarrass himself, probably. And the idea of Natalie Swerdlow in his hands was particularly disturbing, because he would embarrass himself more than ever.

Now she had the ability to tower over him in the monstrous bloom of her grief, could in fact *kill* him if she wanted to, and he would let her. He would simply give in, the way his father had often given in to his mother in moments of domestic conflict, and his grandfather had given in to his grandmother. The Langer men seemed to be under the control of the Langer women, generation after generation, the women strong-willed and outspoken, the men somewhat shrugging and indifferent, their heads buried in a home repair manual, or, in Adam's case, a *Playbill*. Adam had never wanted to go head-to-head with a woman; he and Sara had had a kind of ease that kept them from arguing very often. There was no one else with whom he had such ease; certainly he didn't have it with Shawn, for sex created its own set of complications. And certainly he didn't have it with Sara's mother. But he wasn't sure what he did have with her; sitting here beside her now, eating her over-sweet offerings, he realized that he felt slightly better than he had since the accident.

Natalie was smoking a cigarette and crying quietly, steadily. "I might just as well walk into the water," she said. "What's the difference? My child is dead, and that is the worst thing that can happen to a person. You spend your whole life saying to yourself: *Don't let that happen,* and now it has. Now I'm one of *them,* those mothers. The ones you can't even make eye contact with, because it's just too sad." She sighed. "Carol says I should join one of those groups. I knew this woman whose husband died and she threw herself into this organization; it was actually called 'Lost My Partner, What'll I Do?' And it became her life. I don't want some awful group to become my life. I don't want to meet other people and hear their sob stories. I couldn't bear it, I swear I couldn't." She put her head down. "But I can't bear this either," she said. "So I don't know what's next." She paused. "Our 'Surrender, Dorothy' thing—we'll never do it again."

Adam knew that their "Surrender, Dorothy" thing was a telephone routine that she and Sara had been doing for years. After Natalie's marriage had ended, Sara had developed a sudden, odd fear that her mother might be taken from her and replaced with an impostor. She and Natalie decided that whenever one of them telephoned the other, she would have to say, "Surrender, Dorothy," to prove authenticity. They considered *The Wizard of Oz their* movie, for they had watched it together repeatedly over the years. It was an adventure tale that both of them could relate to; poor Dorothy, Sara had always thought—lost in the world. What would Sara have done if she had lost her mother? Would she have even survived? It seemed doubtful. When Dorothy gazed into the crystal ball and saw the face of her beloved Auntie Em, Sara had wept and wept. And when Natalie watched the movie with Sara, she remembered watching it as a little girl in the Bronx, and so she wept for the loss of her own youth. She was a middle-aged woman whose marriage had become undone. Who would love her, and how could she manage? Mother and daughter hitched their stars to each other, for there was no one else.

"Surrender, Dorothy," they said back and forth on the telephone. After a while, the catchphrase stuck, becoming a tender in-joke, a reflex that began all calls. Adam had always thought this little routine was strange, and did not really understand Sara's intimacy with Natalie, forged in the roomy, manless house so many years earlier.

"I just want to die," Natalie said now. "I'll walk into the water, that's what I'll do."

"Don't walk into the water," said Adam. "Please don't do anything like that. It would be really stupid, and really sad."

"I'll do what I want," she said. "Back in New Jersey, I have a houseful of pills, you know. The medicine cabinets are packed: old tranquilizers, antihistamines, although they probably expired in 1968, and even the pinworm medicine our cocker spaniel Triscuit used to take. I'm sure I could do it with them."

"Look," said Adam, "I don't know what you should do, but I know you definitely shouldn't go back to New Jersey." He paused, as an idea formed. It was a bad idea, certainly, but it was now too late, for he had started to say it: "You could stay here," he said. "In Sara's room."

"Oh, I couldn't," Natalie said.

"Yes, you could," he said dutifully, continuing what he had begun.

"I guess," she said, "maybe you're right. Maybe I could. I have no clothes with me, but I could wear Sara's. We wore the same size."

At first he thought his suggestion had sprung purely from a well of altruism, but now he realized he was also looking out for himself and his friends. In some way the idea excited him too, as though having Sara's mother in the house might save them all. But how could she save them? She was in worse shape than they were. Since the accident there was a sluggishness to the household, which Adam thought must be what old age feels like. In past summers, they would all stand in the kitchen cooking big, sloppy dinners, smoking and drinking and listening to loud music. They would wash lettuce and chop carrots and get nicely buzzed on bottled beer. Sara would cook a big Japanese meal for them once a summer, spending hours in the kitchen by herself, occasionally drafting someone to help her unroll the fragile, vaguely smelly sheets of seaweed. They would drink sake with dinner, which had a surprising potency to it, so that by the end of the evening they were all helplessly drunk and no one could bear to clean up the kitchen until the morning. Late at night Sara would come to Adam's room and sit at the foot of his bed while he read aloud to her from his work. Adam had loved those nights, those summers; they had been a predictable part of his life that he craved during the rest of the year. Now here he was, without her, and it was just misery and sorrow. They had agreed to stay in the house for the rest of the month, but at times he was sorry. How did they think it could be manageable? How could they find a way to live with this?

"I think it's a good idea," he told Natalie. "You can stay until you're back on your feet."

But he knew that this was a meaningless nod toward her childless future. Grieving parents never found their footing, never found their feet, never even found their *shoes,* but simply stayed in bed forever. In junior high, his best friend, Seth McCandless, had died of leukemia. It was a long, slow slippage, with hair loss and transfusions and a seventh-grade benefit performance of *The King and I,* and in the end the McCandlesses had emptied their son's locker, weeping as they knelt in front of the gun metal gray compartment, retrieving the stuff of youth: gym shoes, a Spanish textbook called *Usted Y Yo,* and the smelly remains of what had once been a turkey roll sandwich. The McCandlesses had, by all accounts, turned weird after Seth died, keeping their house shuttered and the yard unshorn. Seth's room had remained a shrine to the dead boy; on the windowsill, his once-busy ant farm had been left untouched, the ants eventually transmogrifying into a snaking, fossilized traffic jam. Mrs. McCandless had "let herself go," according to Adam's mother, which really only meant that she stopped dyeing her hair and sometimes spent whole days in her nightgown, so that on Halloween the neighborhood children called the McCandless home "the witch's house," and egged the porch with a vengeance. Eventually the house was sold and the couple disappeared from the neighborhood, perhaps from the edge of the world.

Anything was possible when a child died. Poor Seth had a head of chick-fuzz in his final days, and he had joked with the nurses and orderlies that he should only be charged half of the daily rate for the TV rental, because he was now blind in one eye. All the kids from the drama club came to visit, gathering in a sober circle around his bed and trying to cheer him up with stories of what plays the club might be performing in the fall.

"Well," said Beth Gershon, serious and homely, "we're trying to get Mr. Lavery to agree to *The Bald Soprano,* but you know how conventional he is. We'll probably end up doing *The Crucible* for the umpteenth time. And I'll have to be Goody Proctor again." Seth had listened attentively, hanging on to these last details of what had once been his world, his life, until it had been so unceremoniously snapped away.

After Seth's funeral, Adam became quiet and stayed in his room reading a mortality doubleheader of *Death Be Not Proud* and *A Separate Peace.* He also, at that time, began writing, scrawling agonized adolescent free-associations in a spiral notebook. Later, these became fragments of dialogue and, later still, plays. So maybe poor Seth McCandless, now long dead, had turned Adam into a writer.

But Sara's death wouldn't make him turn into anything; he was almost thirty years old, and had already turned. Her mother was another story; a mother could change, could transform into the witch in the witch's house, or go wild with grief and lose her job, her property, her hold on the world. Adam was frightened for Natalie, and he thought that if he let her go back to her house and her dead dog's pinworm medicine, he would never see her again.

"Listen, I can't stay with you and your friends," said Natalie vaguely. "You young people. I'm sure you all want to be alone."

"No, we don't," he said quickly. "Everything changed when Sara was killed. We don't really know what to do with ourselves. We're completely fucked up."

Sara's mother studied him, and he let himself be watched. In the distance he saw the small fires of people with less on their minds, and he wished he could join them, unpeel the silver foil from a roasted potato and eat it among friends, laughing. A Frisbee would be flung, the kind that glowed in the dark, and it would sail freely across the sky. Wine would be drunk, nostalgic, stirring folk songs sung. Instead, he was sitting on a dune with the mother of his dead best friend, inviting her to move in. And somehow, she was saying yes.

6

Smiling Buddha

For days and days Natalie slept like a baby, while the real baby in the house almost never slept at all. Real babies wanted to take it all in, they didn't want to miss a minute, whereas a woman whose child has died can afford a long absence from life.

Natalie lay in Sara's bed, having no idea what time of day it was, and not particularly wanting to get up and walk across the room to consult her watch, which lay quietly ticking on Sara's bureau. Occasionally she glanced through Sara's red leather notebook, which Sara had filled with Japanese characters, probably notes for her dissertation, Natalie thought. She had a fantasy of someday being able to translate these words, being able to read what her daughter had written. There were Berlitz tapes in the drawer, and when Natalie could bear to get up and move around more, she planned on listening to them in order to learn Sara's second language. For now, she comforted herself with the tiny, delicate Japanese characters that Sara had painstakingly written. She kept the notebook beside her in bed as she moved in and out of sleep, holding it against her like a pillow or a stuffed animal.

Why not sleep all day and night? At the house in New Jersey after the funeral, Natalie had been continually wired and awake. But the house in the Hamptons had a distinctly soporific effect. Dr. Chatterjee would have diagnosed clinical depression, no doubt, and would have prescribed some drug that would have monkeyed with the serotonin levels in her brain. Yes, she was alarmingly depressed, but she knew it wasn't depression that was causing all this sleep.

No: it was comfort. The bed, with all its associations, and the room that contained that bed, provided a sense of follow-the-dot continuity. She could picture Sara here, could see her standing before the warped mirror brushing her hair, and lying down in bed, folding up her long limbs. Natalie wasn't sure how many days she had been lying here in Sara's room—one, two—when there was a sharp knocking on the flimsy door. "Mrs. Swerdlow?" came a worried female voice. "It's Maddy."

Natalie did not know what to say; she would have liked to simply draw the thin blanket up around her shoulders and not reply, but the knocking came again. "May I come in?" the girl asked. And then, because there was no lock on the door, the knob turned and the door swung open and there stood Sara's friend Maddy Wernick, looking terribly worried.

"What's the matter?" was all Natalie could say.

"We were getting a little concerned," Maddy said, "because you haven't come downstairs to eat. I mean, we heard you going across the hall to use the bathroom, so we knew you weren't swinging from the rafters up here, ha ha, but we were getting spooked. So we chose someone to come up here and check. And I was the one."

"Oh," said Natalie. "Well, you can tell your friends I'm just very sleepy, if that's all right." She thought that that would be that, and in anticipation of Maddy's departure she lay her head back against the pillow.

But Sara's friend simply stood in the doorway, unwilling to leave. "Mrs. Swerdlow," she said softly, "I'd really rather that you didn't go back to sleep, if that's okay with you." Her voice threaded into vagueness and an absence of nerve.

"Pardon?" said Natalie, sitting up once again.

"Well," said Maddy, "I'm not just here to make sure you're okay. We also decided that maybe somehow we could get you out of bed, too. You've just been sleeping and sleeping, and not eating at all. That can't be very good for you."

This young woman was practically poking Natalie with a cattle prod, ordering her to move, when all she wanted to do was lie here and stew in the soft nearness of her daughter's presence. "Whether it's good for me or not," Natalie said evenly, "I'm twenty years older than you, and I don't think it's any of your business."

Maddy blushed. "We promised your friend," she said.

"My friend?" said Natalie. "Carol? You promised her *what*?"

Maddy shifted unhappily from foot to foot. "We promised her that we would take care of you. Right before you sent her off on the bus, she took us aside and basically told us that you were in bad shape and needed to be watched. Which," Maddy added quickly, "is totally understandable, considering."

Natalie sat looking at her, realizing how uncomfortable she was making this girl, and how it would be possible to make her much more uncomfortable, to even make her cry, if the standoff went on much longer. She didn't want to do that; Maddy Wernick had been Sara's best female friend, someone Sara had relied on over the years. Natalie had never known Maddy well, but Sara had loved her. Wasn't that enough? Natalie sighed once, deeply, and then she swung her legs over the side of the bed, planting her bare feet on the floor. "All right," she said. "I'll get up."

The others were all sitting downstairs in the kitchen; it

appeared to be dinnertime, because a big pot of water was boiling on the filthy stove, and a box of Ronzoni spaghetti lay on the counter beside a jar of sauce. The electric sunburst clock over the stove showed the time to be 5:30. That would be P.M., Natalie thought, marveling at how she'd drifted in and out of sleep for over a day. Natalie walked into the middle of the kitchen. "Good morning," she said, and she saw them exchange troubled glances.

"It's evening, actually, Mrs. Swerdlow," said Adam calmly.

"I know that," said Natalie. "It was just an expression." She was aware of how awful she must look in this bathrobe, her body so thin and worn, no makeup rescuing her face.

"We're glad you've joined us," said Peter. "Do you want some dinner? It's nothing much, but we haven't really shopped or anything. In fact, we've barely eaten, either, since we've been here."

Natalie nodded, suddenly grateful, and she sank into a Naugahyde chair at the table and waited like everyone else for the water to boil. The baby babbled, clanging a spoon against the plastic tray of his high chair, and the voices in the room all rose up and joined together in some peculiar, soothing song. Natalie put out a finger for the baby to hold, and he agreeably grabbed it.

"When Sara was a baby she used to sit in her high chair looking out the window for the longest time," Natalie said.

"Oh?" said Adam.

"Yes," said Natalie. "I worried that she was autistic, she was so quiet. The food would get cold while Sara sat and looked outside. But she was just taking her time, because that was the way she was."

"It never stopped," said Adam. "At Wesleyan we'd all be cramming for exams and we'd be hysterical, pulling out our hair, drinking Jolt Cola. And Sara would be sort of above it all, looking over her Japanese books and then gazing out the window."

"I wish I could have been as bright as Sara," said Maddy wistfully.

"You know, I had her tested when she was seven," said

Natalie. "She had a 160 I.Q. That's genius. But I never felt she'd really put it to good use. And now she never will." There was a pained, respectful silence. "I don't know how to think about her anymore," Natalie continued. "I feel as though I need more information, more details." She looked from face to face. "I've told you some things," she said. "Now you tell me some."

Adam and Peter and Maddy looked at one another, as if wondering what sorts of things they could tell Sara's mother. What sorts of things, they seemed to be asking silently, were okay to divulge? "I don't know what you want to hear about, Mrs. Swerdlow," said Maddy. "I mean, I don't really know what you knew or didn't know. And I also don't know what would even interest you."

"It all interests me," said Natalie. "Please, fire away. Anything that occurs to you about Sara, anything I might not know."

There was a long silence. "I'm sorry," said Adam, shrugging lightly. "Nothing's occurring to us, I guess. If you could be more specific, that would be helpful."

"Well," said Natalie after a moment, "what about men?"

Men. The friends looked at one another. What was there to say about Sara and men? Or, rather, what was there to say about Sara and men that they could tell her mother? "She told me a great deal, as you may already know," Natalie said. "We weren't shy with each other that way. But I'm certain that there were things she could only tell her friends, things that she wouldn't tell me. And I want to know why her life was the way it was. Her love life. Why she never settled down." Her gaze shifted to Adam.

"Mrs. Swerdlow," he began, "I know you think she was so attached to me that it somehow kept the men from sticking around. But that's not true at all."

"I didn't say it was," said Natalie.

"We were best friends," he went on, "and I wanted her to be in love, if that was what she wanted."

"*Was* it what she wanted?" Natalie asked.

"Sometimes," he said.

The pasta was brought to the table by Shawn in a glossy heap; wine was poured from one of those inexpensive jugs with a sprightly label that showed a busty Italian signorina carrying a basket of grapes. Everyone sat and ate, even Natalie. At first she was aware only of texture: the surprising and even appealing glutinosity of each strand and the lubrication of the sauce, but finally she was aware of taste, too. The food actually had a good taste, and nothing she had eaten in a long time had seemed at all edible to her. The wine, too, cheap though it was, slipped right down her throat, leaving behind an acidity one associated with the kind of wine served at gallery openings in urine sample–sized cups.

"So I guess," said Maddy, "you knew about Sloan."

"Sloan?" said Natalie, and she suddenly recalled that this had been the name of the last man that Sara had been involved with—the environmental lawyer who had eventually gone up to British Columbia. "Oh, right, Sloan. I don't really know that much about him, actually."

"Well," said Maddy, who was herself high on wine and feeling a bit loose, "the first thing about him that Sara told me was that he was a good fuck." There was a shocked silence. "Oh, God," Maddy quickly said. "I kind of forgot who I was talking to here. You'll pardon the expression. I only meant," she hastily went on, "that he was extremely . . . handsome. Handsome in ways that were completely alien to me. I recognized that he was handsome, and I could appreciate that fact, but his handsomeness was totally out of my realm. He was one of those men," she said, "who looks like a brontosaurus. A really big head and teeth. You got the feeling, looking at him, that he could have ripped you apart, totally snacked on you. His muscles were huge, kind of bursting through his shirt, and yet he acted as though he never worked out, as if God had planted those muscles there like seeds, under the skin, and watched them grow." She shook her head. "But you just knew he started his day at five A.M. at the gym, pumping himself up, and went straight from there downtown on his bike, to his do-gooding environmental law office."

Natalie could picture Sara's lover better now; he appeared before her in the light of the kitchen, preening and naked except for a bicycle helmet and knee pads. Of course Sara had wanted that; what was not to want? "How did they meet again?" Natalie asked. "I'm sure she told me, but I forgot."

"They met," Adam said, "at a party I took Sara to. It was in somebody's loft—one of those huge spaces that you stand around in and just feel like your own apartment is inferior the whole night. At least, that was the way it was for me. I forgot that I was supposed to talk to people, or at least pretend to be interested in them. Instead, I kept kneeling down and examining the parquet floors, and looking up at the painted tin ceilings. I was thinking about how I'd never have anything like this loft, and Sara was standing right beside me, like always, and next thing I knew I turned to her and she wasn't there."

Natalie felt as though she was hearing a wondrous adventure tale, in which the heroine was whisked off to a magical land. It struck her, again and again, that she could search the entire earth for Sara and never find her. The magical land was elsewhere, inaccessible to the living. Surely Sara was somewhere, if you looked hard enough. But no, she was nowhere.

The night that she had disappeared in that loft, though, she had merely gone out onto the fire escape to have a smoke with a man who had smiled at her while Adam was examining the intricacies of the woodwork. The man said his name was Sloan, and he and Sara stood on the rusted fire escape looking over the Hudson River, the lit points of their cigarettes punctuating the night. The attraction between them was strong and a little sickening, for it brought with it a knowledge that eventually, perhaps soon, they would be in bed together. There was an innate embarrassment to this fact, Sara had told Adam, because it presupposed even the possibility of modesty. Sloan sucked in the last bits of his cigarette, seeming to smile at the inevitability of a sexual future with this woman he had just met. Sara felt naked already, as though a strong wind had whipped her clothes off and left her undressed beside this imposing man.

They exchanged the usuals: *I'm an environmental lawyer. Oh, really? I'm a graduate student in Japanese.* They talked about how they each hoped to live downtown someday, but how both of them lived on the Upper West Side, a mere four blocks from each other. They frequented the same Szechuan restaurant; probably, Sara commented, they had sat with their separate sets of friends in that brightly lit box of a restaurant wolfing down Double Happiness Chicken at the same moment, but somehow they had never noticed each other.

No, that's not possible, Sloan said. *I would have noticed you.*

To which Sara felt her face heat quickly, the warmth climbing all the way up to the hairline. She didn't know what to say, and she half-turned and saw Adam through the window of the loft. He was watching her with that look on his face that people had when they knew they had been left out of something good.

Sara told Sloan she had to go, and he asked for her telephone number, inquiring whether he could take her out to their "shared Szechuan stomping grounds," as he put it. She said yes, that sounded nice. In a week they had dinner, and soon they were having sex.

Sara's friends didn't use the word "sex" when describing this to Natalie; what they said was this: "In a week they had dinner, and soon she was seeing him all the time." But Natalie knew what it meant. As she sat at the kitchen table and listened and ate spaghetti, she realized she felt jealous of her sexy, charming daughter. Inappropriately jealous of her daughter who now lay in a grave in Queens. Natalie's jealousy brewed inside her like a dirty little secret, but regardless of the jealousy, she wanted to know more. She wanted to know it all. Perhaps, if she stayed here all month, she would uncover everything about Sara that was possible to know. She would become her daughter's hagiographer, and number one fan.

As the days passed, everyone noticed that Natalie was sleeping less and eating more. She showed up at meals, and even began to cook for the rest of the household. When a meal was through she enjoyed cleaning up the kitchen, spending an hour alone in the grimy room, wiping all surfaces hard with a sponge, creating some semblance of order. "Can we help?" Maddy and the others would ask, but she always said no, shooing them out of the room so she could clean up by herself. The place hadn't been thoroughly cleaned in decades, and she announced that she was determined to put an end to the indifferent summer-share squalor. They tried to stop her, insisting that she ought to rest, ought to take it easy while she was here, but she wouldn't listen.

One morning, they were all awakened early to the sound of the Dustbuster and one of Sara's Japanese language tapes booming through the house. *"Where is the bus stop?"* the voice on the tape asked, blaring first in English, then translated into Japanese: *"Basu tei wa doko desuka?"* Then the voice said, *"Do you know what time it is?"* The translation followed: *"Ima wa nanji desuka?"* Sara had kept these tapes for colloquial emergency purposes, but she'd never needed them.

"I wish she would just cool out already," Peter said to Maddy one morning later that week, as they awakened yet again to the sound of the robotic Japanese instructor and the accompaniment of the Dustbuster. "She's in constant motion suddenly. She's acting like a maniac, like Hazel the maid on speed."

"It's therapy for her. And the place needs it anyway," said Maddy, looking around at the vaguely unclean room. The entire house was a study in indifference; Mrs. Moyles didn't ever seem to mop or dust or use a sponge. When Maddy and her friends arrived each August, they weren't about to start cleaning. Maddy recalled that Natalie's own house in New Jersey was a clean acreage of beige rugs, sectional couches, and art posters from Galerie Maeght. The carpeting was pale too, and so were the furniture and the walls. Dirt would have shown itself easily in that house; it would have had no camouflage.

Dirt went against a mother's natural instinct. Some hormone must kick in when you give birth, Maddy thought; no longer can you enjoy the sloth and brazen filth of your childless days. You can't open a bottle of Advil and carelessly leave a few pills scattered on the night table surface, or let a pack of matches fall to the floor unnoticed. Now you have to keep the dirt and dust away from your child, to wipe clean all the windowsills, to vacuum the small, potentially edible thumbtacks and paper clips from their hiding places in the carpeting. When everything finally had the appearance of order, there was always a moment of irrational joy.

Maddy felt this herself whenever she cleaned Duncan's nursery back in the city. She had gone on maternity leave from the law firm, a job she didn't like anyway, in order to be able to stay at home with him. Sometimes she cleaned his room, with its duckling nightshade and its calm, yellow walls, just to cheer herself up. It was easy to see why Sara's mother was cleaning like a dervish, trying to set everything right.

The insanity of the situation, the thing that made no sense, was that although Natalie had lost a child, she was still a mother. Where could she deposit her maternal energy now? Maddy wondered. It was aimless but potent, looking for a place to express itself, like a dog that humps human ankles or the legs of tables. Maddy imagined Sara's mother becoming a peppy volunteer at an orphanage, standing in the middle of a ward with hand puppets jammed onto her hands, making the puppets speak to each other in high-pitched voices that might possibly amuse these thrown-away children.

But here, in this falling-apart summer house, Natalie needed to do *something,* and it wasn't hard for her to figure out what to do: She would clean, clean, clean, restoring the place to a more presentable state. Each day, she could look forward to taking another crack at cleaning Sara's house, the way people look forward to reading another chapter of an exciting but bad novel they have begun, a book in which secret missile siloes are discovered in rustic outposts, and treachery from the wildcard leader of a tiny Middle Eastern nation shakes the Pentagon.

"I think it's good that she's cleaning," Maddy said to Peter, as they lay in bed and listened to the early-morning sounds of Natalie at work. "She can take her mania, as you call it, and put it to use. People need something to do with themselves when a terrible thing happens to them."

"I know what *we* need," he said, and suddenly he put his warm hand on her thigh, as though sex could somehow cure death. But the idea of Sara actually being dead was still foreign and invasive. She couldn't have sex with him now, and in fact had begun to find it intolerable long before Sara had died.

Sex had become problematic shortly after Maddy had become pregnant; there had been little lightning-bolts of pain in her nipples, so the idea of being touched there had been unpleasant. Then the morning sickness rose up in a big wave (a tsunami, Sara had called it), and the closest Maddy let Peter get was to bring her ice chips in the bathroom as she knelt at the toilet.

Later, during the second trimester, when, according to a pregnancy advice book she'd read, "with morning sickness gone, and a new sense of well-being firmly in place, the sex drive may return, in spades. And remember—you still don't need to worry about contraception!" Maddy had felt even more troubled by the idea of sex with Peter. While the book assured her that sex was completely safe, she worried that the tip of his long penis would poke against the soft skull of the baby, causing brain damage. She knew this was ridiculous, and she was too embarrassed to tell Peter or to mention it to her chic female obstetrician, Denise. Instead, she simply put up with sex for a while, letting him blindly thrust inside of her. But she felt no pleasure, simply spirals of worry. She also didn't want to have an orgasm, because it was known to bring about mini-contractions—harmless though they were, according to the book. But Maddy didn't want to risk even the remote possibility of going into premature labor, and all for what? So Peter could have fun? She didn't know what to do, and so, in advance, she discussed the matter with Sara.

They were in a Starbucks at the time, sitting on tall, spindly stools. "I think," said Sara, stirring her *latte* slowly, dreamily, "you should have sex, but you should fake it."

"I have never done that in my life," said Maddy. "That's from another era—our mothers' era. Nobody has to fake it anymore."

Sara shrugged. "All right, then don't fake it," she said. "Tell him you just don't *want* to come, that you don't feel like it."

"It will hurt his feelings," said Maddy.

"You have to take care of yourself, of what you want," said Sara. "Just do what you have to do."

And so, with Sara as her invisible guide, Maddy went to bed with her husband that night, and as soon as she touched him she felt the corresponding pulse and blossom under her hand, like a sponge thrust into water. When he was inside her, there was a hot, sharp streak, and she imagined the baby's head receiving the repeated blows, its tiny eyes closing to withstand the pain. Peter shuddered out his own orgasm. After he had recovered, he moved his hand predictably down under the blanket, the fingers splayed, and tried his usual maneuvers to bring her to orgasm.

Just do what you have to do, she heard Sara saying, and Maddy closed her own eyes and began to utter some small sounds in her throat, letting them build in an operatic fashion, actually beginning to enjoy the craft of the deceit. She closed her legs and scissored them, nearly crushing Peter's caught hand, and then after a couple of small pulsations, her feet flexed, her jaw set in the particular way that it usually did when all this was authentic, she relaxed her entire body. They lay together for a while, Peter stroking her head, the baby safe from uterine contractions, and Maddy thought to herself: *I must call Sara.*

Now, Maddy took Peter's hand off her thigh and uncurled it. "I can't do this," she said. She motioned in the vague direction of the Portacrib, where Duncan lay asleep. "The baby," she added.

"The baby's in dreamland," said Peter.

"Right now he is," Maddy said. "But he could wake up." She paused. "And actually," she went on, "I just don't feel like it. I mean, Sara's *dead,* Peter. It's so recent."

His sex drive was intact, but certainly it had undergone some sort of transformation after witnessing Maddy in labor, when he had seen her howling like a she-wolf on a hilltop. It had been her great mistake to refuse the epidural offered to her by the anesthesiologist, who'd actually seemed disappointed when she turned it down. Then, during pushing, that two-hour period of time during which Maddy began to hallucinate a roll of theater tickets unspooling from her vagina, Peter had seen her cervix open wide, so wide it might destroy him, might swallow him whole, like in some grade-B movie called *Attack of the 10-Centimeter Vagina.* She had shrieked and contorted her face, and although Peter held her hand and whispered to her that she was his beloved, and popped a tape of those singing monks into the cassette player so she could visualize the cool of a church and people in cowls lighting candles, she knew that Peter would always possess an image of her when she appeared before him in their bed: that of a screaming, Munch-like figure with a vagina as vast as a state wildlife preserve. But still, somehow, it did not deter him.

She was vaguely disgusted by his sexual fealty; it seemed excessive to her, even a bit unnatural. In part, this was because she knew she wasn't beautiful. As a teenager with Sara, Maddy had taken on the role of the less attractive but wryly good-natured sister (a role that, in the movies of her parents' era, would have been played by Eve Arden), and it occasionally occurred to her, over the years, that she hated this role. Why didn't some boy write a love letter to *her* about the way her eyes looked in the moonlight or the way her skin was "as smooth as 'abalaster' "? But the roles were firmly established, and there was nothing to do about it except not be Sara's friend. And because Maddy loved Sara, that wasn't a possibility.

An ambient competition encircled the two friends even though they never acknowledged it openly. But it wasn't just competition; it was a slowly revolving, rotisseried rage, at least as far as Maddy was concerned. She was humiliated by her own secret reserve of unkind feeling toward Sara. Whenever they went shopping for clothes they would casually strip together in a dressing room, and Sara would be sure to murmur something like, "God, Maddy, you have such perfect legs. Mine are stumps." Because neither part of that observation was remotely true, Maddy would be forced to accept the remark in unhappy silence, or else beg to differ, which then forced Sara to murmur her dissent and continue the lie.

Rejected now, Peter turned away from Maddy, stepping into pants, and then he slipped silently from the room. When he was gone, Maddy reached into her bottom dresser drawer and pulled out a small, flat bottle of Mrs. Moyles's peach schnapps that she had begun drinking after the accident. This was such a *girl's* drink, as sweet as any children's medicine, but it still provided a familiar ribbon of heat as it went down the gullet, vaguely reminding her of a lunchbox dessert of canned peaches in heavy syrup. Maddy drank only when Peter wasn't looking. Now she tossed her head back and swallowed a warm, clear ounce or so, then she capped the bottle and thrust it back under her shirts in the drawer and stood over the Portacrib, staring down at Duncan.

It shamed her to admit it, but her son made her happiest when he slept. That way, she could be certain nothing bad would befall him; he had moved beyond the frightening window of crib death, and now sleep seemed such a lovely harbor for a baby. When he slept, she could move about the house freely, carrying the monitor receiver with her like a cell phone, glancing at the row of red lights for constant reassurance. It was only when Duncan was awake that she doubted her own skills as a mother, worrying that she would drop him or that he would spike a fever so high it would be unmanageable.

There was a book that Maddy had taken with her to the house this summer and which now convinced her that she was a bad mother. The book was a best-seller written by one Dr. Melanie Blandish, Ed.D., an Australian child development expert. It was called *The Upbeat Baby,* and it had made Maddy feel that her depression over Sara had caused her to be a terrible mother, and that her baby would grow up to be pessimistic and probably even insane. He would develop a classic young-adult onset schizophrenia, in which he would go from being an adorable undergraduate majoring in Semiotics at Brown to a terrified, unshaven beast cowering in his childhood bedroom jabbering in other tongues.

Maddy kept the Melanie Blandish book in her drawer, right beside the peach schnapps, reading surreptitiously when Peter wasn't around. She was like someone poking at a tender, recent injury, causing herself a kind of low-level pain that in its intensity offered a singular pleasure. "Your baby needs your love all the time," wrote Dr. Blandish. "You ought to make yourself available to him, like an all-night chemist's dispensing love. If you seem particularly distracted, believe me, *he will know it.*" This passage haunted Maddy; how often had she seemed this way, how often had the baby seen her cry over Sara, and simply stared at her in utter, helpless perplexity? Dr. Blandish didn't tell you what to do if your best friend had just been killed in a car accident and you were trying to raise a baby; she gave no advice on managing your life, but simply offered premonitions of doom.

Why, Maddy asked herself lately, had she ever decided to have a baby? She wasn't ready for this, and neither was Peter. Very recently, it seemed, they had been staying up late and having lots of sex and eating in a variety of cheap restaurants and going to many movies, and once even going to a tiny jewelry store on Avenue A on a Saturday night to have Maddy's nose pierced. Then, on a whim almost as casual as the nose-piercing decision, they had decided to stop using birth control. She had taken her circular packet of pills one night, put them in an ash tray, and ceremonially burned them, although the plastic had only curled and smoked and stank up the apartment, leaving the pills themselves intact behind their transparent bubble windows.

Sara had been envious at first when Maddy became pregnant so quickly. "You're so lucky," she'd said. "You're like a fertility goddess. Now you get to drink malteds for nine months, and then people give you all those presents, and then you end up with this tiny baby all your own. You get to *continue* yourself, to make a bid for immortality." Sara's envy was an important element to Maddy; she'd welcomed it in a secretive, somewhat triumphant way.

But Sara had really only envied the theoretical baby, not the actual, demanding one. When Duncan was born, Sara brought yellow roses to the apartment and a "family size" bar of chocolate, and then she'd hovered for a few hours, folding doll-sized laundry and screening Maddy's phone calls. Then, when things became too tedious, Sara slipped off to a late showing of an arty, violent Hong Kong action picture at Columbia with some man she'd recently met in a seminar. "Oh, are you sure you don't mind?" she'd asked before she left, and Maddy had answered no, no, of course I don't mind, there's nothing for you to do here anyway, I'm perfectly fine. As Sara watched the movie at midnight while snuggling against the leather-jacketed shoulder of her date, Maddy disappeared into the quicksand of motherhood. Her nose hole became infected, and the doctor scolded her for not having had it pierced under his supervision and for not taking care of it now, and said she had to let it close over. She nursed the baby for hours and sometimes was so weary afterward—her nipples a hotheaded red, her eyes barely open—that she went to bed at eight, while in the meantime Sara kept sleeping with a number of interesting, difficult men. Sara dated and dated, and eventually she met the powerfully handsome Sloan, who kept her occupied for a while. Meanwhile, Maddy nursed her baby around the clock, feeling isolated and alone in a surreal way, even with Peter beside her. Sometimes she felt like a lost astronaut spinning into infinity. Once, at 3 A.M., Maddy ate Sara's chocolate bar by herself, polishing off the entire, formidable block in one sitting.

At night lately, when she nursed the baby in this terrible but familiar summer house, she thought of the people she loved: Sara, who lay dead in a cemetery, and Peter, who slumbered on in their uncomfortable bed, protected from the true tragedy of the situation because he had not been close to Sara. His grief seemed stiff, a little phony. Now, with the sound of Japanese phrases hurling through the air, and with the alcohol making its way down inside her throat and fanning out, Maddy carefully descended the stairs, carrying her baby in her arms.

IN THE KITCHEN, Sara's mother had taken it upon herself to scrub a cabinetful of pots that still bore traces of ancient chicken dinners. She was working with deep, humming concentration, focusing on the pan she held under a blast of hot water, and Maddy thought she looked the way Sara would have eventually looked in middle age, beautiful and melancholic and having seen a little too much sun. She turned to Maddy now, holding the dripping pan in one hand.

"Good morning," said Natalie. "And good morning to you too, Duncan," she added, coming forward to get a good look at the baby, whom Maddy was tucking into his high chair. The baby squirmed and squealed impressively, his little tongue pushing through his lips as though he were trying to taste a falling snowflake. "Just look at him," said Natalie. "He's so tender. May I?" She put down the pan, held out her arms, and Maddy nodded.

Natalie lifted the baby and held him against her, smelling the top of his head, inhaling deeply. "Oh, that smell, it's heaven," she said. "Simply heaven. Baby juice; they ought to bottle it." She paused. "Would you possibly consider letting me take him out in the carriage later?"

"Be my guest," said Maddy.

"We'll go for a stroll," said Natalie, "and take in the sights." She placed the baby back in his chair and picked up another pan to clean. "Oh, I loved having a baby around," she said. "I was so young when Sara was born and God knows I did everything wrong, but who knew back then? I smoked throughout my entire pregnancy, can you believe that? In one hand I held a glass of milk, in the other hand I held a Camel unfiltered. And no one told me not to. No one said a word. I used to smoke in the waiting room of my obstetrician's office; they even had ashtrays there." She shook her head. "Well, the world has changed," she said. "Nothing is the same, nothing at all." Then something caught in her throat and she turned on the water full force and resumed scrubbing.

Maddy went to her then, touching the edge of her sleeve. "Mrs. Swerdlow," she said, "please stop cleaning. Please just take it easy. Give yourself a break."

"Thank you," Natalie said, "but this is what I want to be doing. I'll be fine." She turned back and continued to work, her arm moving rapidly against the pan, grinding a little piece of steel wool into a mush of fibers. Maddy stood watching for a moment, exasperated and helpless, and now Adam and Shawn entered the room, having heard the exchange.

"Mrs. Swerdlow," Adam began. "I think what Maddy's trying to say is—"

Natalie tossed the pan down into the sink and wheeled around. "Look, guys," she said, "I'm doing what makes me feel better. If you really can't stand it, then I'll leave, all right? I'll take a job cleaning rooms at a Holiday Inn. I'll get it out of my system.

But to think of sitting in this place all day, this horrible little house, no offense, and thinking about my Sara and going slowly mad—"

"Nobody wants you to leave," Adam said quickly. "We just want you to slow down a little. You should . . . well, I know it's a cliché, but you should *heal*."

"I thought it would be a good idea to be here," said Natalie, "with Sara's friends, with Sara's things, in the place she lived when she died. My friend Carol thinks I'm crazy, says I should see a bereavement counselor. So I said, Carol, what exactly is this bereavement counselor supposed to tell me: *This is going to be a rough time?* No. The only place to go was here. And I thought it might help if I made the place nicer, if I spruced it up, made it liv-able. It keeps me busy; it keeps me from becoming a bag lady wearing three coats in August, okay? And if you can't stand the sight of a middle-aged lady walking around your house doing what she needs to do, well then, this isn't going to work."

"We'll just have to make it work," Maddy said in the soft cadences of someone talking a person down from a bad drug experience. Now Adam and Shawn joined in like a Greek cho-rus, telling Natalie how much they wanted her here, how they hoped she felt welcome, how she could stay here until Labor Day.

But they were all thinking about what it would really be like having Natalie here for the month, imagining it in a way they had not been able to do when Adam first invited her earlier in the week. They had thought she would languish in Sara's old room under the moth-bitten summer quilt, as she had done at the beginning, crying quietly and being about as demanding as the cactus in the house that no one paid attention to or cared for. But instead she was suddenly everywhere all at once, and the prospect of being indoors with her all month seemed unbearable. They had to get out; they had to leave the confines of this little house.

"Why don't we go to the beach?" Shawn said suddenly, and the rest of them, relieved, readily agreed, dividing up to gather belongings: suits, towels, the old umbrella which had made a big circle of shade for them every August for years. Sara had sat in the weave of that shade, leaning against Adam, laughing, singing backwards, reading one of her Japanese novels that looked as beautiful and elegant as a *bento* box.

Now, after they had moved through the house rounding up their things, and Peter had joined them, they all congregated downstairs to leave for the beach. Natalie planned to follow behind the truck in her own car. "All set," Natalie said, coming downstairs, and Maddy turned and looked at her as she descended the steps. Maddy inhaled hard, startled.

Natalie was wearing Sara's blue beach hat, the one that Sara had worn every summer for years. With the hat on her head Natalie looked so much like Sara that the eye was almost fooled, and the heart leapt in response. There would be many small episodes like this one: moments in which people averted tears by running out of the house, putting a hand over the mouth, or a hand across the eyes, or even both hands over the entire face.

"Oh, the hat," Natalie said, lifting a hand up to her head and touching the edge of the crinkled brim. "I'm sorry, I'll take it off."

"No, don't," said Peter. "Leave it on. It's yours now." Then he hoisted a cooler full of beer and sandwiches, and headed out to the truck.

"I'll go with you in the car, Natalie. You shouldn't ride alone," Maddy offered. "We'll meet you at the beach!" she called out to the others.

This was how it would be, too; someone would accompany Natalie everywhere, like a child in need of a chaperone. Maddy moved the baby seat into the back of Natalie's car, set Duncan in place, and they were off. They drove along the main road in silence. Outside, a muted haze of greenery scrolled past, punctuated by the bright colors of people on vacation. Women wore white T-shirts with hot pink writing across the front, and cars carried surfboards on their roofs, lime green and purple. The sky here was wide and unstreaked, one big, clean window. The car went past million-dollar homes with broad porches and candy-striped awnings and croquet mallets lying, forgotten, in damp grass. Who owned these homes? West Coast movie stars on vacation, Wall Street robber barons, Queen Noor and her husband, the king of wherever it was he was from. Everything here seemed to be about leisure. It would have been idyllic if you were young and unencumbered, as Maddy used to be. If that were the case, you might actually spend the summer here in luxury, sitting on a chaise reading thrillers, or just painting and repainting your nails, both finger and toe. But the beauty of the area was unsettling to Maddy now, and the perfection of the day seemed overbearing and relentless.

"Tell me," Natalie said as the two women drove. "There's something I guess I forgot to ask at the time, for obvious reasons. Sara died, so who cares about a goddamn car, right? But what did they do with it, anyway?"

"With what?" asked Maddy.

"The car. That she was driving," said Natalie. "*My* car."

"Good question. I'm not sure," said Maddy. "There's a place out here where a lot of cars that don't work anymore, and cars that have been in accidents, are taken to. It's over at the edge of town; you can't miss it. I don't know for a fact that they took your car there, but that's what I'd guess."

"Well, I'd like to go there now," said Natalie. "Before the beach, if that's okay."

"Mrs. Swerdlow," said Maddy, "I know it's none of my business, but why torture yourself?"

"Because it comes naturally to me," Natalie said quickly. "Always has. When I was little, and I'd just seen a horror movie, I used to force myself to think about it at night before I went to sleep. That way, I'd totally lose myself in it, and then eventually it wouldn't be so bad. Eventually I'd be sick of all the gory details, and they'd go away."

"So you're going to do that this summer?" said Maddy. "Think about Sara until you go insane? And then hope you come back out the other side?"

"Oh, something like that," said Natalie.

"Actually, I'd like to do that too," said Maddy. "Because I think about her all the time, and it's not as though I can really discuss it with Peter in a way that he'd understand. He and Sara weren't that close." She paused and added, "Sometimes I get this desire to see her, and it's so strong that I think I will die."

"Would you say," said Natalie, "that Sara was a generally happy person? After all, she was alone in the world. She didn't have a man, the way you have Peter."

"She had Adam."

"Well, hardly," said Natalie.

"I know you think it's not the same," Maddy said, "but she took great comfort from him." She paused, smiling slightly, then she added, "She told me that he even passed the vomit test."

"The what?"

"A long time ago Sara and I both decided," said Maddy, "that the true measure of how comfortable you are with a person is whether or not you could let them be in the room while you're vomiting. Whether you'd let them hold your hair out of your face and pat your back, and just generally be right there, watching you heave and go through the whole horrible process. Or whether you'd *never* want them to see you that way, whether it would be too humiliating. You'd be feeling really nauseated, but you'd want them out of the room, out of earshot. Sara felt that Adam could be right there beside her, no matter what happened."

"Well, that's because there wasn't any sexual tension between them," said Natalie. "If he had been a man she was involved with, a *straight* man, then she would have wanted him far, far away. Believe me, that's the way it always is."

"But why should it *have* to be that way?" said Maddy. "Why should we have to hide from the men we sleep with? Isn't it possible to have sexual tension with someone *and* total comfort?"

"Do you and Peter have that?" asked Natalie.

"Well, no," said Maddy. "When I was pregnant with Duncan, I threw up every morning in the beginning, and I was very embarrassed that when Peter kissed me he'd start to think of how I looked when I was throwing up. But now," she said, with a hard little laugh, "it's not as though it matters, really. We don't kiss very much anymore."

"Oh, you're young," said Natalie vaguely. "You're both young people. You have no idea of what will happen to either of you. Everything will change."

On impulse, Maddy directed Natalie to turn the car to the left, away from the beach and in the direction of the heap of abandoned cars. They drove to the edge of town, to a place that bore no resemblance to the rest of this area. No beaches, no fruitstands, no seductive smells of coconut oil or barbecues. Maddy had Natalie drive toward the mountainous junk heap of cars she had seen summer after summer on the fringe of town. Natalie turned off the main strip and followed along a single-lane road that went past a warehouse filled with snorkeling gear, a factory where tuna fish was canned, an industrial park that indiscreetly belched out a dark roll of fumes, and, finally, the cross-hatching of the railroad tracks.

The train that took passengers all the way here from the city was a long, slow, outdated one. You had to change in Jamaica and stand out on the platform in the stink and heat until another train was ready to take you the rest of the distance, rocking in airlessness the whole way, so that when you arrived you were breathless and weary, with half-moons of perspiration beneath your arms. But still you were *here;* still you'd made it.

The road suddenly fell into shadow, and Natalie and Maddy could see that a huge hill loomed ahead, wavy as an oasis in the

open heat. Natalie slowed the car and squinted to see; the hill was
not a natural occurrence, but a vivid and multicolored mountain
of amputated car parts and abandoned, crashed, collapsed, and
long-dead cars. Everything that made up the mountain had once
been in motion. Natalie slowed her own car and pulled it to a stop
beside the fence.

"I don't think we can go any farther," said Maddy. "There's no
way in."

"Well, we can try," said Natalie. "Who's going to stop us?" She
got out of the car and walked toward the fence.

"Mrs. Swerdlow," said Maddy, following behind, "please wait
up." She unhitched the baby and slipped him into the carrier that
she wore, his big head bobbing like one of those ridiculous toy
dogs people put in the rear windows of cars. The baby didn't complain, but simply made small lip-smacking sounds, which meant
that he would need to nurse again soon. Oh, shit, she thought, and
followed Natalie. With the hill of cars so close, Natalie felt com-
pelled to find Sara's totaled Toyota, as if its remnants might prove
something important, some little-known theory, some conspiracy
thing. But there was nothing to prove, and she knew it. Still,
Natalie placed a tentative foot upon a rung of barbed wire, and
started to scale the fence in her open-toed sandals. "Please, Mrs.
Swerdlow!" Maddy called. "This is an incredibly dumb thing to
do. You'll hurt yourself!"

But once Natalie had begun climbing, it really wasn't very far.
The wire was taut, and Natalie kept her hands away from the
sharp little knots that appeared every six inches or so. Soon she
was throwing her leg over the top and slowly making her way
down the other side.

"Oh, what the fuck," said Maddy to herself, and then, with
one hand marsupially cradling the baby's head, she shakily
climbed the fence too. She was frightened at first, worried that
something would happen, that the baby would drop to the
ground, or that she herself would fall, crushing the baby beneath

her, but after he made it over the top, she knew it would be okay. Duncan was unharmed, blithely looking around him and crowing quietly. Safe on the other side, she and Natalie walked together in silence, circling the great hill of collapsed cars. They saw an Eldorado with its roof bashed in, as though someone had dropped a wrecking ball upon it. They saw one of those vans that suburban families all drove these days, its rear end missing, an infant seat still strapped in place inside.

What had happened there? Maddy wondered. What had happened to any of these cars, and the people who had driven them, or the ones who had ridden in the back seat, innocently looking out the window, the children playing Ghost or Geography, or peering at little beeping Game-Boys in their laps? Natalie saw disaster upon disaster, stacked up as haphazardly as dishware in a busy industrial kitchen. Tires poked out from the pile of cars, and so did license plates folded in half like books, and jagged, loosened fenders. There were sudden, powerful glints of sun caught in the circles of sideview mirrors, and hoods of cars left wide open like monstrous mouths. She saw a dangling pair of furry, fermented green dice, and a fender with an old bumper sticker that read "Go Perot." She walked around and around, searching like someone picking through a weeded-over cemetery to read old headstones with engravings that had faded into shallow illegibility. *Here lies . . . Beloved daughter of . . .*

Suddenly she saw that Natalie had begun to cry, stumbling forward through the tangle of cars. Maddy was spacy from the heat that bounced off all the metal in this already hot day, but she wanted to keep circling the hill until she was done. Nearby, a train was pulling into town, bringing more summer people with their beach umbrellas and portable radios and their simple, collective desire for fun.

"Mrs. Swerdlow," called Maddy over the train's whistle and clatter. "Please, you won't find anything here." She put an arm out and pulled Sara's mother toward her.

But then Natalie saw something. "Oh, look," she said. "Look." Both women bent down. What they saw was small, its silk string wound around a disembodied rearview mirror, and could easily have been taken from some other car entirely, but there it was, a tiny figure of Buddha, smiling knowingly into the sun.

7

The Shopping Trip

At four in the morning, Shawn squinted in the white light of the upstairs bathroom, examining himself again. He had been woken up minutes earlier by the baby, whose funhouse shrieks echoed throughout the rooms. When Duncan woke him up, Shawn usually stayed up for the rest of the night, and whenever that happened, he tended to obsess. He would sit up in bed and start thinking about AIDS, the subject that terrified him most of all.

Then he would climb over Adam and go into the bathroom, proceeding to peer closely at his arms and legs, searching for suspicious spots or marks that might indicate the presence of a virus in his system. Now he saw a strange mole he'd never noticed before. Was it anything to worry about? he wondered. Had it possibly been there his entire life and he'd never paid it any attention, like an unimportant star buried in the night sky?

He had repeatedly resisted being tested, and in fact had somehow managed to stave off true anxiety about the subject, but suddenly, here in this house with death hanging over it, he was frightened. And to top it all off it was August, so his analyst, Dr. Selznick, wasn't available, not even by telephone. Not that Selznick would have been any help; all he was interested in were dreams, and as a result Shawn had begun having dreams that were detailed and confusing and as laden with dead ends as an Escher drawing. Shawn was a low-fee patient (fifteen dollars a pop) whose dreams and fantasies and the specifics of his sex life were shared by Selznick with a senior analyst, discussed in the grimy light of the Institute's tall unclean windows, and most likely given humiliating labels: latent, regressive, pre-Oedipal. Shawn didn't care; for as long as he could remember, he had been waiting for someone to show even a passing interest in his inner life. His parents had always maintained that dreams were basically a pointless gumbo, and that sex was a procreative necessity so excruciatingly embarrassing that you never discussed it with anyone.

Now Shawn was long free of his parents and their provincial notions of shame. He was proudly in analysis four days a week in an age when *no one* was in analysis anymore, but when everyone was sustained by pharmaceuticals, and he was a would-be writer of musicals, in an age when everyone said the musical was dead. But he was also, suddenly, very afraid, and it seemed there was no one to tell his fears to. Everyone in this house was in mourning; they didn't want to hear his fears. He remembered passing a medical office in the next town which, according to an ad in the local paper, promised HIV testing and "reliable, accurate, *anonymous*" results in twenty minutes. Maybe he could bring himself to borrow Natalie's car or Peter's truck and drive to the medical office, but the idea of going alone was even more terrifying than the actual fear of AIDS. He couldn't start discussing this topic with Adam again, for Adam was too sad and distracted. So instead, Shawn kept it to himself, sitting on a closed toilet at four in the morning in the damp bathroom with its dingy aqua seahorse shower curtain, and peering moodily at a mole on his upper arm, wondering if it was a warning of things to come.

Finally he left the bathroom and came back into the bedroom they shared. Adam lay in the ridiculously small bed, which had carvings of squirrels and acorns gouged into the headboard. This had been Mrs. Moyles's son's room a long time ago, probably decorated with soccer trophies and posters from Led Zeppelin and *A Clockwork Orange,* and now it was a boy's room again.

Shawn silently stepped into his pants in the awful little room, then he slipped downstairs and sat at the piano in the half-dark. Quietly his fingers found the yellowed keys and he began to play a melody from his musical.

"That's so pretty," said a voice behind him. Shawn turned, suddenly self-conscious, and there stood Natalie in Sara's kimono.

"I didn't know you were up," he said clumsily.

"Oh, I roam the house at all hours," she said. "I was just reading the paper and having some coffee. Come join me."

He followed her into the dim nighttime kitchen. "Have a section," Natalie said, taking the paper apart and handing him a piece. He was afraid she might give him Business or Sports, and that he would have to politely stare at it for a while, pretending at least a minor degree of interest in some merger or team. To his relief, he saw that Natalie had handed him the Arts section. There were items in here he could actually read for meaning, articles on writers and musicians and performance artists who had experienced some sort of phenomenal success. What was the key to success? Shawn wondered. Was it really who you knew, or was it simply about pure talent? And if that were the case, Shawn wondered if he would really have a chance at a career. No one had ever called him talented; he had played the songs of his musical to an occasional friend, who usually shrugged, muttering that he personally knew nothing about writing, which was undoubtedly true. His friends weren't playwrights; they were actors, waiters, clowns at children's birthday parties, forced to wear red rubber noses and giant, floppy shoes, and give themselves professional names like Flookie the Wonderful Friend, or Bumbo the Magnificent and his Amazing Balloon Animals.

Of the people Shawn knew well, only Adam was a successful writer, and Adam hadn't seemed to like Shawn's musical, which was called *Spinsters!* But Shawn was determined to become a real playwright this summer, and to get someone to like his play, or, if that were impossible, to at least get someone to listen to a few of the songs from it. His fantasy was that Adam's producer would take an interest in his work.

"How's your musical going?" Natalie asked now. "Writing a musical must be so difficult. I really admire you for being able to do something as ambitious as that." He looked up, amazed that she was expressing admiration for him, however unfounded. "I have always envied people with talent," Natalie went on. "I've never had it myself. I don't have a creative bone in my body. I guess that's why I'm a travel agent. You need to enjoy talking on the phone, and you need to have a general sense of geography, but nothing more."

Natalie assumed Shawn had talent because he was here, among all these talented, preoccupied people, and because he shared a bed with Adam. She had no idea of how far removed he was from these other lives. Shawn had always known he was slightly marginal, the one on the sidelines who is allowed into places because he is good-looking and can be charming, but whom no one ever really wants to know.

As a child, Shawn would lie in bed at night and pretend that he was the host of a TV variety show called *Shawn's Spotlight*. He spoke quietly in the dark, introducing the night's guests ("The lovely Rita Moreno!" "A big hand for Helen Reddy!") and sometimes he sang, too. He had written a theme song to *Shawn's Spotlight,* which began, "Music and laughter and singing that's great / are all in store for you on Wednesdays at eight . . ." In the dark he would sing and run through his monologue, until his brothers, Ray and Tom, would complain from across the room, telling him to shut the fuck up and go to sleep. A pillow would sometimes be hurled, or a harder object. But Shawn had swelled with the continual wish to reinvent himself, and he used to swear that he would someday.

He shifted in his chair now, posturing a little, imagining the way a truly talented person would sit in a kitchen chair. He had the inclination to rest one elbow on the opposing knee, but then he realized he was only copying the unlikely pose of Rodin's *Thinker.*

"Talent is a difficult thing," Shawn tried. "Sometimes it's a burden."

"Oh, I would imagine so," said Natalie. "In what particular ways would you say it burdens you?"

"Sometimes," Shawn said, mumbling a little in embarrassment, "you just feel oversensitive. As though there isn't a thing in the world that doesn't interest you, or demand your attention, or make you want to write a song about it." He wasn't making this up; he had always felt distracted by a half-dozen things even when walking across a room. The spines of books called out to him, and even a spool of dental floss seemed to warrant a second look. He had an *eye* for things, yet that didn't mean he had a way to make that eye land on anything significant. But the more meaningful things, the emotions, the ways people spoke to each other in the heat of a moment, these were the difficulties that needed to be addressed when you sat down to write. If you didn't include them, if you forgot all about them, then you were a worthless writer of musicals whose work would never see the light of day.

Spinsters!, while being melodic and accessible, strained to include only what was important. The night that Shawn had met Adam, the night Adam spoke as part of a panel of playwrights about the responsibilities of being a young writer in America, Adam had said one should only write about "what matters." He had sat behind a table onstage, between a young Cree Indian play-wright, author of *The Crunch of Leaves Beneath My Feet,* and an African-American woman playwright with a croupy laugh, author of *Highfalutin'.* Adam had spoken intensely about writing the things that need to be written, regardless of who might read it. He had said you should write as if everyone you knew were dead, as if no one could possibly find fault with you. Then he had knocked over his water glass, sending water cascading across the table and into the lap of the Cree Indian.

Adam's play, *Take Us to Your Leader,* had been a comedy, but it had also dealt with the large issues: family tensions, religious intolerance, even death. The play was hilarious, with jokes about a mother's bad cooking and existential angst, and, of course, a homosexual son character trying to come out of the closet on Mars.

But how did Adam *do* it? Did he possess a gene for talent, which Shawn did not? And could Shawn possibly steal a piece of that talent away from him, perhaps while Adam was sleeping beside him? Could he hover over the imperfect face of the sad boy wonder, and take away something of substance? If you slept with a famous, talented young writer, surely something had to rub off on you, something special and delicate, like the silky powder that came off on your hands when you touched the wing of a moth. With Adam, it wouldn't be silky; it would be something coarser, less beautiful. Adam wasn't handsome or subtle, but he was smart. He was covered in grains of talent; it encrusted him like a breading, and Shawn wanted to pocket just a few grains. No one would ever notice.

"You feel oversensitive?" said Natalie. "That's the way I feel now. As though I can't even get through the day because I'll be too overwhelmed."

"I know that exact feeling," said Shawn. "I've had it all my life."

He felt her approving gaze upon him, and this was so rare and profound an experience that he wanted to enjoy it for a few moments longer, like a dog inclining its head in the hope that someone, anyone, might scratch it.

"You didn't know Sara," she said next, and he was disappointed; he really didn't want to talk about Sara. He could never admit this, but the subject was starting to bore him.

"No," he said. "Only a little. Only from Adam. I met her that night, of course." He paused. "She seemed very nice, though," he lamely added.

"You would have liked her," said Natalie.

"Oh, I'm sure I would have," he said tolerantly.

She looked at him hard, her eyes narrowing. "You've been wearing that shirt a lot," she said. "No offense, Shawn, but don't you have any other clothes with you?"

Shawn blushed. "Actually, no, I don't," he said. "I hadn't planned on staying here more than a day or two. But then Sara, well—*you* know—and I decided to stay on for Adam's benefit. So here I am."

"I shall take you shopping," Natalie announced.

"You don't need to do that," said Shawn. "Thank you, but I really can't afford to buy anything new right now."

"My treat," she said. "I insist."

He shrugged and laughed nervously, then found himself agreeing to let her take him to the store that morning. So a few hours later they drove to town in her car. Shawn enjoyed sitting beside her and listening as she pressed the search button on the radio, little blips of music or talk emerging from the good speakers and then disappearing, passed over in expectation of something better. When they pulled into the parking lot of a men's store called Dover's, he was almost disappointed, and would have preferred just driving around all morning. In the window, mannequins stood with hands on hips, sunglasses on their eyeless faces, bodies hard and perenially tanned. Shawn followed Natalie inside, where a doorbell discreetly chimed at their approach. A middle-aged salesman came over to them and asked, "May I help you?"

"Yes, thank you," said Natalie. "We'd like to find this gentleman a few things. A couple of shirts, maybe a jacket. Trousers. Sandals. He seems to have packed too lightly this summer."

The salesman studied Natalie and Shawn, trying to figure out the situation. Mother and son? Aunt and nephew? Or maybe something slightly sexual and perverted. Shawn enjoyed giving the illusion of being a kept man, someone fawned over by an older woman. In the dressing room, he slipped off his shirt, realizing that it had begun to smell a little bit too human; maybe that was why Natalie had suggested he buy some new clothes. He was mortified. Hygiene had always been important to Shawn; once he had gone to bed with a man named Buddy whose fingernails were embedded with dirt, as though he'd come directly to bed after having spent the day digging up a sewer. Shawn himself tried to be scrupulous. If he couldn't be famous or brilliant or wealthy, at least he could be clean. Now he balled his shirt up and threw it into a corner of the dressing room, slipping a new white shirt over his head. Then he stepped into a pair of linen trousers and observed the effect in the mirror.

"How does it look?" Natalie asked from outside the door.

"I'm not sure," Shawn said, trying to mute the feeling of pleasure that he felt upon looking at himself in good clothes. "Come see." He unlatched the slatted door and let her in. She stepped into doorway of the tiny room tentatively, as though this were an illicit act.

"Oh, you look wonderful," Natalie said. Together they gazed at Shawn in the three mirrors in the dressing room. She came closer to him, and then, with a hesitant hand, reached out and straightened the collar of his shirt. "There," she said. "Perfection."

He looked at himself again, and as he did he noticed in the mirror that her face had changed; she seemed suddenly on the verge of panic. "Natalie?" he said, turning to her. "What's wrong?"

"Sara," she said, her hand to her throat. "I was thinking how I used to take her shopping with me. We'd leave early in the morning, and we wouldn't get home until it was dark outside." She choked on the words. In the near distance, the salesman lurked and bobbed, pretending to be busy among a soft pile of men's sport shirts. Shawn closed the door, blocking the salesman's view, giving himself and Natalie the illusion of privacy, for certainly everything could be heard through this flimsy piece of slatted wood.

"Ooh, I feel dizzy," said Natalie, and Shawn sat her down on the floor. If you looked closely, you could see the occasional straight pin embedded in the field of pale carpeting. She leaned against the mirror and closed her eyes. "Sara and I always turned shopping into a big outing," she said. "At the end of the day, before the department store closed, they would blink the lights, like when an intermission is over at the theater and you're supposed to return to your seats. A voice would come over the intercom telling you that you had fifteen minutes of shopping time left. At that point, we'd just rev it up, as though we were on that old television show *Supermarket Sweep,* where they give you a limited amount of time to buy everything in sight."

Natalie reached into her mesh shoulder bag and began to rummage around, finally fishing out a pack of cigarettes and offering one to Shawn. He accepted, and sat beside her against the mirror. She ran her thumb along the wheel of a lighter and lit first his cigarette, then hers. They smoked silently for a few moments.

"Shopping was a whole different ball game in my family," Shawn finally said. "There were six of us kids back then."

"Were?" said Natalie.

"Yes, now there's five," he continued. "My older brother Ray overdosed on methadone; he'd been in and out of residential treatment. But when we were kids, the six of us would squeeze into the back of the station wagon. We just bounced around in the back of that old car, with our mother or father screaming at us to shut up, to calm down, to stop fighting, whatever. Mostly we wore hand-me-downs—for years I would pretend I was Ray, because I always got his clothes. He was older, cooler, more regular than me, and I'd stand in front of the mirror looking at myself. There was this one shirt—it was in this totally awful seventies style, you know, with a little zipper that went halfway down the front, and the material was some spongy polyester blend. But I loved that shirt, because I could become Ray in it. I could be normal, straight, whatever. And when we all went shopping, I'd pay attention to what Ray was getting, because in a year or two it would be mine. We shopped at this huge store near our house called Kernicky's Value Land," he said. "It was like a warehouse; it not only had clothes, it also sold farm equipment and bizarre things like animal enemas. I said to my mother: I cannot buy a suit from a store that sells animal enemas. But she always said something like: Who are you to complain, you're just one of six kids, so shut your trap."

" 'Shut your trap.' She actually said that? I think that's terrible," said Natalie. "Do you speak to her often now?"

"No," said Shawn. "Almost never. Her secret wish is that I would get AIDS and die so she wouldn't have to deal with me ever again."

"No mother wishes that!" said Natalie. "But you're not sick, Shawn, are you?"

"I don't know, actually," he said. "I haven't been tested, and to tell you the truth, I'm a chicken about it. But some of the people I've slept with, they've already dropped dead. I tried to call one of them just to make sure he was alive, and it turned out his phone had been disconnected. It's freaked me out, I have to say."

"Then you must get tested," said Natalie. "Tell Adam you want him to go with you and hold your hand."

"No, no, I can't," said Shawn. "The subject freaks *him* out too. He was always a little paranoid about it, but now, with Sara and everything, I can't ask him to deal with this, too. It's my concern, not his. He doesn't have to worry; we've only had 'safe sex,' as they say, and he was tested right before we met."

"Then I will go with you myself," said Natalie. "This after-noon. We'll get in the car and we'll—"

"No," said Shawn. "Thank you, but no. It's enough right now that I look halfway good in these clothes. That's enough for today. Let me take it one step at a time." He did look good; he knew it, and he was relieved. To be a gay man at the end of the twentieth century meant having to look good, unless you were Adam Langer, and then you could look sort of bad, but it didn't matter. Usually, the men Shawn became involved with were as handsome as he was; together over dinner or in bed the men looked like an evenly matched set: two gleaming cufflinks, a pair of bookends. But he and these men often shared a kind of desperation, as though they all knew that they needed their looks to carry them through life. Their jobs were uniformly boring: paralegal, word processor, and, in Shawn's case, telemarketing representative. The work lives of these young men were as dull as that of the dullest suburban dad on his way home to Scarsdale or Darien. But they had a secret code that kept them from sinking into despair, a system of flirting and winking and calling each other up and discussing who was fuckable, and who wasn't.

He thought of Natalie's offer to take him for an HIV test, and rejected it again in his mind. Five men he had been sexually involved with over the years had died: Steven H., Steven P., Jonathan from the gym, Andrew, and Donald the bartender at the Bedrock Club. One by one, like characters trapped in an old mansion in a mystery novel, the men had been knocked off. In the beginning, Shawn had assumed that it was a foregone conclusion that he would develop AIDS and die too. He had walked around with palpitations, giddy and expectant. But time kept passing, and to his astonishment there were no symptoms, not even a slight swelling of swollen glands in the neck, or a lingering cold, or fatigue. He knew men who regularly visited a local juice bar called Squeeze, where they ordered wheat grass cocktails, a bright green liquid that was served in tiny plastic cups. The men downed their miniature drinks, silently willing the liquid to provide them with energy and longevity and an invisible shield against infection. But still they fell ill, these men he saw at the gym, or knew from the clubs, or from his unsuccessful stint as a waiter, or from the week he had spent at a friend's share in the Fire Island Pines (in a house that was, for the record, much nicer than this one). And still Shawn stayed healthy. Which didn't necessarily mean it would last. It was entirely possible that one morning, a year from now, he would wake up with a rash, or an odd marking on his leg, and that would be that.

He often imagined his own death, the mourners filing into the funeral, none of them having been particularly close to him. His parents would probably refuse to come in from Michigan, out of some half-baked moral conviction. But his roommates would be there, already wondering who they could get to rent Shawn's room, and a couple of his siblings would make the trip too, as well as the loose grouping of casual friends he had made over the years. But no one would be passionate about him if he died, the way Sara's friends had been about her. No one would be hysterical, or driven half-mad, or endlessly obsessing and even deifying him, the way they did with Sara.

Since Sara Swerdlow died, Shawn's worries about himself had gotten so extreme that he thought Natalie was right: He ought to find out his fate once and for all. As it was, he woke up every day not knowing. It occurred to him that he might suddenly weaken, and that his life might slide into oblivion, and he would die without ever having achieved *anything,* without a single song he had written having ever been sung aloud in a theater by professional actor-singers. But still he behaved as though *not* knowing his HIV status provided him a bright green, protective shield. He kept his boyishness alive, and in fact worked hard to preserve it, although in his heart he knew that this year, this summer perhaps, marked the very end of boyishness for him. And the realization made him long, more than anything, to have his musical produced.

For years, it had been acceptable to say you were a writer of musicals but to still make your living from telemarketing. It wasn't a bad job, really. Most of the people you called hated you, and spoke back in truculent voices. In the background you could hear the clash of dinnerware, for you were invariably getting them smack in the middle of a meal. The overburdened American family had one brief moment of breaking bread together and you arrived to spoil it. *Good evening, ma'am, I'm calling from Advantage America, and we'd like to ask you a few questions about your leisure and entertainment needs.* Often they were bewildered, mouths full of food. *Wht? Fmmf, um, wahl, unh* . . . But sometimes they'd come right out and say, "*Fuck you, asshole!*"

Occasionally, you would stumble upon a deeply lonely person over the telephone who would quickly agree to be interviewed, and then wouldn't let *you* off the phone at the end of your survey. They'd actually invent reasons to keep you on the line, asking you to repeat the last question, or asking what other surveys they might participate in. They pulled you into the jaws of their lonesome misery, and you could easily picture their home: a studio apartment with a hotplate, or else the big, chilly house of a widow in a kelly green cardigan.

When the evening ended, very late (at 11:30 P.M. you could still call homes in the Pacific Time Zone), you and the other telemarketers would close up shop, shutting off the banks of fluorescent lights and heading down together in the elevator of this seedy but clean building in the West Thirties, a nowhere neighborhood dominated by Madison Square Garden and a long, slow crawl of taxicabs outside Penn Station. You'd hop onto the subway, or catch one of those cabs if you were feeling flush, and go back to your own home where, at any given hour, you yourself might get a phone call from a total stranger, asking if you had a few minutes to spare.

Now Shawn was away from the phone, away from his own shared apartment. His two roommates, Dirk and Arthur, one an actor/waiter and one a weight trainer/musician, seemed peeved that Shawn had escaped the city for a good chunk of August, despite the fact that he was all paid up on the rent. No one in New York could stand it when anyone else got a summer reprieve. It wasn't exactly as though this beach house was much of an escape, anyway. The place was terrible, and everyone in it was depressed about their friend Sara's death.

At first, after Sara died, Shawn had decided to bail out, but then he saw how needy Adam was, and how he could easily fill that need. It was pleasurable to make the famous young playwright indebted to him. Shawn brought him meals and rubbed his shoulders and held him in bed at night. How hard would it have been for Shawn to have written *Take Us to Your Leader*? If only Shawn had thought of it! But instead of contemporary, biting social comedy, he had opted for an old-fashioned musical, and everyone knew the musical was dead.

Spinsters! was singable and contained genuine characters, but it had very little chance of ever reaching a Broadway stage. It was a deeply unfashionable play for the nineties, whereas if Shawn had lived in the fifties, he would have been a celebrity in the Rodgers and Hammerstein tradition. Shawn would have been seen all around town, and asked to sit for photo shoots with Cartier-Bresson, and been interviewed by Walter Winchell and eaten shrimp cocktails late at night at Sardi's. But the truth was that Shawn was out of style and no one was interested. Instead, everyone got all hot and bothered over plodding old Adam. So Shawn hung around the beach house, waiting.

And now this woman, Natalie Swerdlow, was here too, and she made everything much more tolerable for him. Her sadness made her seem deeply, soulfully kind; many wounded people appeared that way. Shawn wondered if his own mother would grieve for him if he died. She had once called Shawn up and asked, in her hard, heartland voice, whether he had "the AIDS." There was something almost quaint about that "the." It reminded him of old-fashioned stories, in which people developed "the chilblains." Probably he was being unfair in his assessment of his mother, but in a way he thought she was actually disappointed that he didn't (at least not yet) have the AIDS. For if he had, then she could be rid of him once and for all, then mourn him fiercely and get over it. But they were stuck with each other—the cold, narrow mother and her failed, misunderstood faggot son.

He looked over at Natalie Swerdlow, who sat beside him in the tiny room, and it occurred to him that she was nothing like his mother. She was endlessly tolerant, and that was all anyone really wanted, wasn't it? Natalie was the kind of mother who for some reason was in awe of Shawn Best. Which no one else on earth would ever be.

"You don't want to get all involved in my problems, my HIV status, my pathetic life," he said to her. "You've got enough to deal with."

"I need whatever I can get," said Natalie. "If I just think about Sara and nothing else, I will go wild."

" 'I'm wild again,' " Shawn suddenly began to sing. "Beguiled again / A simpering, whimpering child again . . .'"

" 'Bewitched,' " Natalie joined in, and together their two imperfect voices began to sing, " 'bothered and bewildered / am I . . .' "

They sat comfortably together and smoked and sang. She knew all the same show tunes that he did, and in fact had seen most of the famous shows when she was young. She had seen Ethel Merman in *Gypsy,* and Carol Channing in *Hello, Dolly.* They sang silly songs too, like "I'm Gonna Wash That Man Right Outta My Hair," their voices rising in nostalgic pleasure. The carpeting was surprisingly spongy, and the store was cool, and they might have sat like that for a long time, singing freely and smoking many cigarettes, but suddenly, in the middle of a giddy rendition of the line that went "Rub him outta the roll call / and drum him outta your dreams . . . ," there was a loud knock at the door.

"Excuse me!" called the salesman. "Are you *smoking* in

there?" They were quickly silent, looking at each other with a kind of desperate mirth. Natalie exhaled, filling the room with smoke. "You are!" cried the salesman triumphantly. "You are actually smoking in the dressing room! I'll have to ask you both to leave. Right now."

It hadn't really occurred to either of them that smoking in the dressing room was a transgressive act. Now they quickly stamped out their cigarettes on the heels of their shoes and tried to wave the smoke from the air, but the room was so tiny that the smoke had nowhere to go. When they opened the door, it drifted out into the store. The salesman stood in front of them, rigidly clutching a bunch of wooden hangers. "Please purchase those clothes or remove them immediately," he said. So Natalie went to the cash register and bought Shawn all the items, the credit card verification and the folding of the clothes taking place in haughty silence, and then they left the store. The little doorbell rang lightly once more as they crossed the threshold and went back outside, where they snorted and laughed like the adolescents that they had once both been, a long time ago.

8

Campfire Girls

There was a party one afternoon at a mansion on the water, and Adam was invited. He didn't really want to go, but Shawn worked on him, telling him it would be good for him to get out of the house. This was true, of course, although Shawn's motives surely had to do with his own desire to be at that party. Shawn longed for such invitations, Adam knew, and had rarely been able to edge his way into that world of wealth and canapés and light conversation.

On the day of the party, when Adam and Shawn came downstairs dressed in pale, slightly formal summer clothes, Natalie stood in the kitchen with her head in the refrigerator. She was ferreting through everything on the shelves, extracting ancient bottles and jars. She yanked hard on a bottle that gripped the glass shelf with its own glue. Finally the jar was uprooted, and Natalie peered in to see what it was.

"Chutney," she said aloud to no one in particular. "Major Grey's Peach Chutney. Does anyone know how old this is?"

Adam, standing in the doorway buttoning his cuffs, tried to recall. "Yes," he said after a moment. "We got it three or four summers ago. We had an Indian dinner. I think it was Sara's idea."

Natalie gazed at the bottle with the thoughtful attentiveness of a mother gazing at her daughter's face. "Sara was a chutney person," she said quietly. She cradled the sorry-looking bottle in her hands, and at that moment Adam decided it was essential to get this woman out of the house. Otherwise, he could imagine her standing here forever, the refrigerator door left swinging wide, the chutney held tenderly in her useless hands. "Mrs. Swerdlow," he said. "Finish what you're doing and get dressed. You're coming with us."

THE PARTY WAS held at the home of Paul and Sheila Normandy, noted patrons of the arts. Adam had initially met the couple backstage at a performance of his play; a stream of people often came backstage, including celebrities and friends of Adam's parents ("It's Adele Glucksman! From 15 Bluebird Court!"), as well as the mayor and a loose circle of wealthy friends of the producer, some of them Broadway investors. The Normandys fell into this last category, and while they hadn't invested in his show, there would be future shows needing investors, and his agent, Mel Wolf, had wanted him to be charming backstage.

"But I don't know how to be charming," Adam nervously said to Sara after the curtain had come down one night and the actors were taking their bows. He and Sara sat in one of the tiny cinderblock dressing rooms; she was patiently retying his necktie, which he had knotted poorly, as usual.

"Yes you do," she said. "They just want you to be yourself. The witty gay writer. Come on, you do that very well. You *are* charming, Adam; it's not fake."

Suddenly the Normandys appeared in the doorway of the dressing room, and Adam rose. His tie was neat now, and his hair newly combed. Sara had helped him become presentable, and he was grateful. Women *did* that, he thought; they tied your tie, they flooded you with confidence, and they were wonderful companions. He and Sara never ran out of things to talk about. She had been teaching him Japanese, and he had been reading plays with her. They had recently been through an Aristophanes phase and had just begun Tom Stoppard.

His lack of attraction to her was sometimes a source of frustration. He had never felt particularly bad about being homosexual; this frustration wasn't grounded in self-loathing. Early on, Adam had known exactly what he was, what he liked, what pulled him into deep and tangled and exciting dreams. His parents had been fairly understanding, after a requisite crying jag and an insistence that he spend several sessions with a kindly female therapist in Great Neck. The therapist, Dr. Rachel Kline, was middle-aged and energetic and wore Indian-print dresses. She had found nothing wrong with Adam, and instead the two of them had played Yahtzee and shared a pot of raspberry tea during each chatty, friendly session.

So nothing *was* wrong with him, and that was still true. Sara had always insisted that he was extremely normal, much more so than she was. "I grew up raised by a totally narcissistic mother and no father," she had said. "Where does that leave me?"

"*My* parents were extremely boring," he had told her. "So middle-of-the-road and docile and boring that it probably warped me inside."

"No," she said, "you don't understand. No one wants interesting parents. Interesting parents are a curse." She paused. "My mother is very interesting," she added pointedly. "Parents should be completely dull and ordinary and predictable. You want their relationship to be stable and incredibly boring, as though you would kill yourself if you had to be in that marriage."

Neither Sara nor Adam wanted a boring marriage for themselves, nor did either of them want one of those Bloomsbury-type marriages that involved lots of furious letter-writing in lieu of sex. Sara wouldn't settle for such a thing; she was deeply attracted to men—men who were attracted to her right back—and she would always seek them out and then report back to Adam. He, in turn, would sleep with men and report back to *her.*

A few weeks after initially meeting the Normandys, Adam was invited to a dinner party at their Manhattan home, and he brought Sara as his date. The Normandys and their friends were so unlike the people he and Sara knew, whose idea of a dinner party was often potluck, with guests bringing falafel and brownies. But the Normandys had invited dozens of people, who were seated that evening around small, formal tables lit with rosy candles. He and Sara walked in arm in arm, and their mouths opened at the same moment. The opulence was too much for them, too stimulating.

Paul Normandy was squat and friendly and seemed to be waiting for his first heart attack to happen, while his wife was built like a praying mantis and draped in jewels. "Look at the way their skin shines," Sara had whispered that night. "That's not oil or sweat glands. It's wealth; they've got the money glow." Artwork could be found everywhere in the apartment, which was adorned with giant cracking canvases of eighteenth-century milkmaids and recent, disturbing oil paintings of dogs with their throats slashed. When canapés circulated, Sara and Adam tried to engage the waiters and waitresses in conversation, for who else was there to talk to? Who else was in their league?

Eventually, when Sheila Normandy came over to say hello, Adam became overcome by discomfort. "Hey, thanks for inviting us," he'd said, giving his hostess's hand a shake and crushing her fingers with their hard, pointy rings. Sheila winced, and Adam pulled back in apology. Then he proceeded to drop a piece of salmon-and-chervil roulade down the front of his dinner jacket, and excused himself to go clean himself up, leaving Sara to fend for herself.

In the Normandys' bathroom, frantically dabbing at the stain with a wet yard of toilet paper, he'd looked in the mirror and seen himself as he was: not the gay Neil Simon at all, but instead an ordinary-looking person who had no business here in this bathroom that was as big as his entire apartment, with gold faucets shaped like fish. All he could think of, looking at the fish faucets with their wide-open mouths, was fellatio. He fantasized about lowering his pants and letting some man—the Normandys' butler, perhaps, a cute British guy—take Adam's penis in his mouth. When he emerged from the bathroom, embarrassed by his own thoughts and spattered with water, Sara pulled him aside, yanking him into an alcove beneath a lesser Seurat; they were so close to it that all colors had separated into a field of discrete dots, and they couldn't even see what the image was supposed to be.

"You've left me here for hours," she said.

"It hasn't been hours."

"Yes it has," she said, her voice petulant, but he decided to forgive her. Everyone always forgave Sara.

"Well," Adam said, "I'm here to rescue you." He took Sara's arm, feeling the reassuring brush of velvet sleeve against his wrist as they went in to dinner.

Now, walking up the driveway of the Normandys' summer home without Sara, Adam thought of how, if she were here, she would quiet his anxieties. He was barely half himself without her; he was small, shriveled, joyless, abstracted. Her mother was beside him instead, and everything was out of alignment. He suddenly felt on the verge of weeping as he glanced over at this woman who was like Sara but not—this woman who had given birth to the woman he loved. All around them, valets directed cars into parking spots and guests approached the house, the women dressed in pale linen and clutching purses no bigger than summer fruit, the men sauntering casually up the steps. Just as reluctance threatened to overtake him, Natalie turned and said, "I don't want to do this. I want to go home."

"Me too," said Adam. "So let's go."

"No, wait, it'll be fine, you guys," Shawn said quickly. "We'll have drinks. We won't have to talk to anyone but ourselves." He was almost pleading, so much did he want to be at this party. "Please," he said. "It'll do us all some good." And so they kept walking. As they headed toward the house, Adam gazed at the grounds. Somewhere out back, he had heard, there was a helicopter, resting silently on its own launch pad. He mounted the wide porch steps numbly, wondering if he would ever take pleasure in anything again, if he would ever feel comfortable in the world without Sara.

Inside the house, a butler quickly appeared with a tray of peach bellinis, and a sprightly female caterer appeared with a tray of hors d'oeuvres cut to the size of nickels. The living room was as big as a beach, and filled with people. In the corner, at a massive white piano, a well-known cabaret entertainer was playing standards; the word "love" kept trilling into the air. Unnoticed, Adam, Shawn, and Natalie wandered lost through the room. No one noticed them, and no one showed an interest in talking to them.

Suddenly there was a distraction in the large room, a rustle of interest elsewhere, and Adam looked upward to see Paul Normandy and his wife, Sheila, descending the wide stairway. Clasped around Paul Normandy's left ankle was a thick metal manacle. Having been convicted recently of a securities swindle, he had been placed on house arrest all summer, which meant that he was forced to remain in the splendor of his beach home until the fall, an electronic monitoring cuff attached to his ankle. In September, back in Manhattan, he would begin a certain number of hours of community service. The house was undeniably a good place to be imprisoned. Except for the fact that Paul Normandy was unseasonably pale, he seemed none the worse for wear now, making the rounds of guests, shaking hands and slapping backs, while his tanned wife gave other wives air-kisses, not even attempting to touch lips to cheek but simply aiming for the approximate vicinity of the other person.

"Look, Adam, the wife is coming over here," Shawn whispered. "She seems to be coming right over to *us*. Oh, Jesus."

"What's wrong?" said Adam.

"What's wrong is that I don't know what you're supposed to talk about in situations like this. I practically grew up in Dogpatch."

"Well, I don't know what you're supposed to say either," said Adam. "Sara always said I should fake it," he added, as Sheila Normandy strode directly toward their little cluster. Adam and Shawn turned and gave her identical party smiles. "Adam Langer," she said, positioning herself before him and taking his hands in hers. "I heard that you were involved in that terrible car accident. I'm so sorry about your loss." Before Adam could answer, he saw that Sheila had moved her gaze over to Natalie, and that the two women were observing each other in a peculiar, narrow-eyed way. For a long moment neither of them said anything.

"Wait a minute," Natalie finally said to her. "I know you."

"And I know *you*," said Sheila.

There was another pause, and then Natalie began to sing in a tentative voice, "Sit around the campfire . . . join the Campfire Girls."

"Sing wo-he-lo, sing wo-he-lo," sang Sheila.

"Work . . . health . . . love!" the two women sang together.

After the song, they shrieked and lunged for each other, embracing furiously. "Sheila Carmucci?" said Natalie.

"Natalie Wall?" cried Sheila. "I can't believe it. You look exactly the way you used to look; I can still see it in your face."

"I don't have braids anymore," said Natalie.

"And I had my teeth straightened," said Sheila. "And later on

I had everything enhanced with collagen, but that's another story."

"It's still you," said Natalie.

"Yes," said Sheila. "It still is. I don't think anything can change that, can it?"

The women regarded each other with astonishing tenderness. Natalie later explained everything to Adam and Shawn: how she and Sheila had been Campfire Girls together as children, going on overnights to the woods just north of the city. The shriek and the embrace were visceral on Sheila Normandy's part; in truth, she didn't want anyone to know of her modest background, that she was the daughter of a man who ran a poultry warehouse in the Bronx. But she never lied about her past on the odd occasion when it rose to the surface, and when she saw Natalie for the first time in almost thirty years, it was a moment of true pleasure.

"I had no idea you'd become so prominent," said Natalie, gesturing around the room. "This is unbelievable."

"And you," said Sheila, leading Natalie by the arm away from the now-forgotten and bewildered Adam and Shawn. "I want you to tell me everything."

LATER, AFTER the party was over and Natalie was driving them down the gravel road of the mansion and back to their own house, she suddenly asked if there was anywhere to get a drink. She certainly didn't need any more alcohol, but Adam felt that he could hardly deny her something that would deaden pain. Besides, it seemed especially bleak to return to the house right now, having just come from such splendor.

"A drink sounds great," said Shawn. "You know what's around here, Adam. This is your territory, not ours."

"I can't think of anywhere, really," said Adam. "I mean, there's the Gangplank, but obviously we wouldn't want to go there."

"What's the Gangplank?" asked Natalie.

"A gay bar," said Adam. "I shouldn't have mentioned it. I think you'd feel kind of uncomfortable there, Mrs. Swerdlow."

"No I wouldn't," she said, and so he directed her there. The street in front of the bar was packed with cars, some parked the wrong way, a few even on the grass. Men leaned against trees, smoking and flirting. From inside the bar came the tinny drone of technopop. Adam had never thrown himself into dancing, or into the excitement that accompanied it. Instead, he had always been there on the sidelines, watching crowds of writhing dancers like an anthropologist doing field work. The music belonged to *them,* not him. It had belonged to extroverted men in gay bars, and it had belonged to Sara, who sometimes spent evenings with men Adam never met. Her independence had sometimes defeated him, left him feeling like a child lost and quietly suffused with panic in the middle of a department store. She had not belonged to Adam: she had had her own tastes and desires that had nothing to do with him.

What they shared was often a general sense of the hopelessness of love, its near-unavailability, as though love was a rare bird spotted in a wilderness preserve only one day in any year. You had to stake it out with binoculars, quiet and patient; if you moved too soon, or leapt up in excited pleasure, it would fly off in a shudder of feathers.

"I don't think I even know who the supposedly contented people are," Adam had said to her. "I mean the truly and consistently contented ones. The ones who aren't walking around with some artificial happiness manufactured by Prozac or Paxil. I wish the genuinely happy people would just raise their hands and identify themselves, and then we can ask them what their secret is."

"You know something? I really love you," Sara suddenly said.

"I love you too," he had replied, something he'd never said to a man.

The way it was supposed to have gone, this joint life of theirs, was like this: Sara would complain a lot but ultimately marry one of her dashing boyfriends and have children with him. Adam would complain a lot and date men occasionally, but would always live alone. He would be the godfather to Sara's children, dedicating plays to them, becoming a delightful Sunday uncle who would be eternally playful and indulgent in ways that their own parents could not be. And throughout Adam and Sara's separate but deeply interlaced lives, they would both feel longings for a merged life, for perfection and union and lying in bed again without the problems that sex always brought.

He looked around him at the various men now, feeling himself withdraw, changing into a meek reference librarian in a movie, his shoulders becoming rounded, his chest seeming to turn concave. Men came from all over the area to this bar, crowding into the cinderblock building and drinking and talking intimately in corners. From inside now came the persistent and persuasive thump of dance music.

Once inside the door, Adam paid for himself and let a strange man jam a rubber stamp that read ENTER onto the back of his hand. His hand blazed from the touch of the stamper; that was all it took to excite him. That, and the music rising and the hordes of men he could glimpse inside, all of them presumably men who had sex with other men. Adam felt himself grow tense and alert the way he always did when he entered a room full of men. Instinctively, he put an arm on Natalie's back, as if to link himself up with her, the way he had always done when he had come here with Sara, as if to say: *Save me from the world of men.*

"God, look at you," said Shawn as they walked down the dark hallway and into the main room.

"I'm not good in bars," said Adam. Shawn, however, seemed right at home here, having spent hundreds of nights in gay bars of all kinds, and when they arrived in the main room he leaned over the warm, sloping glass of a jukebox and dropped in quarters. Immediately, a man came over to Shawn, ostensibly to see what songs he had picked. Adam felt defeated as he walked to the long bar and ordered a Sprite. But then Natalie appeared beside him, tapping her foot to the music and trying to look as though she remotely fit in. There were no other women in the bar. She was as nervous as he was; together they were like two freshmen at a college mixer, both waiting to see if anyone would be attracted to them, if they would ever be loved. Natalie ordered herself a Stinger and drank it quickly.

"Look," she said, peering over the top of her glass, "I think you have a couple of admirers." Adam looked, noticing two men in their late thirties in tank tops who actually seemed to be staring intently at him.

The men approached. "Excuse me," said one, "are you Adam Langer?"

"Yes," said Adam, feeling heat in his face.

"It's the gay Neil Simon," said the other man. "We thought so. We just wanted to tell you how much we like your work. My mother even likes your work. I took her to your play, and she actually laughed. And this is a woman with no sense of humor; they removed it with her thyroid."

"Well, thank you. Thank you," said Adam.

"Are you working on something new?" asked the first man.

"Oh, he works all the time," Natalie said. "Nonstop, all day. I can hear his little computer clicking away. It sounds like a dog's toenails on linoleum."

He cringed at her lie. His work was going poorly; he couldn't focus on writing at all, but still it was pleasurable to have these men admire him. On his own and unknown in a bar, Adam usually felt miserable, but once someone knew who he was and allowed him to be excused from the normal requirements of true attractiveness, he did very well. The two men, whose names were Henry and Armand, seemed genuinely excited to be in his presence. Natalie had begun a conversation with Armand, and she was now advising him on making hotel reservations in Greece. He looked interested as she talked, and after a while a couple of

Armand's friends came over to join in the talk. It was as though she drew them to her with her otherness, her solemn and older femaleness in the midst of all these men. "There's not much choice on Crete," she was saying. "You might do better on Corfu."

Tonight she seemed to be the mother these men hadn't had, the one who was understanding and tolerant of who they had become. She was standing and chatting with a whole group of men, her eyes bright as she offered sound, motherly advice, answering their travel questions and telling them details about herself. The music grew very loud and Adam could no longer hear much of the conversation, but he could read her lips as she spoke to a tall man with nipple rings. "Her name was Sara," he saw her tell him. "She was thirty when she died." Soon the man asked her to dance. She reached out a hand for Adam to come join in too, as if this were a three-way dance, a game of ring-around-the-rosy, but he vigorously shook his head no. He wasn't a good dancer, and never had been. Everyone said dancing was like sex; if you made two characters dance in a play, then that was always a symbolic prelude to their lovemaking. He saw the tiny lights of joints as they were inhaled and passed among shirtless dancing men. For a moment he saw Shawn, who was now dancing with the man from the jukebox. And then, startled, he saw Natalie, who was now inhaling someone's joint, her eyes closed, her body loosely moving. She exhaled and passed the joint to someone else, her expression newly dreamy. Adam marveled at the way she was able to give in to the cluttered warmth of the evening and make herself comfortable in the midst of all these limbs and the heat they generated. As the dance floor filled, the place smelled like a locker room, the peculiarly sour smell of large groups of men which, for some reason he couldn't explain, he really liked.

In the middle of the dance floor, Natalie was trying to become someone else, someone who could actually dance without thinking of death. She was a surprisingly good dancer, flexible and fluid. Then Adam was startled to see that Natalie was taking her blouse off, joining the shirtless crowd, undoing her buttons and tossing her blouse to the side. Soon there she was in her bra. He felt tremendously sad and anxious for Sara's stoned, dancing mother. But in this mass of half-naked bodies she seemed merely another eccentric, throwing an interesting and even exotic female note into the mix. She was the lone woman in this sea of men. More men pounded into the bar, pushing in a group out onto the dance floor. Unlike Natalie, Adam would never take off his shirt; he would continue to shuffle through life all covered up.

Suddenly he pulled off his jacket and clomped onto the dance floor, saying "Excuse me, excuse me, sorry," as he made his way through the crowd. When he reached Natalie he held his jacket out to her like a suburban husband approaching his wife at the end of an evening with her fur coat in hand, gallantly holding the sleeve-holes open so she could slip in her slender, pale arms. Natalie stared at him and his jacket, confused. "Here," he said. "Why don't you put it on?" he suggested. She started to protest, and then something made her change her mind, for she stepped in front of him, facing away, and let first one arm fall into a sleeve, and then the other. Then she looked at him in a serious, grateful manner, and disappeared back into the crowd, where she was enveloped by men, dancing with her eyes closed, for one night forgetting.

9

Thrilling in Bed

I n the thick of death, why does love survive? No, that wasn't
the interesting question, Peter thought. The interesting
question was: In the thick of death, why does desire survive?
For it was desire he felt for Maddy at one in the morning, even as
she turned away from him in her sorrow and distraction. Sara
was dead, and everyone was overcome with sadness, but still, in
the late-night confines of this room, Peter remembered exactly
what the smooth taffy-pull of sex felt like, and he wanted it again.

But there was no place for sex anymore in this marriage.
Slowly, sex had been elbowed out, starting with the pregnancy
and culminating in the death of Sara. When he reached for
Maddy now, at one in the morning, she shook her head and whispered, "The *baby's* awake."

"Oh, he's not looking," Peter whispered back. "This won't
traumatize him."

"You never know," said Maddy. "It's the 'primal scene,' right? It's a really big deal. Dr. Blandish has a whole chapter on how important it is to be modest around your children."

"I'm so sick of Dr. Blandish," said Peter. "Who does she think she is? And besides, *I* witnessed the so-called 'primal scene,' and it didn't screw me up for life."

"You did?" said Maddy. "What exactly did you see?"

"I was six," he said. "I had a nightmare; I think it was about being chased by big yellow shoes, and I left my bedroom and walked right in on my parents. My father, who as you know is a pretty substantial guy, was lying right on top of my mother. I figured, with the way he was lying, she'd have to be dead. But she wasn't, she was breathing hard. No one noticed me, and I just stood there in the darkness at the foot of their bed, wondering how she could breathe like that with my father on top of her. Finally they saw me, and all three of us screamed at once."

"Well, I don't want Duncan to see us," Maddy said.

"*You* don't want to see us," said Peter. "Or feel us. Or anything."

"You're right," she admitted finally. "I guess I don't anymore."

His sex drive had always been more powerful than hers, but that hadn't troubled him. He had associated his interest in sex with his maleness, considering it strictly a gonad issue. Back when he was single and unattached, he would sometimes lie on his futon in his burglar-friendly East Village apartment, located directly above a Jamaican head shop where the reggae played day and night, and the potent spice and flower smell of sinsemilla wafted up through the vents. Peter would sprawl on his back, listening to the music and getting a contact high from the smoke, which he topped off with a beer and a few broken-off rectangles of Ghirardelli chocolate, and he would think about having sex with an assortment of women—admirable ones such as social workers or lawyers for the disadvantaged, and lurid ones such as lap dancers with strategic beauty marks. He used to think about his sister Dana, whose breasts tormented him in adolescence with their proximity—both to him and to each other.

In recent years, he masturbated to the image of a girl named Arquetia who had been one of the students in his homeroom class at the school where he taught, and whose skin was of a profound, almost waxed shade of black. "Fuck me, Arquetia," he once heard himself whispering into his pillow. Sometimes he masturbated to Maddy's image, a stand-in for her real self which had become inert and unwilling. Occasionally he masturbated over Sara, an activity that had begun as soon as he met her in college, and which continued on, to his embarrassment, after her death.

Sometimes at night now, lying beside the infinitely sad and unwilling Maddy, he thought of Sara and became excited. One night last week, after Maddy had refused him again and turned over and went to sleep, he allowed a single hand to creep down and grab himself. Then swiftly, neatly, he had a silent orgasm, Sara's face hovering above him, her phantom hand resting lightly on his.

ONE NIGHT IN the middle of the month, the entire household went to the summer carnival, a corny annual affair set up in the Caldor parking lot. There were roulette wheels, zeppole and sausage stands, and a big glass cotton-candy machine in which sugar was spun into billows of flyaway, pale blue hair. There were the usual rides, too, including the Spider, a truck with bumper cars on it, and a surprisingly big Ferris wheel hovering above everything. They wandered through the carnival in a group, idle and hot.

Peter stood beside Maddy and Duncan at a shooting gallery, aiming his air rifle at a row of tin ducks that clacked mechanically past. One by one he knocked them down; his aim was sure, and the man behind the counter presented him with a large green stuffed animal that was supposed to be either a dog or a bear, it was unclear which. Duncan liked the ambiguous animal, and immediately reached out for it, so Peter handed it to him.

Shawn and Adam were having temporary tattoos applied to their arms, and Natalie stood alone off to the side, gazing up at the Ferris wheel. "I used to ride Ferris wheels all the time when I was growing up," she said. "The bigger the better."

Peter decided that he would make a friendly gesture toward Natalie now; it seemed to be the right thing to do, especially since Maddy had always complained that he hadn't liked Sara, which of course wasn't true. But the truth could not be told. "Mrs. Swerdlow," he asked, "would you like to go up?"

So up they went, onto the Ferris wheel, sitting side by side in a small, swinging car that hung suspended above the parking lot and the crowds below. He never quite knew what to say to Sara's mother; it was always somewhat awkward. "So," he said now. "It's quite a view."

"Yes," she said. Then her capacity for small talk was used up. "You don't like to talk about your relationship with Sara, do you?"

"There's not much to say," Peter said. "She was mainly Maddy's friend."

"Oh, cut the crap," said Natalie.

He stared at her. "*Excuse* me?" he said.

"I know what went on between you two," she said. "Did you think I didn't?"

Peter was horrified. He couldn't imagine what he should say next; there was no etiquette book to instruct him. "But you're her mother," was all he said, breathless suddenly.

"You're damn right I'm her mother," she said. "And she told me things she told no one else. I know all about you."

Before he could even think of a reply, the Ferris wheel suddenly stopped moving and their car was left swaying near the top of the sphere. For a few minutes there was nothing—no sound, no movement—and Natalie and Peter didn't say a word. Finally there came a loud squeal of feedback from below, and then an announcer's voice began to speak over the P.A. system. "Due to a mechanical error," the voice said, "the Ferris wheel is temporarily stalled. Will all people on the ride please remain calm. Do not try to exit the Ferris wheel at this time."

"My God, we're trapped," Natalie said.

"Oh, this happens every summer," Peter said. A crowd was forming below, and he could see Adam and Shawn, and then Maddy, with Duncan strapped to her back. The big stuffed animal was still in the baby's arms, a blob of green. Maddy waved to Peter, and he lifted his arm obediently in response.

"I'm starting to feel a little dizzy," Natalie said. "Like I might faint, or throw up or something." She did seem rattled, her face sweaty and pale. Perspiration collected in the little vertical groove above her lip—the philtrum, that place was called; he remembered this obscure fact from studying a chart of the human body. Oddly, he thought that she had a beautiful philtrum, a perfect, tiny column.

"Don't look down, Mrs. Swerdlow," said Peter. "Look at me. Only me." She obeyed him, turning her gaze fully to his face. He saw again how pretty she was and how delicate her features were, as Sara's had been. She looked right at him, unblinking, and he perceived a gratefulness in her expression. The sudden vertigo seemed to pass, or at least to shift. "There," he said. "You're doing fine. Are you feeling better?"

She seemed to think about it, realizing they were suspended in air but that nothing bad was going to happen; no freak carnival accident, the top story on the local news. "Yes," said Natalie. "Yes, I am. Thank you," she added softly. "Peter?" she continued. "I didn't mean to upset you before. I would never tell Maddy, you know."

"She would hate me," he said simply.

"I didn't say it as a threat," she said. "It's just that, talking about Sara, knowing everything about her . . . it's the only way I can keep her around."

"I know what you mean," he said, for this was exactly the way he experienced Sara, too. In his case, though, he kept Sara alive through his silent thoughts, his nocturnal fantasies, the elegant pornography he drummed up for himself in which he and Sara lay twined on her couch, the radiator spurting heat into that already overheated living room.

"She thought you had beautiful blue eyes," Natalie said now. "Like little swimming pools. And you do." Peter felt himself grow flushed. "And also," Natalie continued, "she said that you were . . . well, I probably shouldn't say this . . ." Her voice faltered.

"What?" said Peter. "Tell me." Nothing could surprise him now. They were swaying in the metal car of a carnival ride, and it was as though they might never come down; they were stuck up there forever. They could say anything, and none of it would matter later.

"She also said," Natalie went on, "that you were thrilling in bed."

Peter felt the blush deepen, darken. "She really said that?" he asked. "Thrilling?"

Natalie nodded, and Peter stared out over the side of the car, waving vaguely again at his wife and child. A vain pleasure coursed through him, his entire body somehow weakened at the idea of Sara thinking this about him. *Thrilling.* His heart sang in response. He wanted to reach out and hug Sara's mother in gratitude for telling him this detail, but he didn't dare move. He suddenly imagined embracing Natalie Swerdlow, their bodies colliding high above the ground. *Thrilling,* he thought, confused and happy, as the ride was suddenly jolted to life, and the big wheel began to turn, bringing them slowly down to earth.

MADDY BOUGHT A Ouija board at the Toys "R" Us out off the highway. Inside the huge store, mothers and fathers dragged plastic wading pools across the floor, while their children scattered, lost in the hangar-sized existential void. Maddy felt lost too, disoriented in this formless space, wheeling her cart around with its snap-in baby seat, then standing on line behind a family and their own shopping cart that was stuffed with toys that would forever require an expensive dependence on AA batteries. Duncan began to flail and emit his little cat mewl, and she fished around in her purse and found his pacifier. It had a single hair wrapped around it, which she whisked away and then plugged the thing into the baby's mouth. Who knew whose hair that was? And anyway, if she kept giving him pacifiers now, the baby would need his mouth jammed with plastic for years to come. He would develop a stunned, vacant expression that would never leave his face. She was obviously a bad mother.

Maddy waited, gripping the cart, while the family in front of her emptied their cart so each ugly or violent item could be dragged across the price scanner. Then it was her turn, and the cashier rang up the Ouija board and handed it back to her in a big plastic bag. Once outside the store, she pulled the bag off. If she could have, she would have tried to use this thing right here in the parking lot, so powerful was her desire to speak to Sara again. But it was raining outside, a light drizzle that sent families scurrying like chicks to their family-sized vans. Maddy lifted the baby into the old red pickup truck and belted him into his Fisher-Price seat. Then she took the wheel and headed back to the house, thinking only of Sara, and how soon, in some insane way, she would be speaking to her.

Maddy had never believed in the supernatural; all things that involved "eerie" coincidence had seemed to her merely random and dull. But grief quickly turned you into a believer. Maddy had spent a series of nights lying in bed thinking about Sara, imagining the two of them sitting by the lake at Camp Ojibway, sharing those first, hesitant confidences. What had they talked about? Other girls, of course—which one was mean, which one was a psycho, which one a hopeless, pathetic loser. They talked about the books they liked, usually novels about troubled young women who are committed to mental institutions. And they talked about boys, too, whispering confidences to each other, describing what their different experiences had actually felt like. Sara had told her of how a boy's hand, grazing across the convex surface of her breast, had made her almost want to die with happiness. Maddy had listened attentively, imagining that there might be a time in the future when a boy would touch her own breast, and when she too might experience such sensations. She had admired Sara for being the one to try out all these experiences first, for being the royal taster, the first girl she knew who had actually been touched all over, and who had let herself be finger-fucked, as they so indelicately called it then, by an older, deeply excitable boy.

But that afternoon by the lake had taken place so long ago that it had become an antique, a quaint, irrelevant fragment. Maddy wanted Sara back so badly that she would have taken any version of her: the young girl by the lake, the college student, the scholar of Japanese, the desirable woman ringed by a corona of men. Sara, who had always generated in Maddy a sequence of jealousy and guilt. Of course Maddy had loved Sara, and Sara loved her; who else could she really, really talk to?

But love would not end with this death, and neither would jealousy. It all stayed alive and vivid and disturbing, except it had no place to go, no vessel to be poured into. So the Ouija board could be that vessel, a quick fix. In childhood, she and her brothers had played with a Ouija board, and it remained Maddy's only conceivable conduit to the dead. She carried the flat box home in the truck, then took it upstairs discreetly, not wanting anyone to see.

Maddy pulled open her dresser drawer now and hid the Ouija board there, under all her clothes and beside the latest bottle of sweet-tasting liquor she had stashed there. This time it was Cointreau. Maddy took a long drink from the bottle, and then another. She had a low tolerance for alcohol, and pretty soon she felt a responding fluidity in her legs and a flush in her cheeks. She capped the bottle and stuffed it back beside the Ouija board, noticing the copy of *The Upbeat Baby* beneath it. These were all secret, embarrassing objects. The drinking felt illicit because she did it surreptitiously; it was medicinal and necessary and private. So, in its own way, was the Ouija board. Peter would have made fun of her if he had seen it, so she decided she wouldn't show it to him. Instead, she would simply use it by herself in the middle of the night, while everyone else was fast asleep.

But tonight, as it turned out, everyone was wide awake in the middle of the night. Adam had another one of his sleepwalking episodes, rising from his bed as if summoned by Sirens, and stumbling around in the upstairs hallway. "Oh, shit," said Peter, rolling over in bed. "He's walking again." Peter and Maddy opened the door of their room and peered out; Adam was moving through the hall in that clumsy drunken gait, and they watched as he opened the door of Sara's room and marched in. There he saw a sleeping woman in the bed. He regarded her for a moment, and then he lay down beside her. Opening her eyes, Natalie let out a squeal, and within a second Maddy and Peter and Shawn were all packed into the room. A light was turned on, and everyone tried to comfort Natalie and awaken Adam at the same time. Adam was confused and embarrassed, apologizing to Natalie repeatedly, until she asked him to stop. Finally Shawn walked him back to their room and put him to bed. Maddy stayed with Natalie, waiting there until she was completely calm, and Peter hung back uselessly, then finally retreated.

"Can I get you some water?" Maddy asked Natalie, as the two women sat on the edge of the bed. Sara's mother nodded, so Maddy went downstairs and returned with a glass of midnight water, warm and served in one of Mrs. Moyles's chipped mugs. Natalie drank gratefully, gulping it down like a child.

"He really frightened me," said Natalie when she was done. "I thought for a second that maybe Sara really *was* here in the bed."

"Mrs. Swerdlow," Maddy began carefully, "have you ever

thought about trying to contact her?" Then she told Natalie about
the Ouija board that was hidden in her dresser drawer.

"I can't believe you would waste your money like that," said
Natalie. Then there was a pause. "Although I suppose," Natalie
added, "there's no harm in trying it."

So Maddy crept back into her bedroom, where Peter was
again asleep, and she slipped the board from her drawer, and the
two women went downstairs to the kitchen. The only light in the
room emanated from the sunburst clock. Natalie and Maddy sat
at the table, which gleamed in the dim light and was still slightly
sticky from dinner.

"Oh, look at this," Natalie murmured, running her hand
across the surface, and she couldn't resist finding a sponge and
wiping the offending spot of tomato sauce away. Then the table
was clean and damp and shining, and Maddy spread out the
Ouija board, which looked somehow cheaper and flimsier than
the way she remembered it from childhood. Back then, she and
her brothers had asked the board ridiculous questions, such as:
Will I get a good grade on my book report? Or: *Will Dad let me go to
Steve Belletti's party this weekend, even though his parents are away?*
And once, when she was alone with the board, she asked it in a
whisper: *Will I ever get breasts?*

The Ouija board was fashioned out of wood pulp, and had the
alphabet written out in an appealing style, graced by a little sun
and moon. Natalie and Sara sat across from each other, resting
their fingertips on the marker that was shaped like a teardrop.
The marker was plastic, and it too seemed cheaper than the way
she remembered it, but everything in the world had been scaled
down since her childhood: all toys, diversions, expectations. It
made sense that the secret line of communication to the afterlife
would be made of wood pulp and plastic and probably manufactured by abused, underage workers in Taiwan. Life continued to
disappoint, but you took what you could get. These two grown
women, who did not believe in the afterlife, who did not believe

in the spirit-world or in the presence of ghosts, now sat with their fingers lightly and reverently touching plastic.

"So what are we supposed to do here?" Natalie asked nervously.

"My brothers and I used to do this all the time," explained Maddy. "You can ask it anything you like."

"Like what?"

"Like . . . well, 'Who am I talking to?' " said Maddy.

"All right," said Natalie. Then, in a loud, self-conscious voice, she said, "Who am I talking to?"

The women waited. They heard the minute hand on the sunburst clock click quietly, and Maddy felt her pulse jump lightly in her neck. At first, there was nothing, just the clock, just the pulse. They waited, and no one spoke. Natalie cleared her throat. Then, slowly, the plastic marker began to shift, sluggishly at first, then with more persistence, scraping silently across the board, inching itself over to the letter *S*.

"Yes," Natalie said softly, under her breath, as the marker moved with divine obedience to each of the remaining letters in Sara's first name. Then, for good measure, it added "JANE," which had been Sara's middle name. Maddy felt a quickening, her breathing becoming more exerted, the same excitement that she had felt in childhood in front of her family's older, sturdier version of a Ouija board. If she looked in the mirror right now, she thought, most likely her pupils would have been dilated.

"Now you ask it something," said Natalie.

"All right," said Maddy. She felt oddly anxious. "Sara," Maddy said aloud, "how are you?"

For a short while, there was again nothing. Then, finally, "OK." But the marker was moving on its own now, skidding like a puck on ice over to the letter *D*.

"DONT WORRY," spelled the marker, with painful deliberation. Then it added, "I AM YOURS FOREVER."

Natalie and Maddy lifted their fingers at the same moment,

stunned, pleased, knowing this game was finished. It was wonderful to think that they might have Sara forever, to think that
somehow she would be there in the atmosphere, and that even
though no one else would know she was there, they both would.
They had willed these words, but they had willed them together;
they had jointly approved of them, had had them somehow spiri-
tually notarized, Maddy thought, remembering the conversation
about Notary Publics that first evening at the house, that final
evening with Sara.

Natalie's eyes were flooded, shining. She and Maddy held
hands across the board, while the rest of the house slept, and
somewhere above them all, Sara stirred.

NEITHER WOMAN could sleep for the rest of the night, so they settled in at the kitchen table, the baby monitor perched like an
essential icon on the counter, even though Peter was still upstairs
asleep a few feet from Duncan. In some way, Maddy trusted only
herself with the baby, saw herself as the only one who could take
care of him. Maddy poured herself a drink, and Natalie brewed
some coffee. They had just eased into conversation when loud
squawking sounds came from the monitor, and the row of
red lights flashed. "Oh, well," Maddy said, pushing back her
chair. "I'm being summoned."

"Why don't you go get him and bring him down here?" said
Natalie. "I'd love to see him."

Natalie loved Duncan, responded to him deeply. In part, this
was because she knew she would never have her own grandchil-
dren. There had been no baby for Sara, but there had been an
abortion, performed at seven weeks. This had taken place over a
year earlier, and the circumstances surrounding the procedure
had caused Sara to make her mother swear never to tell anyone. It
had begun with a phone call from Sara to Natalie late one night.
It had seemed typical enough at first; they'd done their "Surren-

der, Dorothy" bit, and had laughed together. Then Sara's voice suddenly changed. "Listen, I have to talk to you, Mom," she said. "You know Maddy's husband?"

"Of course I do. That cute boy Peter, with the nice eyes."

"Right. Well, you know Maddy is in London, working with that barrister, whatever that means. It sounds like something on public TV," said Sara. "So I invited Peter over—we all take turns with him—and I made him this entire Japanese dinner, but we never got around to it because, well, because we ended up in bed. Actually," she corrected, "we ended up in *couch*. On the couch, I mean."

Natalie took in a breath. "And?" she said.

"And, well, things sort of happened. Maddy is my oldest friend. What was I thinking of? Oh, Mom, I must be a terrible person, the kind of woman who hates other women, a total piece of shit."

"That is not true," Natalie had said. "You're a wonderful girl. Now listen to me. You must never tell your friend Maddy. Don't think that it's the 'right' thing to do, the morally correct thing, because it's not. It will only make everyone's life worse. Trust me on this one, sweetie; I've been alive for a long time."

So Sara was silent about it; she never confessed to Maddy, and she didn't talk much about it with her mother until weeks later when she called Natalie again, and in another despairing voice told her that as a result of her one encounter with Peter, she had become pregnant.

"And you're absolutely sure about this?"

"I took the test," said Sara. "A pink cross is supposed to show up if you're pregnant. Mine turned into a red crucifix."

"I meant," said Natalie, "you're absolutely sure it's from him?"

"There was no one else then," said Sara, full of sorrow.

Three days later, Natalie took her daughter for an abortion at her gynecological group practice in New Jersey. The procedure was performed by the avuncular Dr. Myron Bronstein. Everyone in the office was sympathetic and discreet; it wasn't like going to a clinic and lying on a cot among knocked-up ninth-graders, which, God knew, Sara would have done in the city if Natalie hadn't offered to pay for the abortion. The procedure itself was surprisingly painful, and afterward Natalie took Sara home, letting her sprawl out in the back of the car, dazed from the IV Valium they had given her. Sara lay down in her childhood canopy bed, sleeping soundly under the bed's white arching roof. Natalie walked past the room and heard her daughter's breathing, steady and slow.

That night they watched *The Wizard of Oz* again, for what must have been the twentieth time. With Sara beside her on the couch, the two of them methodically cracking open pistachio nuts with their teeth as they watched, Natalie realized how much she longed to have her daughter living with her again in the house. The music swelled, and poor, doomed, big-girl Judy Garland sang her song of longing, and mother and daughter sat very close, knowing that while the world was difficult, this moment between them was pure, complete. To sit together in total ease, watching this movie—their movie—was there anything better? Natalie felt useful with Sara back in the house; the only times she was able to feel useful lately were when she found a dirt-cheap fare for a nice couple to get to Aruba for their silver wedding anniversary. That was useful, but it wasn't essential. There were other travel agents in the world, but there were no other mothers, at least not yours.

Now, long past those events, long past a pregnancy, an abortion, a violent death, Natalie watched as Maddy brought Duncan downstairs and proceeded to nurse him. The baby kept one hand grasping the edges of his mother's hair, tugging lightly as though her hair was a tassel you would pull to get a butler to come. Natalie noticed the way Maddy looked peaceful only during nursing; as soon as the baby was done and wanted to stand and bounce in his mother's lap, Maddy seemed to become worried, and her grip on Duncan grew excessive, agitated.

"Why don't you let him play a little bit?" Natalie asked. "He seems to want to jump around. They all do."

Maddy gazed at Duncan. "It's late," she said. "I don't want to get him all worked up. He needs to go back to sleep."

"That's true," said Natalie. "But couldn't he play for a minute? I mean, just look at him." The baby's legs were pumping excitedly; the milk, rather than calming him, seemed to have whipped him into a frenzy. "Could I take him for a minute?" Natalie asked, and Maddy handed her child over, although Natalie could see her reluctance. "Hello, there," Natalie said, standing him up in her lap and moving her knees up and down. The baby immediately began to laugh, a simple, crowing noise. "Oh, this is so gratifying," said Natalie.

"You're very natural with him," observed Maddy.

"Well, I've done it before," Natalie said. "It was very long ago, but I remember. You never forget."

"I can't be natural like that," said Maddy. "I worry all the time that something will happen to him. That I'll drop him on his head and he'll become brain-dead, or that he'll be hit by a car, or that he'll suddenly stop developing. That happened to the baby of someone I know. He was perfectly fine until he was ten months old, and then suddenly everything *stopped*. Now he's three, and in an institution. He never learned to walk or talk. He's going to wear diapers his entire life."

"Duncan is a wonderful baby," said Natalie. "Nothing's going to happen to him."

"No one knows things like that," said Maddy.

"Well, of course that's true," said Natalie. "But you have to pretend things are always going to be fine. And you have to go easy."

"No offense, Mrs. Swerdlow, but I don't know how you can say that," said Maddy. "You, of all people."

Natalie shrugged. "You have children and you watch them grow," she said quietly. "When they're teenagers and they go out for the night, you sit up in bed waiting for the key in the lock. You sit there, hour after hour, just to hear their footsteps."

"It's so unfair," Maddy suddenly blurted out. "She was only thirty. Dr. Blandish says you should never let your child out of your sight, that the world is too unpredictable."

"Dr. *who?*" asked Natalie.

Maddy proceeded to tell her about a book that had apparently sold millions of copies by sending susceptible, hormone-charged new mothers into paroxysms of guilt about their failed parenting skills. Maddy was in tears now, relaying all the details that, according to Dr. Blandish, she had done wrong.

"I've been reading this book every day," said Maddy, "and I feel like I should practically give Duncan away to foster parents, people who are very relaxed around children. Something awful's going to happen, I just know it is."

"Let me see this bible of motherhood," said Natalie, and Maddy obediently went upstairs and scrabbled around in the drawer until she'd found it. She brought it down and Natalie flipped through the pages, making little grunting sounds and clucks of disapproval. "Oh, this is the most ridiculous thing I have ever read," said Natalie, and she closed the book and tossed it onto the table. From the photograph on the back of the jacket, Dr. Blandish smiled coldly, flanked by her two small, perenially upbeat children. "It's so controlling," said Natalie. "She's trying to scare the shit out of young mothers, and frankly, it's working. Dr. Melanie Blandish can screw herself. You want to know how to relax?" Maddy looked at her with desperate eyes, nodding. "Just *enjoy* him," said Natalie. Then Natalie held Duncan out to his mother. "Here, take him," she said. "For God's sake, enjoy him. This is the fun part. Let him fool around more. Swing him in the air."

"I heard they can get baby whiplash," said Maddy in nearly a whisper.

"Not if you're gentle."

Natalie looked at the baby, who was unfinished, blurry, the soft spot on his head apparent under the pale layer of down. Natalie thought of Sara at this age; she remembered a particular sundress, and shining patent leather Mary Janes, and glass bottles that had to be sterilized and filled with warm beige formula poured from a can. The doctor had discouraged Natalie from nursing Sara. "You'll be overwhelmed," he had said. But she had been overwhelmed anyway, and wasn't that the point?

"You don't think I've screwed him up for life?" Maddy asked.

"Not yet," said Natalie. "But I'd say you've still got plenty of time."

Maddy pressed her face to Duncan's head and inhaled hard. The scent of Johnson & Johnson products coupled with something caramelized was all over that head, Natalie knew; he was like a *tarte tatin* sprinkled with baby powder. He wasn't edible, although he seemed it, but he was knowable, he was a person. Natalie watched as Maddy tentatively swung Duncan in her arms. Then, becoming more sure of herself, Maddy swung him again. His little sprig of hair flew up, and his eyes caught onto hers, startled and wide.

10

Golden Boy

Melville Wolf came to take Adam to dinner one night, which really meant that Melville Wolf came to spy. He was staying in the area all week, and he took Adam out to determine whether Adam was writing, and whether what he was writing was any good. Not that he would know. Melville Wolf wasn't an artist or a critic but a theatrical producer, a thick-chested, sweating man whose shirts were made of striped cotton and were invariably dripping at the end of one of his long, emotional days at the office. He was well-dressed, with the purplish-blue complexion of underlying heart disease, and he loved the theater in a big, wrenching way. He loved comedy—tragedy was great, too. Make him laugh, make him cry; it didn't matter which.

The producer had taken a chance a few years earlier with *Take*

Us to Your Leader, and Adam's play had made him lots of money. Whenever he saw Adam now, he reached out and messed up his hair, as though to say: *Oh, you kid.* Mel Wolf had produced many hits, and had been attached to productions of great importance and lesser ones which generated immense revenues. If there was money in it, he was your best friend, and would reach out and mess up your hair forever. If it failed but the reviews were favorable, he was gently philosophical about the situation, touching your shoulder lightly, sadly, giving you another chance to prove yourself to him. If the whole enterprise was a disaster, then his entire persona turned as cold and crass as that of a businessman on a bad day—a vinyl flooring manufacturer who has lost millions. This was what Adam feared most from Mel. He wanted the producer to love him forever, to take him out to dinner so they could plot future productions, the boy wonder and his rich, jovial uncle.

This evening Mel was coming to take Adam out to a nearby expensive restaurant called Shoes of the Fisherman, where you could look dreamily out over the bay as you ate lobster with a tiny fork. Shawn wanted to join them, was openly asking to do so, but Adam put him off. "I'm sorry, it's not appropriate," Adam said as he got dressed for dinner. Shawn lay across the bed in the small room, fretting and studying something on his arm.

"If you were straight, and I was your girlfriend, then I guarantee you'd bring me in a second," said Shawn.

"That's not it," said Adam. "This isn't some self-hating homophobia at work."

"Then what is it?"

"It's not about you," said Adam. "And it's not about us. It's just about *me.*"

"Like everything else," said Shawn.

"I thought you liked that I'm successful," said Adam. "I thought you actually liked that fact about me. You certainly liked it when we met, when you came up to me at that playwrights' thing, and when you sent me your tape."

"Well, I don't like it when you flaunt it," said Shawn. "When you show off about it, and make it seem like it's the most important thing in the world."

"I'm hardly sitting in this house thinking about being famous," said Adam. "I'm thinking about Sara. You didn't know her, and you didn't know anything about my friendship with her, but I am suffering, okay? So don't make me out to be this spoiled person."

"Look, I'm sorry," Shawn said after a moment. "I know things aren't good. I just feel that you get to do pretty much whatever you want, and that I always have to hold myself back."

Adam turned to him in irritation. "What is it you want?" he asked. "You want to make contact with Melville Wolf, is that it? So you can play him your tape?"

"Yes," said Shawn. "Would that be so bad?"

"Actually, yes, it would be inappropriate," said Adam. "I'd rather you didn't mention it to him. I don't have this cozy relationship with Mel. Maybe later on, in a year or so."

There was a silence; both of them knew they might not know each other in a year. "It would be nice," said Shawn, "if you could demonstrate a little interest in my work occasionally."

"I do," said Adam.

"You never ask me how the musical's going," said Shawn.

"I'm sorry. So how's it going?"

"Like shit," said Shawn.

"Well, welcome to the club," Adam said. Then he went to the bureau where Shawn kept his belongings, and picked up a yellow folder lying on top, marked *Spinsters!*

"Leave that," said Shawn, grabbing for it.

"No," said Adam. "I want to look at it. You tell me I don't take you seriously, so let me prove that's not true."

Holding it out of Shawn's reach, he opened to the first page and read aloud:

" 'Act One, Scene One. A typical Roman fountain quietly
burbles in the distance. It is dusk. A woman enters stage L.
She is DIANA ROWLAND, mid-fifties, American, dressed like
a tourist. She sits down on the lip of the fountain and
begins to sing the following song, "Meet Me at the Trevi":

DIANA
Oh, I have no energy
and oh my aching dogs
I sat in the trattoria
and ate like a hog . . .

"I said give me that!" said Shawn, and he grabbed the folder
back.

"I thought you wanted me to see it," said Adam.

"I changed my mind," said Shawn.

"Look," said Adam quietly, "I have to go. My producer's waiting." He left swiftly. All Shawn wanted was a producer, someone
who was willing to stand behind him, to read his work as soon as
it slid out of the printer, someone waiting to see what he was capable of doing. Which was exactly what Adam had.

Adam drove Peter's truck to Shoes of the Fisherman, and saw
that Mel's Lexus was already in the parking lot, with its bumper
sticker that read "Honk If You Love Strindberg." Inside the din-
ing room, which was as pink as a nursery, waiters carried trays
high above their heads, and the room resonated with the clatter of
silverware and spirited conversation. At a table in the corner, Mel
had systematically eaten almost the entire basket of bread before
Adam arrived, leaving behind a vaguely unappealing pumper-
nickel roll.

"Adam!" Mel cried, and he stood up to hug him. When they
sat down, the two men began an ardent conversation about theater in general and then about Adam's play in specific. "So tell me
about the follow-up to *Take Us to Your Leader.* What's it going to

be?" Mel asked. "Something equally funny? Or maybe something darker. I know you've had a tough time this summer; I heard all about it. My sympathies." He patted Adam's hand and there was a nervous moment of silence; Mel Wolf was the last person you would ever want to have console you. But then the moment was abruptly over. "Please," Mel continued, "promise me one thing." Adam nodded. "Promise me that you won't get too dark all of a sudden, you know? Don't start getting like Woody Allen did in *Interiors.* All serious and self-conscious and trying to be a fucking Scandinavian. You wouldn't pull a Scandinavian number on me, would you, Adam?"

"Scandinavia? Never heard of the place," said Adam.

"Good," said Mel. "Let's keep it that way. Your strength lies in light, funny, ethnic comedy. That's where you belong. So tell me, what's the new play about? Enquiring minds want to know."

"Death," said Adam.

Mel smiled a tough businessman's smile. "You trying to kill me?" he said. "Is that it? Because, you know, I went for a stress test last week and I failed it. So your death play better have a little humor attached."

"It will, it will," mumbled Adam.

"Where does it take place?" asked Mel.

"A summer camp in the Adirondacks," Adam said. "The year that Nixon resigned. Watergate seen through the eyes of a child."

"I'm loving it," said Mel. "A backdrop of major upheaval. Who dies? Not a kid, I hope. I'll kill you if it's a kid."

"No, a counselor," said Adam. "College age, bad skin. You'll hardly miss him."

"A counselor's okay," said Mel, waving his hand magnanimously. "Just as long as it's not a kid. Audiences do not want to see that, I'm telling you. There is nothing funny in the death of a kid. We tried to do a musical of *Death Be Not Proud*—couldn't get backers."

Despite Adam's protests, Mel followed him back to the house

after lunch so he could see the place. "I want to see the environ-
ment my young star is working in," Mel said, and Adam blush-
ingly led him inside the house. Mel stood in the middle of the
living room and stared. "This?" he said. "This is it? Broadway's
great gay hope is writing his plays in a trailer park?"

"It's not a trailer," Adam said. "It's a house."

"Theoretically, it's a house," said Mel. "I'll give you that. But
Adam, you deserve more than this."

Just then, Shawn came into the living room, clutching the
score to his musical. "Oh, hi," he said, observing Adam and Mel
with wide, innocent eyes. Adam muttered introductions, understanding that from the upstairs window Shawn had seen Adam
and Mel coming into the house, and that Shawn was trying, desperately, to make himself appear on Melville Wolf's radar. Shawn
sat down at the old piano in the corner, arranging his music in
front of him, and softly began to play "Meet Me at the Trevi," the
opening number to *Spinsters!* Adam closed his eyes in embarrassment as Shawn played; the music was as unobtrusive as something heard in a cocktail lounge, but the intensity behind it, the
ambition and the desire and the need to be discovered, were so
apparent that Adam wanted to apologize to Mel. But when he
looked at Mel, he saw that Mel did not seem annoyed by Shawn's
music; he didn't seem to feel he was being set up. In fact, he didn't
seem to hear the music at all. Shawn kept glancing up quickly
from the piano to see whether Mel had any response, but Mel was
gazing, transfixed, across the room into the doorway that led to
the kitchen.

"Adam, who's that?" Mel whispered as Shawn began his next
number, "Chianti for Two."

Adam looked into the kitchen and saw what Mel had been
staring at: Natalie at the counter, washing a head of lettuce. Her
hair was pulled back off her face, but a few strands had separated
themselves out, and fell into her eyes. Her face was flushed with
exertion, and she looked young and fragile and particularly beau-

tiful. "That's Sara's mother," he said. "Her name is Natalie Swerdlow." Mel continued to contemplate Natalie, gazing at her in shy admiration. Natalie sensed that she was being looked at and she turned, brushing the hair from her face. In the background, Shawn played his medley of moody songs.

"Hello," said Natalie, and she shut off the taps and stepped forward, her hands spattering water to the floor. Adam introduced her to Mel, and she shook his hand with her own wet hand, creating a moment of awkward humor, sealing this introduction in water. "Whoops, I'm sorry," she said. "I got you all wet."

"Ah, it's nothing," said Mel. "Now I'm baptized."

Behind them, Shawn stood up, done with his attempts to get Mel to listen. He headed outside without saying a word. Adam didn't go after him, didn't even consider it; he was mesmerized by watching Mel and Natalie. Flirtation was different between men and women than it was between men. When men and women observed each other, it was as if across a great and wary divide, while men tended to respond to other men with locker-room/pup tent/collegial familiarity. Heterosexuality held real mystery to Adam, and always would. He had never been able to understand what his parents had had to say to each other all those years when he lived in their house, what they discussed in bed at night when he wasn't there; his imagination failed him on this point, and he finally decided that the only thing his parents discussed when they were alone was *him*. He pictured them lying in their bed with the padded headboard, the television yakking softly across the room, talking to each other about Adam's report card, or his lack of skill in sports, or the impressive but vaguely disturbing fact that he had memorized all the lyrics from the cast album of *Man of La Mancha* and would often walk around in a dreamy state, stretching out his arm as he sang, his mouth full of Mallomars, "To love . . . pure and chaste from afar . . ." But perhaps there was more to his parents than he had ever gathered; perhaps they had an entire underworld teeming with secret passions and interests.

He used to ask Sara what she liked about men, and she would reel off a list of the qualities that had attracted her to a variety of men over the years. There was no consistency to her list; one man was admired for his long, muscular back, another for his impression of the Beatles singing "Komm, Gib Mir Deine Hand" at their Hamburg concert. It wasn't that Sara felt a commonality with men; she simply liked being around them, liked being touched by them. And Natalie was the same way, Sara had always said. "My mother is totally into men," were Sara's words. "She never kept this fact from me. Which, now that I think about it, I kind of wished she had."

"Look, Natalie," Mel was saying, and Adam realized that in the few moments that he hadn't been listening, Natalie and Mel had progressed very nicely into an actual conversation, unassisted by him. "I'm in the area for a while," Mel continued, "and maybe I could take you out for lunch or something."

"Sure, fine," she said, with neither genuine enthusiasm nor resistance.

"Then I'll call," said Mel, and he reached out to shake Natalie's hand good-bye. "All dry," he murmured, looking at her hand, and then he was gone.

Adam went upstairs to his computer, flicked on the screen, and sat in front of the shimmering square of light, staring at the most recent scene he'd written. It wasn't good, and he knew it. He felt himself sinking into some kind of failed existence, his own version of what Shawn felt. If Sara hadn't died, Adam could still be funny. He would have someone to be funny *for;* he could call her up, as he always did, and read her his latest pages, and she would laugh hard, or let him know when a joke was bad. She was his ideal listener, the perpetual loop of laugh track in his head. He'd once read an article about Lucille Ball which said that the actress's mother was often in the audience at tapings of *I Love Lucy,* and that her laughter was so distinctive that Lucy could always single it out when she watched the show on television.

Years later, after her mother had died, Lucy had sat and watched the old shows just to hear her mother's laughter.

Sara's laugh had always rung out in Adam's head, too, except it hadn't been preserved in television amber, and now it was gone. The idea of being funny, of writing something that Melville Wolf would like, something that his willing matinee audiences would embrace, seemed impossible now. Instead, Adam imagined himself turning into a one-hit wonder; he saw himself teaching a theater class at a second-rate liberal arts college in Pennsylvania. He would be their playwright-in-residence, their faded coup in corduroy jackets and elbow patches, living by himself in a crumbling Victorian fixer-upper on the edge of campus, and none of his semiliterate students could have ever imagined that their vague and befuddled professor had ever been considered precocious. The youth would have drained from him, and would now belong only to them. But it was too painful to think that his career would end this way—the brightly flaming comet, its diminishing tail.

SHAWN HAD GONE outside in a useless rage. The heat was nauseatingly strong, making him wonder what he was doing out on the front lawn, and what he was even doing here at this house. He paced back and forth on the grass, waiting to see if Adam would follow him outside, but knowing somehow that he wouldn't. Adam was in there with his *producer;* the word formed itself into an irrational snarl, something to be mocked, loathed—something unavailable to Shawn forever. Melville Wolf's green Lexus sat in the driveway, incongruous beside the awful house. He walked over and placed both hands flat on the blazingly hot hood. Inside the car, on the passenger seat, Shawn could see a few Playbills: *Waxworks, The Loss of Hannah,* and that new imported British sex farce, *Charmed, I'm Sure.* Swiftly, barely giving it any thought, Shawn opened the car door. From within came the sounds of gentle chimes. He ducked into the car, slipped the cassette tape of his

musical from his pants pocket, and placed it on top of the pile of
Playbills. Then, using the pen he always carried, he dashed off a
note on the cover of *Charmed, I'm Sure.*

"Mr. Wolf," he wrote, "we met today at Adam's. Here are a
few songs from a musical I'm writing. Enjoy!" Then Shawn
signed his name, stood up, and closed the car door, stunned by his
own nerve, the way he had felt the day he'd sent a copy of this tape
to Adam that first day. He'd had a lifetime of nervy acts, although
each time he performed one, he felt breathlessly guilty. He had
once masturbated discreetly beneath his desk during social stud-
ies, while the class was watching a filmstrip about the Industrial
Revolution. He had saved his tiny moans for each time the filmstrip emitted a loud beep, signaling the teacher to click over to the
next frame. And throughout high school, he and a creepy,
strangely silent friend named Roger Gladney had shoplifted constantly: magazines, clothing, watches, anything that appealed to
them.

But he had never felt as criminal as in this moment; in his
entire life he had never transgressed in as complete a way as he
had just done. His songs now lay in the car of a Broadway producer; all Melville Wolf had to do was put the tape in his cassette
player and let the music roll across him. Shawn could imagine the
producer nodding gently as he listened to *Spinsters!* while driving.
The music would seduce him, and Shawn's life might be changed
forever.

He walked back to the house now, his pocket empty, his heart
beating more quickly, the terror within him playing over and over
like the world's catchiest Broadway tune.

I I

Sara in the Sky

The mushrooms were furry and shriveled with age, like dried morels at the back of a shelf in a Korean market, left untouched behind some packages of instant MSG-filled ramen noodles for months or even years. "I brought these with me to the house," Shawn announced as he carried a plate of them onto the deck, "and forgot all about them because of Sara and everything. But this morning I came across them in my bag and thought maybe this just might improve the morale of the troops."

"God," said Peter, "I don't know, Shawn. We haven't done them in years. Everything was different then."

"I can't do mushrooms," said Maddy. "I have a baby here, remember? But I could babysit for the rest of you." They looked from one to the other, shrugging, considering the offer. "By the way, where's Natalie?" she asked. "She can't be around for this."

"She's cleaning upstairs," said Adam. "Totally occupied. I heard the Dustbuster going. And the Japanese language tape is on. She'll be busy up there for hours."

"Are you sure you don't mind if we do this?" Peter asked Maddy. "You'll be okay with Duncan?"

"I'll be fine. Go right ahead," she said. "Just go, all of you." She shooed them off as though they were going on a fishing or hunting trip and she, the lone woman, was staying behind.

Back in their days of drug-taking, Adam had always been the one holdout, the hallucination chaperone for all the others. Sara had enjoyed taking the occasional drug; it wasn't that she would ever deliberately seek it out, but if it was offered, she would ingest it happily, easily. Not Adam. It had taken him so long simply to create a self he could tolerate, that the idea of losing that self frightened him enormously. So over the years he had always sat and watched as everyone else swallowed whatever it was they were swallowing at the time: psilocybin mushrooms, or benign, white aspirin-like tablets of Ecstasy, or, for a brief stint after college, a flurry of cocaine, which as far as Adam could tell made everyone seem somehow more ambitious and focused than they really were, as though they had just spent a lengthy and rigorous session with a career counselor.

Now Peter and Shawn had begun to pull apart the black and gray barnacled mushrooms and put them in their mouths. "Mmm," said Peter, tilting his head to the side like someone assessing a wine. "A subtle taste, fruity yet strong."

"I sense a hint of elderberry," said Shawn, "with an undercurrent of . . . currant."

They laughed and chewed away on the rubbery mushrooms like two puppies gnawing on a shoe. Adam imagined them disappearing under the effects of the drug, and he saw himself as more alone than ever, stranded here away from his friends, out of the loop, left to do childcare duties with Maddy. This was too much to take; more than anything now, he didn't want to be alone.

There were two mushrooms left on the plate, curled and runty, and Adam picked one up between his fingers, like someone selecting a crudité, a soggy uncooked mushroom to dip into a pool of ranch dressing on someone's summer patio. He watched his own hand lift the mushroom from the plate, and he was scared. His friends *liked* being scared. They liked the plunge and ascension of roller coasters, while he liked kiddie cars, a simple and repetitive revolution that never took him from the earth. He didn't try to talk himself out of it now, but simply lifted the spongy mushroom and deposited it in his mouth.

The mushroom tasted of hiking trails and bad cooking. His body told him to spit it out, but Adam chewed on diligently, with the effort you might expend eating calamari, and then he swallowed hard, feeling the toxins go down his throat, imagining the way they would disperse, entering his cells and changing them for a while. He had felt similarly the first time he had ever given a blow job. His heart had sped that time, telling him that this was all wrong, that he should stop right now. But then he had thought about how often he had imagined this moment when he was younger, how often he'd thought about doing exactly this to some of the boys he'd grown up with, and how, in his thoughts, it had seemed, amazingly, okay. It had seemed, in fact, to be a good match; there was a symmetry about it: a mouth on a penis, both men groaning in shared, connected happiness. The taste, he'd imagined, would be rubbery, flavorless, saline, human. Not unlike a mushroom. Now he chewed on and on, and then swallowed hard in an exaggerated, gulping way.

"How long does this take?" Adam asked, suddenly worried. "When will it kick in?"

"Twenty minutes, maybe," said Maddy. "Just relax, Adam. You'll like it; you'll see." But he felt his jaw going stiff, and he began to pace around the deck. Other than the jaw sensation, nothing happened; maybe this batch was so old that it had lost its powers. He was immediately relieved at the idea. Perhaps he would remain a mushroom virgin, and spend the rest of the day working on his unfunny new Watergate-summer comedy.

Elsewhere in the neighborhood, children splashed and tormented each other in a backyard pool. The bell of an ice cream truck jangled quaintly, a lone bird sang. Adam realized, listening to the individual sounds, that he had crossed over the threshold and was now genuinely tripping. It had really begun. His eyes narrowed, adjusting to the new brightness of the day. He rubbed at his forehead, for it itched as though he were pollen-sensitive. He turned to Maddy to say something, but instead of speaking, he collapsed into unexpected laughter.

Then the door to the house opened, and Natalie emerged. *Oh shit,* he thought, for it was as though they had been busted, or as though they were all teenagers and she was the mother of one of them who would call all the other mothers, and they would be grounded until the millennium. Back when they were adolescents, there had actually been mothers who purchased special spy kits to make sure their children weren't using drugs, mothers who dusted the surfaces of their teenagers' dressers with a special powder that would show whether traces of pot or cocaine or even heroin had graced the premises. There were mothers who dunked little dipsticks in the unflushed toilets that their adolescent sons had recently peed into, the toilet seats still thoughtlessly left up. There were spying, lying, hyper-vigilant mothers with magnifying glasses and deerstalkers' hats. But Natalie was smiling benignly, her arms spread wide. "This is wonderful," she said to everyone. "Just wonderful!"

Adam and Maddy and Peter stared at her. "What's wonderful?" Adam asked in a quiet voice.

"I ate a mushroom," she said. "Shawn gave it to me." They all stared in horror.

"You *what?*" Adam said.

"I ate a mushroom."

"Natalie," said Adam, and he stood and put his hands on her shoulders, as if preparing her for more bad news. "I have to tell you something. Those weren't normal mushrooms. They weren't shiitake, or even portobello."

"They weren't?" she said.

"No, they were hallucinogens," said Adam. "You start to . . . trip on these. You know, to see things. Like with LSD."

"No, no! I can't believe it," she said, and then she broke into a smile and began to laugh. Everyone stared. "Oh, Adam, how dumb do you think I am?" Natalie said. "Of course I know what these are. I ate the last one on the plate. Shawn said I should try it, and you know, usually I'm against drugs. I've been on a Mothers Against Drugs steering committee, and I helped decorate their fundraiser, and my travel agency even donated a trip to Bermuda for the raffle, but that was then. Now I'm . . . I guess I'm . . ." She giggled. "I guess I'm *tripping,*" she said.

"I guess you are," said Adam.

"I was scared at first," she continued. "But then I thought, maybe I can hallucinate and see Sara. I hate drugs; I don't even like extra-strength Tylenol. But I would do anything in the world to see her again."

"It's not like that," said Peter. "You don't just *see* things that aren't there. You don't suddenly see an object that doesn't exist."

Natalie went and sat in the sun with a drink in her hand, peering upward into the light. She didn't know what she was getting herself into, but then again, neither did Adam. And now, looking at her, seeing the good bones of her face, the ascendant thrust of her neck, the vulnerable clavicle below, he felt afraid.

What had possessed Shawn to give a mushroom to Natalie? Who wanted to trip with someone's *mother?* The idea was shocking, perverse in its own way. To bring a mother along on a drug trip was like bringing a chaperone with you on a hot date. But Natalie's eyes were already strange; she sat in the sun and stared up at nothing. There was an art show going on in that patch of sunlight; the white, blank sky was filled with scrawls, confusing and urgent as graffiti on a subway car.

Shawn came out of the house now, and Adam collared him.

"What's wrong with you?" he whispered harshly. "Why did you give mushrooms to that woman?"

"She's not 'that woman,' " said Shawn. "She's Mrs. Swerdlow, and she was hoping to 'see' Sara again, and I thought it was only fair to let her. Do you have a problem with that?"

"Yes, I have a problem with that," said Adam. "And so do the rest of us. Because she is Sara's mother, she's not our friend, she's a . . . she's a grown-up."

"And so are you," said Shawn. "At least, you're supposed to be. If thirty isn't grown up, then what is? Forty? Ninety? You going to hang on to being young even while you're collecting Social Security? To being a 'young' playwright? 'Precocious'?"

"No," said Adam. "But if I had known that Natalie was going to be joining us on this little adventure, I might have—" Suddenly he became quiet, because he had begun to see a series of starbursts. He stood up straight, respectful of their presence. The mushrooms had arrived at the entrance to his brain, at Huxley's doors of perception, and were exploding there and multiplying.

"Oh, forget it," he said. "Tell Natalie she can come," he added, and then he sank back into his chair.

THE AFTERNOON pushed on in equal measures of amazement and annoyance. Adam went inside for a breather and sat in the rocker in the corner, focusing intently on the illustrations on the upholstery. Betsy Ross's eyes actually seemed to flick toward Paul Revere's, and the silversmith seemed to smile in response. Perhaps he was smirking at the way her head looked in that bonnet, Adam thought, for in fact Betsy Ross's head did resemble a pan of Jiffy Pop, filled to bursting. What am I thinking? he wondered to himself, realizing his thoughts were both trivial and bizarre. Betsy Ross and Paul Revere couldn't talk; they were merely pictures on the fabric of a rocking chair. He stood shakily and went outside again to join the others, feeling an intense need to be among his friends, to find a way to enjoy these odd little miniature hallucinations. Outside, Peter lay on the lawn with his eyes shut. Clouds were moving fast above him, and the sky opened up into its full width. Natalie came and lay beside him; together they stared up at the sky. "That's Cumulus," Peter said, "and over there is Nimbus."

"The narrow ones?" said Natalie. "Yes, I see." They lay with their arms touching, completely without self-consciousness. There was a heat moving between them and demanding to be noticed, a heat that came with a sparkling edge. All Peter wanted was to kiss and touch her; was there any way to do that and get away with it? He felt a little bit in love with this difficult fifty-year-old woman. He had to remind himself now that it was the drugs talking, and to keep himself from leaning above Natalie and running a single finger along her lips. Peter had to blink several times to dim down his vision. His arm against hers felt alive, pulsing with fibers and cells and a silent swoosh of blood. Natalie's own arm lay passive but equally alive, and the cells that made up her tissue were genetically responsible for the collection of cells that had made up Sara.

He thought of poor lost Sara on the sofa in her apartment, the way she had opened her blouse and he had pushed himself against her, shocked at the urgency, at the way he could so easily be unfaithful. It had been like a game of "Scissors, Paper, Stone." His marriage was stone, but Sara was paper, and she could easily cover stone, fluttering over it, eclipsing it completely. The connection to Sara was now overwhelming, and he suddenly felt the need to touch her mother. Bravely, he reached out and held her hand. Beside him, Natalie turned to him, arching an eyebrow.

"Feeling comfortable?" she asked with some irony, and he started to untwine his hand from hers, but she trapped it in her grasp. "No, it's fine," she said. "Don't move. We can watch the clouds." So they lay there, thrillingly, secretly holding hands, the clouds traveling above them. Nobody cared, nobody saw, everyone was involved in his or her own private screening. Adam was inordinately involved with the weave of the fabric on one of the chaises, while Shawn was running his finger back and forth through the flame on his Druid candle, which had been lit for the occasion. Nearby, Maddy was clear-headed and capable, trying to burp Duncan, holding him over her shoulder and rubbing his back in an upward motion. Every once in a while she peered over to see if anyone needed her, which no one did, at least not yet. She'd been feeling much better since that night with Natalie, when she'd swung Duncan in her arms. She'd been less hesitant with the baby, more eager to let him loose, and as a result she too felt looser-limbed, less prone to tears.

Adam was stationed on the chaise now, watching the colors vibrate and thinking about how much he loved these people, and how it might actually be a good idea for them to live together forever; the house no longer looked poor and ratty to him. Natalie had cleaned it furiously, and as a result the place now shone with a new light. Even the outside shone, right through its coat of dismal, mustard-colored paint. A light burned beneath that paint, creating the illusion of a ceramic glaze. It was the light of Sara smiling, Adam thought. And then he felt that they ought to devote this trip to celebrating Sara. He looked at Natalie, who lay beside Peter, the two of them appearing for all the world like a married couple lying easily together. He walked across the soggy grass, for it had rained lightly last night and everything seemed especially damp and soft and pearlescent today. "Natalie," he said, standing over her. "Natalie, we should perform a ritual for Sara; she would have liked that. Some kind of Japanese thing."

Sara's mother looked up at him. "Yes, I think that's a good idea," she said.

The celebration took the form of a full-scale, mock Japanese tea party out on the lawn. They spread out a blanket and laid out Mrs. Moyles's chipped teacups and dishes. Natalie wore Sara's kimono, and Shawn brought over his Druid candle, and Peter poured the tea. They set out various objects that had belonged to Sara, including her red leather notebook in which she'd written in Japanese, and the Berlitz tape of the man speaking Japanese, and the small gong that she'd bought in Tokyo. Adam banged on the gong and all at once, without rehearsal, they bowed to each other.

"*Konnichiwa,*" the man on the tape said.

"*Konnichiwa,*" everyone repeated. They sat down in unison and drank the tea brewed from Mrs. Moyles's teabags. They all sat out on the blanket with the candle lit and the Japanese man droning, and the tea cooling in their cups and Sara's belongings all around them.

Peter raised a cup of tea and said, "To Sara," and everyone followed suit.

"To Sara," they said, and then they drank. The tea was weak and tasteless; Adam had never liked tea, because it seemed to him like drinking a mouthful of bathwater. Now he swallowed it in one long, slow gulp and he imagined Sara sliding down a waterfall, Sara in Tokyo, splashing in a rock pool. Peter banged the gong with its mallet.

On the deck of the house, Maddy stood holding Duncan, and she shook her head and called out, "You guys are so fucked up." She carried the baby back into the house. The chanting and the gong and the tape recorder were playing so loud that at one point Adam looked up and saw the next-door neighbor, a scraggly, widowed man in his seventies who stood with a spray bottle of weed killer.

"Excuse me," he said. "I'd appreciate it if you could turn down the noise. This is a family neighborhood." They stared at him for a few seconds, this man who had no family, and then they began falling against each other and spurting into helpless, collective laughter. "Does Mrs. Moyles know what you're like?" the old man asked. "Because she ought to. She ought to see who she's renting to. She ought to know."

"We're sorry," said Maddy, suddenly stepping forward to take charge. "They've been in the sun too long," she said, "and I think they're a little giddy. I'll make sure they're quiet."

The man shook his head. "*Summer people,*" he said with contempt, and then he retreated into a narrow space between two bushes.

It was clear that it was time to go somewhere; this always happened at some point during drug trips. In the absence of the ability to crawl out of your skin, you crawled out of the house. There was a pizza place called Sonny's in town with red booths patched up with electrical tape, and fountain Cokes that tasted syrupy and made you nostalgic for an era that you hadn't even lived through. Because none of them could possibly drive now, Maddy took them to Sonny's in the truck, the baby strapped in beside her, and the trippers remanded to the back like convicts or farm animals.

At the restaurant they ate hungrily, jammed into a booth. The waitress eyed them with suspicion, clearly assuming they were drunk, while Maddy primly ordered for everyone and tried to behave as though nothing was strange at all.

The pizza, Adam noticed, was a masterpiece of color and texture. Natalie was staring at her slice too, and so was Peter. Shawn, however, was lost in the Formica grain, which appeared to be swimming like one-celled animals under a microscope.

After the pizza, everyone went back outside, and there in the parking lot behind the restaurant, under the summer sky, Natalie stared upward and said, "Look up there. You can see it, can't you?" They looked up dutifully; the sky was pale, easing into evening. But as Natalie gazed upward, the clouds seemed to join together and form letters like skywriting. "SURRENDER DOROTHY," the letters said. She could hear Sara's voice on the telephone, uttering this familiar phrase, and now she felt the ache of wanting to hear that voice once again. If she closed her eyes she heard it; if she opened them she saw the words.

The others stood and watched Natalie. Maddy walked up to

her and put a hand on her shoulder. "Listen, Mrs. Swerdlow," she said. "It's the drug. That's what's going on here."

Natalie shrugged away. "You were the one with the Ouija board," she said. "So now here I am, looking up and seeing words there, and you're telling me it's the drug?"

"Well, I wanted to think there was some sign of her too," said Maddy. "Even in a metaphorical way."

"There is nothing metaphorical when a child dies," said Natalie. She glanced up at the skywriting again, and saw that the letters had collapsed back into clouds. Suddenly Natalie felt overcome by nausea, and she ran toward a Dumpster and let herself vomit into it. Behind her, Natalie could hear Maddy saying that this often happened on mushrooms, that it was just a disgusting and inconvenient side-effect. Natalie knew that tomorrow she would be embarrassed, that she would try to make a few jokes about what had happened. But really, she told herself, what was the big deal about vomiting in front of other people? It really didn't matter anymore; they could see her vomit, they could see her do anything; she no longer cared what anyone thought of her. She vomited endlessly, tasting the earthenness of the mushrooms again. Sara had disappeared, was receding into the sky, into the periphery of her mother's sight, the way children always did, eventually.

Nausea had struck Peter now too, and he was leaning over another Dumpster across the way. "She's not here anymore," Natalie said to herself. There were still a few lights twirling on the periphery of her vision, but none of them had anything to do with Sara. A busboy was standing out back having a smoke, and he observed these vomiting people coolly.

They vomited, one by one, like those Baptists in the news who had gone to a church picnic in the Midwest and had all been poisoned by a tainted ham. Afterward now, everyone wiped their faces almost daintily. Then they piled back into the truck and let Maddy drive them home, their mouths still sour, feeling a collective exhaustion they had never known before. Natalie closed her eyes, no longer willing to think about what had happened over the course of the day: the mushrooms that had been swallowed, the tea that had been poured, the gong that had been struck, and the hand of that boy Peter that she had held so tightly in hers.

12

In the Blood

One afternoon while Natalie was mopping the floors, Melville Wolf returned to the house, not to see Adam, not to hear Shawn's music, but to whisk Natalie off in his Lexus. She didn't resist, but simply left the mop in its bucket of gray water and went off with him. In the car, he put a tape into the player and said to her, "Tell me what you think of this."

Music played. It was strangely familiar, both the melody and the plaintive, imperfect male voice that sang. "What is this?" she asked.

"Adam's friend," said Mel. "He slipped me his tape last time. I forgot all about it until today, when I was coming over here."

"And?" said Natalie.

"And," said Mel, "I'm afraid I don't think the kid has any talent." They traveled and listened; Natalie felt particularly protective of Shawn, and for a moment she wanted not to believe that Mel's words were true. But she agreed; the kid didn't have any discernible talent. The music was clunky, wooden, a bit shrill. The two spinsters in Rome sang their songs, and when Mel put a finger on the stop button, Natalie was relieved. Poor Shawn, she thought, as Mel ejected the tape. "Would you give it back to him for me?" he asked, not unkindly. "Tell him I said thanks for letting me listen."

Natalie slipped the cassette into her straw bag, feeling sad for Shawn, embarrassed at his efforts and their unequivocal rejection. But soon she forgot about him and his musical, for Mel drove her out to the tip of the island to an outdoor lunch stand. There, at a table in the shade, he ate fried things heartily, and she picked at steamed things delicately. What did he want from her? She wasn't sure, and yet she knew that it was a relief to be here with him, away from the house, from Sara's friends. Since the recent afternoon of the mushrooms, there had been an increased claustrophobia among everyone. With Peter, she felt an odd and inevitable strain. He was extremely handsome, this boy, and this unnerved her. It was comforting now to be away from that, out here with this solid, brooding, blustery man, with whom there was no subtext.

So here she sat, eating lunch with Melville Wolf, who told her theater anecdotes from a past that was long gone. He mentioned all the greats, spoke of calming Chita Rivera's nerves with a foot rub before a performance of *West Side Story,* and he even told a touching story about the time that an extremely young and grateful Barbra Streisand had asked him for a lozenge. "You're not eating," he noted at one point during the meal. "It's because the things on your plate have all been steamed. Nothing's been fried. Nothing on your plate tastes good."

"I don't eat much anymore," she murmured.

"During my divorce I was under so much stress, and food saved me," said Mel. "My wife left me and I learned to eat. Here, try this." He dunked a fried scallop into red sauce, and held it out to her.

"Really, no," she said.

"I insist," said Mel. "Just taste it. Close your eyes, and think only about the taste, nothing else."

"I can't block out the facts of my life," said Natalie. But he kept the scallop in the air, and she tasted it. He was right; it was cooked perfectly, hot and crisp and glistening with oil. Inside was the peculiar oversweetness of the scallop itself. He was right that when she tasted the scallop she thought only about what she was tasting, and not at all about Sara. The food covered up everything else; it made the rest of her life seem far away, a rapidly fading backdrop. "May I?" Natalie asked, reaching for another scallop.

He nodded eagerly, and then waved his hand for the waitress. "Miss! Miss! Another Fisherman's Platter," he said. The additional food arrived and they ate and ate; Natalie lost herself in all the breading, all the sauce, and the scent of deep-frying that she and Mel now seemed to be doused with for good. By the time the meal was over, she felt sated, as though she could nap. They slowly left the restaurant and sat together on a bench at the pier. Without much fanfare, he put an arm around her. It felt warm and thick, and she leaned into him, knowing that her slight body was barely registering against his more substantial self. To her surprise, she napped. Lately, sleep was a difficult, elusive thing, but now, stunned by the kind of food she never ate, she fell shamelessly asleep against the sweater of a man she barely knew.

When she woke up, it was with a start. Embarrassed, Natalie sat up quickly and smoothed out her hair. "Oh, God, I can't believe I took a nap," she said.

"Relax," said Mel. "It was adorable." But he shook out his arm, which had apparently gone to pins and needles from the pressure of Natalie's head. They walked along the pier a while, and Mel spoke about Adam. "He's a good kid," Mel said.

"Yes," offered Natalie mildly, "he is."

"Your daughter—she and Adam were best friends, right?" said Mel, and Natalie could only nod. "She must have been someone special," he said. "Someone who could put up with that kid's insecurities."

"She was wonderful," said Natalie, and she liked the idea that Mel had not known Sara, had only met her a couple of times in large social situations, but had no fixed, definitive view of her. With Mel, Natalie could shape that view. She could present her daughter any way she liked. "My daughter," Natalie continued, "was a very complicated girl. She liked to be around Adam, and took great solace from him, but she was very popular among regular, I mean *straight* men. She had Adam to fall back on, and he had her. I can't say I understood it."

"Young people today," said Mel. "They bore the hell out of me. Their problems! They think they're so interesting, but actually, I want to cry out of dullness, listening to what they have to say. Generation X. What the hell does that mean? X-tremely annoying?" He paused. "If our generation was assigned a letter, what would it be?"

"*P,*" said Natalie. "For polyps."

"And Prozac," said Mel. "And prostate."

She laughed easily, and he reached out and put an arm around her again. Through the aura of fish and frying oil, he also smelled of a long-extinguished cigar, and she imagined him in his office in New York, with framed posters from Broadway shows on the walls, his shiny, good shoes up on his desk, his head trapped inside a nimbus of cigar fumes, chatting away happily on the telephone, the way Natalie did at Seven Seas Travel. All day long she discussed fares to Barbados, while he discussed grosses. Still, there was a similarity, a familiar feeling.

"Listen, Natalie," he said, "I'd really like to have dinner with you in the city, after the summer's over. There's this place on the east side that serves seven-course Hungarian feasts."

"That would be nice," she said politely.

"No. You don't mean it," he said. "You can't. With what you're going through, how could you think about me, how could you care if you see me again? I couldn't ask you to care. Not now." There was a delicate pause. "But I'm warning you: I'm going to ask you sometime," he said.

They walked together in silence. With his arm against her she actually felt a thin strand of pleasure, followed by a reflexive thought: *I must tell Sara.*

LATER THAT afternoon, Shawn asked Natalie to go with him to the beach. A team of Japanese surfers would be there, and he promised her they would put on a great show. But when they got to the beach, the waves were tame, and the Japanese surfers were waiting impatiently on the beach for the wind to pick up. Their bodies were beautiful and hairless, and they called out to each other in their language. Occasionally, Natalie thought she could actually pick out a word someone had said.

"God, look at them," Shawn said, and together they gazed openly at the cluster of gorgeous young men in bathing trunks.

Then, as if through the powers of sheer will and desire, Shawn lured one of the surfers over and began to ask him questions about his designer surfboard, which was decorated with an illustration of a rising sun. "I made it myself," the surfer said. "I drew picture of sun."

"You speak English well," said Shawn, and the surfer, who said his name was Kenji, seemed pleased.

"I study a long time," Kenji told him. "My goal? To move to Southern California and start business there. Maybe in three, four years, when my body is too old for the big waves."

"Too old?" said Shawn, amused. "How old are you now?"

"Nineteen."

"Well, you look at least twenty-one," said Shawn.

"Really?" said Kenji, pleased. He didn't seem to know that

184 | Meg Wolitzer

Shawn was flirting with him. For the first time, Natalie saw
Shawn as a possible predator, as someone with power, which he
lacked back in the shabby light of the little house.

"You'll have to come over sometime," Shawn said. Kenji
appeared bewildered, then pleased.

"Sure," he said. "Great!"

Then one of the other surfers called to him, and he waved a
quick good-bye to Shawn and turned and sprang off toward the
water. Natalie and Shawn watched as he waded in, the surfboard
under his arm, then paddled like a dog, his shining black head
above the water, catching the sun. What kind of person would
want to ride a wave? Natalie wondered, marveling at how
unknowable they were, these handsome surfers from another part
of the world.

"Look at them go," said Shawn. "Amazing."

"Truly," agreed Natalie.

"Attraction to other people used to be this easy thing," said
Shawn. "You saw someone you liked. A surfer, maybe, a bartender, a repairman; it didn't matter who he was. He just had to
appeal to you, and to think you were appealing, too. And you'd go
somewhere, back to someone's apartment, and that would be that.
It was so wonderful. I miss those days, I really do. Now sex is
totally different. There's this potential skull-and-crossbones in the
air; you have to pretend it isn't there, but it is. You can't really
relax. You keep thinking about body fluids, and it makes you
insane, it really does."

"Shawn," said Natalie, "let's get you tested. Right now."

"What? No, no, I really can't," he said, his voice tightening.

"I see you walking around like you're dying," said Natalie. "I
see what you're thinking about all the time. You're young," she
said. "You're a writer, you're filled with life. You shouldn't have to
be obsessed with death."

"I'm scared," he said simply. "What if it's positive? Then I'll
just become this totally terrified person."

"But what if it's *negative?*" she said. "Then you can live your life a little." She was surprised at the urgency in her own voice. She felt suddenly zealous about this whole project. And her zeal somehow convinced him, and off they went, along the highway to the next town, to the medical office that had HIV tests and results back very quickly. They walked up the narrow flight of stairs in an undistinguished medical arts building and into a bland waiting room where a receptionist in beachwear sat behind a desk. Natalie explained that they had no appointment, but asked if it was possible to get a blood test anyway, and the woman said it was. So they sat for a while, flipping through old issues of *National Geographic* and trying to relax.

When Shawn was called in, Natalie went with him. He sat in the office not of a doctor but a registered nurse, dressed in shorts and sandals and an "I Gave Blood" pin, who told him that since all blood test results needed to be reported to the Department of Health, he was free to use a pseudonym.

Shawn thought about this for a moment. "Oscar Hammerstein," he said, and the nurse did not register any recognition. Then Shawn rolled up his shirtsleeve and held out his slender arm. Wet cotton was rubbed across it, and the nurse waved her hand to fan it dry. Natalie sat on the chair beside him, not saying a word. Shawn looked at her; he and Natalie kept their gaze locked onto each other as a needle was procured and suddenly its hot point was under his skin at that delicate place, and the pain was like a long sizzle, making him bite his lip. Then the nurse removed the needle and pressed a piece of cotton onto the spot. Shawn turned to look as she held up the vial she had been holding, which was filled with his own warm, dark blood. He watched as she carefully wrote the words "Oscar Hammerstein" on the label, and then carried the vial out of the room, off to some centrifuge where it could be whipped and shaken, and then she could return with an answer for him, either good or bad.

They sat in the waiting room together again, not looking at

each other for a while. Shawn told her about going with his mother to the local G.P.'s office when one of the kids in his family was sick, sitting with a raw throat in the no-frills waiting room of ancient Dr. Hempel, who never bothered to warm his stethoscope before an exam. His mother always seemed somewhat betrayed if a kid's sickness was real and required medicine. They could barely afford the pink liquid antibiotics that Hempel always dispensed for strep or an ear infection, and on the way home in the car she would drive with a grim expression, as if quietly angry about the inconvenience and cost of the illness. At home the kid would be put in bed for the day, and Shawn remembered that when he was the sick one, he would lie in his bottom bunk hearing his sisters and brothers playing and shouting in the distance, and would feel an anxiety that he wasn't among them, a feverish need to be up and about, so as not to create more work for his already overworked mother.

With Natalie, he felt that he could be very sick and it would somehow be all right; he could have a lurking sickness, still confined to the bloodstream, not yet loosed on the rest of him, and she wouldn't point a finger at him, reminding him that sex with men had brought this on, as though the cause mattered now. He told Natalie that it amazed him that she didn't seem to care that he had had sex with men; she clearly wasn't interested in that, she was only interested in what his blood revealed. To his surprise, she was most concerned with making him feel better, which he understood was what a mother was supposed to do, at least in theory. She was supposed to be someone who would *accompany* you to difficult places, and simply sit there quietly. Someone who would offer you Tic Tacs as you waited, or hold your frozen hand if you liked, or occasionally look up from her magazine and offer a quick, worried smile and a few platitudes.

"You know," said Natalie, "whatever it is, this thing, we'll deal with it."

"I doubt it," said Shawn. "You can't deal with something like this. You just have to let yourself be swept up into it. And I've seen it up close, Natalie. The protease inhibitors you have to take, and how if you miss a dose you're screwed, and the little beepers that go off to remind you, and the terrible taste in your mouth, and the intestinal problems, and how everyone knows exactly what's wrong with you and you can't hide it. And how everyone is afraid to sleep with you. So maybe your life is saved, but you become one of the living dead."

"No," said Natalie firmly. "People do deal with these things. In their own, strange ways, they really do. I know you can't believe that right now, but it's true."

The nurse poked her head into the waiting room. "Mr. Hammerstein?" she said without any irony. "Oscar, would you come with me?"

Shawn and Natalie followed her back into the tiny examination room. They all sat down, and the nurse looked at him with a steady gaze, and then said, "Mr. Hammerstein, your blood test revealed that there were no antibodies present for the HIV virus."

For a brief moment neither he nor Natalie understood, but then they did. He was negative. He was spared. "Oh my God," he said. "I'm okay? I'm really okay?"

"For now," said the nurse. He was about to leap up from his chair but she put out a hand. "Of course," she said, "it's important that you continue to practice safe sex procedures, and to have yourself tested every six months if you think you might have taken part in any risk behavior. And I'd like you to have a copy of this to read at your leisure." She reached into a drawer and pulled out what appeared to be a comic book. Shawn took it from her and glanced at the cover. In lurid colors, a Hispanic man and a white woman were locked in a clinch, thought bubbles floating above their heads. The woman was thinking to herself, "Hmmm, José's really cute, but I want him to use a condom . . ." And the man was thinking, "Lisa better not ask me to use a condom. I hate those things! I'll pretend that I know I'm clean . . ."

Shawn stood up suddenly. Natalie thought he appeared transformed by his good news; his eyes were glowing, his skin pink with excitement. "Look, thank you very much," he said to the nurse. "This is really wonderful. You have no idea."

"Oh, I think I do," she said.

Together he and Natalie left the medical office, going back down the narrow stairs and out into the strong sun, which he suddenly turned to as if in a kind of tropism, his face lifted. "I'm okay!" he said. "I'm really okay!" He was in tears, she saw, and then he reached out and hugged her fiercely. She was happy for him, almost painfully so, this person she barely knew, this person who would not become a successful writer of musicals, whose life was not flooding with hope and promise, but merely with life.

"Congratulations, Mr. Hammerstein," she said to him, and he grabbed her again, so exciting was it to be young and alive and immortal, at least for now.

13

A Mother's Kisses

What was it about men with babies that excited women like nothing else could? In the city, when Peter took Duncan out for a walk, women stopped him on the street, actually planted themselves in his path to comment on the adorableness of the baby and also tacitly, he felt, the father. He thought that women lusted after men with babies because they wanted to be having sex with the father and cuddling the child. They became completely turned on by the whole package; it created two kinds of desire in them, a potent house-blend of aphrodisiacs.

Peter thought of this now, out on the deck one night late in the month with Duncan and Natalie. Maddy was inside taking a long shower, the water pounding on and on. Once again he had initiated the topic of making love, and once again she had said no.

Then she got out of bed and said she wanted to shower. Soon she had gone into the bathroom and the water had been turned on, and the fruity smells of her shampoo and soap wafted out into the hall. She might well be in there for a long time; there was no point in waiting for her. Duncan suddenly awakened, and Peter carried him downstairs, aware of how rarely he did this. Usually, whenever the baby made a sound, Maddy was upon him before Peter even had a chance.

Now, out on the deck in the warm night air, he took pleasure from this moment with his son, and more pleasure from the fact that Natalie was watching him. Peter realized that he was putting on a little fatherhood show for her, a display of his brand of masculine tenderness. He was setting the power of his huge arms into relief against the tiny, unformed body of his son. He twirled with the baby now, and as he did, he watched Natalie smoking and observing him.

He remembered the first time he had seen Sara look at him in such a critical, interested way. It took place months before that one afternoon of sex at her apartment. Adam, Sara, Maddy, and Peter had gone to the movies together. Just before they went inside, Peter stopped at the water fountain for a drink, and when he turned around, wiping his wet chin with the back of a hand, he saw that Sara was looking at him. She was standing by the concessions stand, leaning against the popcorn machine. Peter was embarrassed that his chin was wet, and he hoped he didn't seem sloppy. He strode across the red carpeting of the lobby toward her, as if drawn by the scent of the popcorn, as if she herself were dipped in butter and waiting. But when he reached her, she swiftly turned away from him and toward Maddy, who was coming out of the ladies room. "No toilet paper," Maddy was saying. "I practically had to use a credit card receipt in my purse." Sara shook her head in commiseration. Had he only imagined that she had been looking at him? Was he so full of himself, so inflated that he thought all women desired him? He was fairly certain he hadn't hallucinated her interest, just as now he was almost sure that Natalie felt something for him. He *wanted* her to feel something; he wanted to preen for her, and he wasn't above using the baby as a prop. From inside the house, he could hear Adam's computer clicking slowly and fitfully, and Shawn at the piano, composing. Peter also heard Maddy's shower still going.

"I have to get Duncan to sleep somehow," said Peter. "I'm going to take him for a walk, I think."

"Want some company?" Natalie asked, as he'd hoped she would.

"Sure," he said carelessly, and he felt the muscles in his face tighten. He went inside and poked his head into the bathroom. "I'm taking Duncan out!" he called into the mist, and then he didn't even wait for Maddy's reply.

THEY WALKED in silence through the dark, quiet streets, the carriage creaking a little on its springs. The neighbor was out walking his tiny, frail dog, who stopped to sniff and select a perfect place to lift his wishbone of a leg. The old man pretended that he hadn't seen Peter and Natalie, and actually turned his head as they passed him. Eventually there were no more houses, and no street lamps either. The road became absolutely dark as they approached the entrance to the beach.

"Oh, I can't see at all," Natalie said.

"Here, take my hand," said Peter, and she did. They had held hands before, on the afternoon of mushrooms, so it was a familiar sensation. They walked through the parking lot, and he saw the approximate shapes of two parked cars. Ahead, on the beach, some people had lit torches and stuck them into the sand. An informal nighttime volleyball game was taking place, the ball thwapping back and forth over a vaguely visible net. When Peter and Natalie stepped onto the beach, the wheels of the carriage instantly slowed. Peter pushed on, until finally the effort was too great, and that was where they stopped. In the distance, the volley-ball players kept the ball aloft. Someone shouted out, "Spike it!"

"Do you want to sit down?" Natalie asked. They sat a few yards from the water, side by side, Duncan now fast asleep in the carriage.

"We all used to come here at night," he said to her.

"Sara too?"

"Yeah," he said. "Her hair would keep blowing in her face, kind of covering it. She'd keep pushing it back." He looked at Natalie, whose own hair was blowing in her face. You look so much like her, you know," Peter said.

"I'm a lot older."

"Well, you don't look it."

"You're very sweet," Natalie said.

"No, I'm not, actually," Peter said, and then he didn't know what to say next, had completely run out of anything to say that seemed remotely natural. After a moment he realized she had quietly begun to sing, and the strangeness of the song made him turn to her.

"Uoy t'nod rebmemer em, tub I rebmemer uoy . . . ," she was singing: Sara's backwards song. "Ti t'nsaw gnol oga, / uoy ekorb ym traeh ni owt / sraet no ym wollip / niap ni ym traeh / desuac yb uoy / uoy, uoy uoy uoy . . ." He just stared at her for a moment and then moved forward so that she was in his arms. She came to him easily; her shoulders were as narrow and lovely as a girl's. She took his hand and brought it to her mouth, kissing the fingertips. The sky overhead was dark, and they could see each other in the dim torchlight of the volleyball game. She let go of his hand, and then he turned slightly, and Natalie's mouth landed against his. They both waited to see what would happen, if the kiss would stay innocent and childlike, if mouths would stay closed, if eyes would stay open. He needed to see if he was imagining her desire for him, if perhaps she scattered sexuality carelessly in the vicinity of men.

But then she opened her mouth against his, and his questions abruptly ended in the stun of warmth. This was all insanely arousing; they pulled apart for a moment in order to mumble and groan at the excitement of it all, and then they kissed again.

"You don't know how much I've wanted to do this," he said to her, and they were poised in that tremendous moment, when you're not sure what will happen, how far this will go, where it will take you, or even why it is happening. Down the shore, a man trolled for coins with a divining rod, moving it listlessly back and forth like a janitor with a vacuum at the end of a long day. Someone else was in the water; there was splashing and laughter. The volleyball kept going back and forth over the ghostly net. Peter's breathing came quickly, and his desire for Natalie had become as big as his desire for Sara that afternoon on her couch. He knew he would do anything now.

But then there was the sound of crying, a sudden, car-alarm baby screech. Peter sprang away from Natalie. In the carriage, Duncan was sobbing, staring indignantly out at Natalie and Peter as though with a kind of knowledgeable fury. A strange sensation rippled across Peter: his seven-month-old baby knew this was all wrong, and was stopping them from going any further. Shakily, Peter unbelted Duncan from his T-strap, and once in his arms the baby became calmer, hiccuping as his crying ceased. Natalie and Peter smiled tensely at each other over the baby's head and shrugged, trying to turn the moment into something humorous, when in fact they both felt a dizzying tilt, the bewilderment that follows interrupted arousal—a tug of gravity from the real world.

"I guess it's a sign from God," she said, smoothing out her blouse. Then she added, "I'm glad."

"Me too," he said, and suddenly he was. Giddy and disoriented, an absurd slogan came to his mind: "I made out with Sara's mother . . . and all I got was this stupid T-shirt." The situation was wild; he wished she could laugh with him about it, but he knew she couldn't. He watched her straightening her collar with her delicate hands. "It's like we're open to any crazy thing that comes along," he said. "It's like we're completely up for grabs."

"I think I know what you mean," she said.

"You are very beautiful," he told her.

"Oh, don't," she said, holding up a hand.

"But I want to tell you this."

"Peter, don't say anything else," she said. "No offense, but just shut up a little, okay?"

So he did, and they stayed for a while longer on the beach, pretending to watch the volleyball game. Peter's breathing began to slow, his arousal began to dissipate, and his heart, just doing what it was told, returned to its uneventful, day-to-day thud. Held fast in his father's arms, the baby seemed to smile in triumph—or was it gas?

They walked back to the house together, the carriage groaning and squeaking. In the living room, Maddy was now sitting and watching television. Her hair was still wet from the shower, plastered down against her head, and she was in a robe. She looked up when they came in, her face neutral and unreadable. "I'll bring Duncan upstairs and change him," Peter said to her, and she nodded. He lifted the baby from the carriage and carried him up the steps. Natalie followed; he assumed she was just going into her room, but instead she trailed behind him and walked into his room. He lay the baby down on the bed and began to open his diaper, the tape making an adhesive sucking sound. He unscrewed a jar of A&D ointment, filling the room with that familiar nursery smell, and he waited for Natalie to say something, for clearly she wanted to. But she said nothing, so he spoke first.

"I don't regret it, you know," he said quietly.

"Do you regret Sara?" she asked.

"I don't know," Peter said. "People's lives are very weird. Things happen—unbelievable things."

"She felt very guilty about you," said Natalie, "because of

Maddy. She didn't want to hurt her; they were such great friends. She knew that it wasn't the kind of thing you should do to a friend, and yet she said there was something in her that afternoon that overrode that idea. She called me up that day and said, 'Mom, I've done a terrible thing.' And then she was crying so hard I couldn't understand her."

In the room, the conversation was muted and the baby rolled and played with a squeak toy on the bed. What had risen up between Peter and Sara's mother was settling down, returning to earth.

But below the bedroom, one flight down in the living room, Maddy sat in silence on the couch, holding the baby monitor in her hand, everything said by Peter and Natalie being transmitted with stunning clarity, and the row of red lights jumping as the words were spoken.

MADDY MADE A decision then and there that she would not respond, would not freak out. She decided she would simply endure the rest of the time here in the house, keeping to herself, losing herself completely in Duncan. The next afternoon everyone went to the beach, and while they were all setting up blankets and towels and driving the post of the umbrella into the sand, Maddy took Duncan farther down the shore. She sat with him a few feet from the water, letting him play nearby. He loved to dig in the sand with a plastic cup and spoon. A big hat shielded his face, and she had slathered him with sunblock, so he was safe. Maddy sat watching him, trying not to think about Peter and Natalie, or Peter and Sara, but she was no dope, she knew it all now.

After Labor Day, when they had to go back to the city, she would announce that she wanted a separation. Peter would look shocked, would attempt to appear innocent, but she would not be swayed. She and Duncan would move to one of those one-bed-room boxy apartments in a high-rise. The crib would go right in the middle of the living room, surrounded by Maddy's law texts and papers. She would become one of those overworked, single professional mothers, whose children are starved for attention. Fuck Peter, she thought. He did this to us. He did it. She closed her eyes and cried in silence—for the loss of her marriage, for how she had been betrayed, for how Sara had betrayed her too, and how Maddy could never confront her about it. It was as though her life had caved in and there was no way to reconstruct it around herself. Work might help, and being with Duncan, but apart from those arenas she would grow bitter; no one would want to be near her. Men would avoid her, not that they'd ever flocked to her to begin with.

What had Sara needed Peter for, anyway? Was it just because Sara had needed *everything,* had needed to taste it all and try it all and be at the center of everyone's interest? Sara had experienced remorse, according to a few words spoken by her mother over a plastic baby monitor; well, big deal, remorse wasn't enough. Maddy cried and cried now, her head in her hands, lost in the fantasy of herself and Sara at Camp Ojibway, sitting among the trees, never imagining the direction that everything would take, never understanding that lives *took* directions—thinking merely that life was an adventure, a long walk in the woods taken by two young girls.

She looked up now to check on Duncan, but he wasn't there. Maddy's heart began to flutter; she stood up on the sand, thinking she might pass out. How could this have happened, when Duncan couldn't even crawl?

"What's the matter?" a man with a bucket asked her.

"My *baby's* gone," she said in a voice of plaintive helplessness, and surely these were the most pathetic words in the world. In the next few moments there was a great swirl of action around her, everyone talking and gesturing and becoming involved. Voices echoed to one other: "Her baby . . ." she heard, and "Missing." In the middle of the fuss and noise there was a sudden new activity, and Maddy looked up to see the crowd part and Natalie come striding through, holding Duncan. He was fine, blinking and looking around him in surprise. Maddy screamed—a single, brief syllable—then she took him from Natalie's arms, burying her head in the creases of her baby's neck, feeling an enormous, animal relief. There was an acid taste in her mouth, and a sudden drenching of sweat in the hollows under her arms.

"He crawled along the shore," Natalie was saying. "I saw him go—he was like a little sand crab, and I just scooped him up and brought him back."

"Duncan doesn't crawl," said Maddy.

"He does now," Natalie said. "Very fast, too."

Peter appeared then, and behind him were Shawn and Adam, and quickly everything was explained and re-explained. "Thank you," Peter said quietly to Natalie. "My God, he might have drowned. What would we have done?"

"Yes, thank you," Maddy said flatly. But she couldn't even look at Natalie. The circle of watchers had broken up, going back to their blankets, their radios, their places in the sun, since there was no real drama here after all. "You saved his life," she added, and then she wrapped her arms tighter around Duncan, her baby who now crawled, who would soon walk, who would need to be watched more closely—her baby who would soon be off into the world.

14

Spinsters!

At the end of the season that had come to be known as the summer of Sara's death, the house seemed to outlive its usefulness. No one wanted to be there now, but no one knew how to move. There was a geometry of bad feelings in the air—none of it referred to directly. The only sounds of pleasure and comfort came from Maddy and Duncan, a mother and child who played together these days with ease.

Natalie was searching for a pack of matches in her straw bag, when she came across the tape of Shawn's songs that Mel Wolf had returned to her. "Oh, Shawn, I completely forgot," she said, taking out the tape. "Mel Wolf asked me to give you this, and to say thank you for letting him listen to it."

Shawn took the tape without saying a word, but Adam, who was watching the transaction, blinked a few times and said, "What's all this?"

And so the story of Shawn's secret tape was revealed to Adam, whose face took on a squinting expression of incredulity. "You gave my producer your tape?" he said. "Without my permission?"

"Your permission? Give me a fucking break. You're not in charge," said Shawn, his hand shaking a little as he thrust the tape back into his pocket.

"No, but I distinctly told you it would make me uncomfortable," said Adam.

"He was just trying to get Mel to listen," said Natalie. "Come on, Adam, lighten up."

Adam swung around to stare at Natalie. "You don't know what you're saying," he said. "So please stay out of this."

"Shawn didn't mean anything," she insisted.

"Yes he did, and don't protect him," Adam said. "You're not his mother." His voice was resoundingly loud and inappropriate, but he didn't care. "You're not my mother either, or the mother of any of us," he went on. Everyone else just sat and stared. No one had ever raised their voice to Natalie; she was a grieving mother, she was exempt.

"I never said I was," said Natalie.

"Oh, that is completely untrue," he said. "You came here—I mean, you just showed up on our doorstep like an orphan—and what were we supposed to do, turn you away? No, we let you in because we felt sorry for you—"

"Don't do me any favors," said Natalie.

"So you became the big mother in the household. We were used to being the kids, and it felt right. But you got really into it, didn't you?"

Natalie seemed to have sunk into her chair, to become smaller, old. Peter stood up in her vague defense, unsure of what to do. "Can you just stop this?" he asked Adam. "I think it's enough already."

"Oh, you're one to talk," said Maddy. "You're the paragon of virtue, aren't you?"

Peter turned to his wife. "I'm not a paragon of anything," he said. "I know I'm not." He moved toward Maddy, but she flinched away from him.

"Please don't," she said. "I've been putting up with this, I've been living in this house because I don't know what else to do, but don't make me pretend everything is okay."

Shawn glanced back and forth between Maddy and Peter, puzzled. "Is there something going on here that I don't know about?" he said. "I mean, I snuck my tape to Melville Wolf, I put it in his car; what does that have to do with anybody else?"

"It's not about you, Shawn," said Maddy.

"Then what is it about?" he asked.

"Sara," she said simply.

"Sara?" said Shawn. "I didn't even know her. I met her the night of the accident."

"Exactly," Maddy said. "But it doesn't matter. It extends forever and ever. Her reach. Her influence. I mean," she continued, "who the hell was she? This person who we confided in, who we lived with. Look at us—we're so pathetic. Dwelling on her, trapped here with each other." She stood up, trembly suddenly, and said, "I wish I'd never met her."

Now Natalie, as though signaled by some maternalistic satellite, sprang into defensive words. "She was a wonderful girl. She was. I knew her like no one else." She broke off her own speech, because she had begun to cry. Fumbling in her bag for a tissue, she blew her nose very hard, and then said, weakly, "I am in mourning here, you know. I am the person who's grieving."

"We all are," said Adam.

"No," she said. "I'm the mother. *I'm the mother.*"

"Of course you are," said Adam. "But we count too."

"You were her friends, not her family," Natalie said.

"I am so sick of that distinction," Adam said. "Family is everything, and friends are nothing. Why wouldn't you let us come to the funeral?"

"I already told you."

"Tell me again. Don't we have any rights? We wanted to say

good-bye. But no good-byes were allowed. Instead, we get you instead."

"You invited me," said Natalie.

"We were desperate," Adam said.

"I'll say you were," Natalie said.

"Sara was a part of our lives," said Adam. "Not just yours. I loved her. We didn't have a password we'd say on the phone—we didn't have a little 'Surrender, Dorothy' shtick; we had something completely different. A friendship. Which," he continued, inhaling hard, raggedly, "you don't give me any credit for. Because I'm the 'gay friend,' and I wasn't her lover—I wasn't like goddamn phony Sloan, or one of those other men who wouldn't have made her happy—so I have no right to be hysterical about her." He paused, feeling so far out of his element that it temporarily emboldened him. "But I am hysterical," he said. "We all are. This whole house is hysterical." She kept staring at him. "Look," he said, lowering his voice, "I know it's the hardest thing in the world to lose a child."

"Oh, don't give me your platitudes," said Natalie. "You don't know anything about having a child."

"No," he said. "But I know about Sara."

"She was my daughter," said Natalie.

"It's not a contest." But of course it was, a heated, furious competition, and the theme of it was: Who owned this broken girl now, her mother or her closest friends? There were no rules, no reference book in which to look up the answer. "We all loved her," he said. "And I think that it's made us a little insane."

"Are you just about done?" said Natalie.

"Yes," said Adam. "I am."

"All right then," she said in a prim voice, and then Natalie strode across the porch and walked out onto the lawn, going around the side of the house. In a moment they heard her car ignition starting. Everyone stared at each other; no one knew what to say.

"What's this about?" said Shawn after a moment. He looked

at Maddy and Peter. "Why are you so angry at each other? What is going on that I should know about?"

"No offense, but there's nothing you should know about," said Peter. "This is private. You don't even know us."

"No, I don't," said Shawn. "And it's just as well." He was tired of them, tired of their wearying solipsism, their unhappiness. He was also tired of their disappointing house, and tired of Adam, who had a connection to a dead girl who still wouldn't die. He was tired of all the talk that went on here; in this crowd, talk was such a big deal. For them, conversation was a form of high entertainment. But he was done with the talk, the late nights in the kitchen with the sunburst clock, and all the dawns in the narrow bed next to Adam, that mouth-breathing, sleepwalking boy genius. Shawn shouldn't have come here at all; right now, he should have been in his apartment in Hell's Kitchen with his two roommates, the actor/waiter and the weight trainer/musician, complaining about the heat and the grime, going to Sunday tea dances at Kimo Sabe and meeting men with good bodies, men who were fun to be with.

"Just tell me one thing," Shawn said to Adam when the others had gone inside. "How come you get everything?"

"I don't get everything."

"How come," Shawn went on, "there are some people who just know how to *get* things in life? It's like there's this whole breed of people who can't win enough prizes. Other people want to keep *giving* them stuff, making dinners in their honor, handing them fucking plaques with their names engraved on them. Really, how come everyone is interested in what *you* have to say? Why should that be? It's not as though you're exactly a man of experience. Although I suppose you'd say that Sara's death has given you experience, has opened you up or something. But you haven't been around the world, or worked on a tramp steamer, or spent a year living in a ghetto. It's not as though you have life experience, Adam. I mean, almost anyone has more of that than you. Even *I* do! I've gone to bed with more people, and I've worked at jobs you wouldn't dream of doing, and I've been places that would give you a heart attack. I've been down by the docks in the city, and to a coke deal in Harlem with my fucked-up actor friend who had just gotten his first commercial—that margarine thing where he had to dress up like cholesterol—and he spent his entire paycheck on coke. I've done all these things, and I'm not stupid, either. So why can't I have what you have? I know I'm not the greatest writer in the world, but do I really have to be? Is that what it takes? Is that what makes it happen, this golden thing that happened to you?"

"Two writers," Adam said, helplessly. "It never works. We'll always be looking over each other's shoulder. It's a mistake, it really is."

Shawn nodded. After a moment he said, "I'm going to go now."

"Go where?" asked Adam.

"Home. I'll take the Jitney back to the city," said Shawn, and he turned and walked into the house. He climbed the stairs slowly, waiting for the sound of the screen door opening, and Adam rushing in. But it didn't happen; the house was silent and hot and as claustrophobic as ever. He hated Adam for wanting to hold him back, and he hated Melville Wolf for not liking his music. And he hated himself for not being able to make something happen, for not being able to charm everyone into giving him what he wanted. He needed to leave. He would miss Natalie; she was the only one. She would be puzzled when she returned and found him gone, but there was no other way. It had been a great relief to have a mother for a while. He wanted nothing more, right now, than to be in the dressing room of that men's store with her again, dressed in finery and singing show tunes.

Shawn went into the bedroom, where his belongings mingled with Adam's in haphazard maleness: waterproof watches with thick black straps; Jockey shorts; a stick of Arrid for Men, unscented; a box, largely untouched, of Trojans; and the beautiful clothes Natalie had bought him. Shawn shoved all his things into his shoulder bag and hurried back downstairs. By the telephone in the kitchen was a list of numbers: Fire, Hospital, the Police, and, finally, a number that was to be saved for emergencies. "Mrs. Hope Moyles," Shawn read, and then suddenly, impulsively, he picked up the receiver on the wall phone and dialed the number.

The landlady's sister answered and put Mrs. Moyles on; Shawn had heard plenty about her, that she was an old drunk, and bitter. She sounded a little slurred now, but still she seemed to listen with attention when he spoke. "Mrs. Moyles," he said in a clear, slow voice, "I am currently visiting your house at 17 Diller Way, and I feel it is my duty to report what has been going on here."

"What do you mean?" she asked.

"I mean," he said, "they've trashed your house. Totally. The place is a disgusting wreck." He paused, then added, "And they've taken drugs here, too. Ask your next-door neighbor, he'll tell you. Actually," he said, "I think you should get here as soon as you can." And before she could say anything, Shawn hung up. He was gone from the house within minutes, pausing to stand out front briefly to remind himself once again how ugly this place was, and how he wouldn't miss it. The only thing he left behind was the gift he had brought that first day: the bayberry candle that flickered out on the back porch, in the kind of chilly breeze that always signifies the end of summer.

WITH SHAWN GONE and Natalie off in her car, the house was quiet. Maddy sat with Duncan on the grass, listening attentively for the sound of Natalie's car pulling up out front. Hours went by; no car came. It was astonishing to realize that she loved Sara's mother; she loved her like a mother. After everything that had happened, she couldn't hate Natalie Swerdlow, just as she couldn't hate Sara. All the hatred had been dismantled piece by piece, and Maddy felt only very tired now. Duncan was crawling in pursuit of a butterfly—one of those small, pale yellow ones that fluttered especially quickly and desperately. She loved being with her baby, ever since her late-night talk with Natalie. She loved Duncan in a way that took her by surprise. She knew that even if she and Peter broke up, she would have Duncan, and she would be okay. She would bury herself into him, devoting all her thoughts and energy to him. What else was there, after all? She had no best friend anymore, and she could not trust her husband. If Peter moved out, she would be as lonely as Natalie, lying alone in the center of the bed at night and pacing the rooms she lived in, forever.

Now Maddy went upstairs and made her way onto the roof, which seemed the right place to be. Out there, smoking again, she leaned against the warm shingles and thought of how much she wanted her life back. She wanted to be just meeting Sara by the lake, just falling in love with Peter in college, just starting the hopeful rise instead of the premature descent. Nearby, a window squeaked open and Peter stepped outside.

"Hey," he said. "What are you doing out here?"

"Smoking," she said.

"Come inside."

"No," she said, although she wanted to come inside more than anything.

"I love you, Maddy," he tried.

"More than you love Sara? Or her mother?"

"What?" he said. "I don't love them. You know I don't. You're the one; that's the total truth. It's very simple."

She looked at him warily. "I guess you do love me," she said. "But it's not simple, and it's not good enough. It doesn't take care of everything." She imagined letting herself simply slide down off the roof as if on a flume ride at a water park, her arms at her sides, her legs straight out in front of her, closing her eyes as she was shunted off into the end of her life. It would be so easy to do that now.

"I don't know what you know," he said. "Or where you heard it, or whether it's true, but—"

"It *is* true," she cut him off. "But I don't want to hear about it. Not a single word, ever. And as far as *how* I know—" She broke off. "I don't feel like telling you," she said. "And maybe I never will. It will keep you on your toes."

"All right," he said. "I've fucked up, I know that. I'm a big fuck-up." She nodded; at last they agreed on something. "For God's sake," he said. "You want to have this conversation out here? You're too close to the edge; are you trying to prove something?" She didn't say anything. "Don't do this," he said. "Please don't. Look, can we at least go inside?"

She thought for a moment, bits of ash drifting into the air. Did she want to stay out here, suspended in some haze of nostalgia, fantasizing about dying, about sliding neatly down onto the lawn, or did she want to go with Peter, who was imperfect and unfaithful and full of regret? Despite all the reasons not to, she loved him still, had loved him since the day they first slept together at Dyke House at Wesleyan, when she was so happy to have something—someone—that was her own. He was hers, he *was,* despite everything. He wasn't Sara's. That knowledge gave comfort now. She was sleepy; she thought she could sleep against him tonight, thought she could almost imagine a time when touching him would not be a burden. She remembered her earlier self, shy at first and then thrilled to be in bed with him, noting, early on, the way one of her shaved legs was thrown over one of his hairy legs—the peculiar, complementary nature of it. There was the quiet of being in bed with him, and the noise too, unabashed and ordinary, and very much theirs. She didn't want to lose that, to let it turn into something else, a calcified marriage, a tacit hostile arrangement, or even a phlegmatic if cheerful partnership in which husband and wife lay side by side reading their complementary male-female magazines every night. She just wanted it to go back to what it had been before: before Sara died, before Duncan was born, before all the shifting and resettling. Maddy crushed the cigarette against the roof and took the hand that Peter offered, letting him help her into the window, as though it were a threshold and he were swiftly carrying her through.

NATALIE'S CAR pounded down the narrow roads, roads she had driven with extra care since she had been here, thinking of Sara in her car during the accident. Now Natalie was driving much faster than usual. She was reckless, thinking that she wanted to die, reaching over to light a cigarette with the little circle of heat on the end of the car lighter, her hand shaking as she increased the speed and inhaled a full throatful of rolling smoke.

It didn't matter if she were killed in her own car accident now; why should she preserve herself, what for? Did the world care if Natalie Swerdlow went on and on? She had spent weeks in the house of her daughter's friends, doing everything she could to stay in motion, to connect, to take care of these children, to find life bearable, to both believe the terrible truth and somehow not have to believe it at all, and finally she was tired of these tasks, which seemed to her both Herculean and absurd.

Out on the road, cars were honking at Natalie. Still she went faster, trying to remember exactly how to get to the place where Sara had been killed. Maybe there would be no traffic there; maybe she could just apply more and more pressure on the gas pedal, feeling a surge as the car dumbly responded to her command. Natalie drove and drove, and for some reason she could not find the spot. She saw only the same safe, slow curvature of road.

Then, several yards up ahead, Natalie suddenly came upon the huge neon Fro-Z-Cone sign. She remembered that this was where Sara had gone for ice cream the night she died; this was the last place Sara had ever been. Natalie quickly pulled the car into the parking lot and stepped out. There were a few other cars parked here; teenagers lounged on the hood of someone's father's expensive car, and a family sat at a picnic table eating ice cream in speechless, sybaritic pleasure. Behind the glass of the ice cream stand stood an old man with a beard, wiping the counter with a rag. From this distance he looked effeminate and odd, like a gay Rip Van Winkle. Natalie walked closer toward the counter and saw, with shock, that this wasn't an old man at all, but an old woman with a vague beard.

"You want to order?" the bearded woman asked. She'd probably seen everything from her post behind this sliding glass. She'd seen teenagers come and go, and she'd pumped sauce onto ice cream, spooned out countless servings of a viscous walnut and syrup mixture, dipped a pair of tongs repeatedly into a tub to fetch out cherries saturated in red dye #2. She'd seen Sara here every summer, too, although she'd never known her name, and she'd even given Sara ice cream on her last night.

"A cup of chocolate soft-serve," Natalie said, although she wasn't at all hungry, but felt she ought to order just to be polite. "Small, please."

"Ninety-eight cents," said the bearded woman, and Natalie gave her a handful of coins. The woman went over to a large, silver ice cream machine that was as primitive-looking as a Univac.

"My daughter used to come here," said Natalie, poking her head inside the partition. "She came here with her best friend. She came here the night she died. There was a car accident. Earlier this summer, down the road; maybe you remember. She was very pretty. She had long hair." The bearded woman was holding a cup under the nozzle, and now she squinted out through the partition, not saying anything. "She was my little girl," said Natalie in a voice that was almost a whisper, "and this was the last place she went to. This was *it*. She bought ice cream here and started to drive home with her friend, and she was killed." Natalie choked on the last words and began to cry.

The bearded woman appeared startled. "Oh, my, well . . . well, *here,*" she said to Natalie. "Take these." She thrust a sheaf of napkins at Natalie from the dispenser, and Natalie gratefully blew her nose and dabbed at her eyes. She kept crying for a little while longer and the bearded woman looked on helplessly.

"I'm very sorry," said Natalie. She leaned on the counter, her hands against its cool, dented metal surface. She stayed like that for several seconds, and the bearded woman stayed on the other side, both of them silent and thoughtful. "Well," said Natalie finally, gathering her composure, "I guess I should go. Thank you. Thank you very much. I'm sorry I cried like this. I couldn't help myself."

"Wait," said the bearded woman, and she suddenly thrust a hand out through the opening in the glass and took Natalie's dish of ice cream back. "Here," she said. Then she fiddled around behind the counter and produced a plastic teaspoon. She tipped it into Natalie's dish of ice cream, letting loose a spill of jimmies that rained down in a small storm of many colors.

NATALIE DROVE and drove, driving just to drive, and up ahead she suddenly saw a familiar set of well-tended bushes, and a long gravel road that wound its way up to a house she knew. As if returning to a place visited in a dream, she pulled the car into the driveway, and hoped very hard that her childhood friend Sheila Normandy was home. Sheila Normandy, of immense wealth, deep boredom, and an even deeper tan, was a perfect companion for a mourning mother. Sheila was all about distraction, someone devoted to making her own life remotely compelling, or at least amusing. Natalie arrived at the house uninvited, and a maid answered the door, took one look at this woman with wind-swept hair, a look of anguish on her face, and a cup of ice cream in her hand, and knew that here was another one of Mrs. Normandy's troubled friends. Sheila was home, having her nails done somewhere in the recesses of the house, and she came out to see Natalie, smelling of ketones and waving her drying fingers in the air.

"My God, Natalie, are you all right?" Sheila asked.

"No, I don't think so," Natalie said.

"Well, you came to the right place," said Sheila. "Inez, por favor," she said, turning to the maid, "would you tell Scooter that Mrs. Swerdlow and I would like to go up?"

"Go up?" Natalie repeated.

Going up turned out to mean up in the helicopter, which was waiting on the back lawn, its rotors spinning slowly, a handsome young pilot named Scooter sitting inside. He helped the women inside, and within seconds the big thing had lifted up off the ground, and Natalie stared, slightly open-mouthed, as the gigantic Normandy house became smaller and the vast greenery of the island in summer revealed itself. Scooter gave them headsets so they could hear each other when they talked, and he patiently showed both women what all the different switches on the control panel were for. Mostly, though, Natalie and Sheila sat in the deep seats, drank wine, and gazed out at the acreage that once was made up of potato farms.

Here at the beach, Sheila often found herself feeling melancholic in the middle of another endless afternoon on someone's bleached-wood deck, and so she found herself oddly comforted by Natalie, the only person out here who knew her as the daughter of a poultry man. Together, the two women discovered that in middle age they both enjoyed a good, serious drink. Several drinks. Up in the helicopter they looked down over the tiny houses and stretches of beach, and the alcohol enriched their blood, making them forget why, on land, they both felt so sad.

"I used to get dizzy when I came up here," Sheila said. "But Paul loved it. Boys need their toys, right?" Back in their house, Paul Normandy paced the floor of their living room, his electronic manacle digging its teeth into his ankle, a cellular phone perenially pressed against his ear.

"I have no idea what boys need," said Natalie.

"You don't see anybody?" asked Sheila. "I mean socially?"

"Oh, yes, I've been out with a lot of men," said Natalie. "And I just met someone out here."

"Tell me," said Sheila.

"He's a theatrical agent," said Natalie. "And I felt very comfortable with him; it was strange. But what does it matter now? I don't want to be with anyone. I can't imagine that I'll ever want to."

"No, not now, but later maybe," said Sheila. "There will always be a later."

"So they say," said Natalie. "But I doubt it. The thing is, I need to be alone at night. I can't bear the idea of someone being there with me. I get up and pace, I smoke, I walk around. I just wait for the night to be over half the time." She paused. "Remember when we were Campfire Girls, and we used to lie outside in those smelly sleeping bags?"

"Oh yes," said Sheila. "I thought I'd never get to sleep, it was so cold, and I was so excited being out there in the woods. We'd always sing our little song before bed, and the next thing I knew, I was fast asleep." She began to sing once again. "Sit around the campfire / Join the Campfire Girls / Sing wo-he-lo, sing wo-he-lo . . ."

"Work . . . health . . . love," both women sang together, in fragile, proud voices.

"You know something?" said Natalie. "I always thought 'wo-he-lo' was an Indian word. I never realized it was short for work, health, love." They both laughed lightly. "I can't believe," said Natalie, her voice suddenly small, "that I will never see Sara again. In fact, it's almost as though I *will* see her again; I feel as though I could search the world over and eventually find her, if I try hard enough. I mean, how can someone just leave the earth?"

Sheila looked out her window, at the careful scatter of houses below. "We just did," she said.

"Flying isn't the same as dying," said Natalie, realizing she was drunk.

"Oh, you're a poet," said Sheila. "Little Natalie grew up to be a poet."

"Actually, what I grew up to be is nothing," Natalie said. "A goddamn travel agent. It's not exactly curing cancer."

"No, *I* grew up to be nothing," said Sheila. "A rich man's wife. Someone who shops. What good is that? I'm just taking up space and spending Paul's money, and don't think I don't know it."

Somewhere down below was the mustard-colored house on Diller Way, but Natalie had no idea which one it was. She let herself be carried through the air, swiftly, defying gravity in this deft little hummingbird. "Maybe we'll crash," she said to Sheila over the chopping sound of the rotors, imagining the helicopter plummeting down to the ground, depositing them there forever.

"Oh, Scooter's never crashed, and he never will," said Sheila. "He's too smooth for that. Too capable. Believe me, I know."

She sent Natalie a knowing glance to let her know that she had slept with the pilot. Anyone would be attracted to a man who knew how to steer a helicopter, a man whose arms were bound with muscles and whose nose was created specifically so a pair of Ray-Bans could rest upon it. Although the name, Natalie thought, would have to go. How could you lie underneath this man, raking his back and muttering, "Oh, Scooter. Oh, Scooter"? She thought of the boy Peter, and how they were practically of separate species. The young should have sex with the young, the not-so-young with the not-so-young. Cross-pollination seemed freakish now, unseemly.

Kissing that boy, she had not had the same experience as Sara; she had come no closer to knowing what Sara had felt, for certainly Peter had looked at Sara differently than he had looked at her. What Sara had felt, Natalie tried for too. She could approximate it, but she couldn't come close enough. Always, there was a barrier; always, a divide. She wanted to tell her old friend Sheila all about it, but Sheila couldn't understand. She had no children, and her shackled husband lived only for leveraged buyouts; he would be unshackled soon, but she would always be adrift. Sheila responded not to the specifics of Natalie's anguish, but to the presence of anguish itself. "You and Paul never wanted to have children?" Natalie asked.

"Oh, briefly we did," said Sheila. "Back when I thought my marriage was going to be something other than it really was. There was a period there in the early days, when Paul and I used to talk earnestly about our 'feelings.' God, we were boring. He used to lie on his back in bed and talk to me about his plans: We'd get rich, we'd have a family, we'd travel, we'd never want for anything. So he got rich, but then suddenly he had other plans. I had to appear with him at parties; it was what you did. Most companies even insisted on meeting a man's wife to make sure she would be an asset, not a liability. We'd have to go with clients to remote tropical islands, where the wives and I would lie in the sun and read trashy novels. I thought it was great. But then I remembered that we'd wanted a family, and when I tried to broach the subject again, Paul looked at me like I was crazy. Now he didn't want kids; he wanted to buy art. Jumbo canvases that we'd put up over the couch, so heavy that if they fell, everyone would be killed. And I stopped pining away for kids; actually, I'd never even understood what it would mean to have one."

"Oh, it's wonderful to have one," said Natalie. "Sara and I were closer than close. We told each other everything."

"You can tell *me* everything. Nothing shocks me."

"Death is shocking," said Natalie. "It's the one thing."

"Yes, I guess it is," said Sheila. "I still think about my father all the time. I see him in the henhouse—the eggs, the feathers in the air." She shook her head. "But a child is a different thing, I would imagine," she said. "No, I can't even imagine it, I can't begin to. But I just want to say that if you ever want to talk, or if you want a helicopter ride, or a facial, or anything at all, I am here."

"Thank you," said Natalie softly. She looked out the window at the island below. When a child died there was only one truth: You could not get over it, ever, but still you had to live. Still your body needed food, warmth, distraction. Still you thought about getting a haircut; still you glanced at the TV listings. Still, somehow, you went on. Now she thought of her bed, Sara's bed, and suddenly what she wanted was not to die, but simply to be in that narrow bed right now. "Sheila, I'd like to go home, if that's all right," she said, managing only a weak voice.

"Scooter," called Sheila. "Do you think you can take Mrs. Swerdlow directly to her house? I believe there's a little lawn there to land on."

"Sure thing," said Scooter. "What's the address?"

"It's 17 Diller Way," said Natalie. "But how can you just . . . take me to my house? Can this thing just land anywhere?"

"Scooter grew up on this island," said Sheila. "He's a native and he knows everything. He's amazing. I'll have someone drive your car back tomorrow, Natalie. Just relax." So Natalie sat back against the seat while the helicopter hovered, searching for the little house. On Diller Way, people came out on their front porches to see what was happening. The next-door neighbor peered through his screen to see what all the commotion was about. Men and women shielded their eyes to watch as the helicopter stumbled and dipped and bumped down softly.

"Wo-he-lo," Sheila said.

"Wo-he-lo," said Natalie, and she stepped out onto the grass.

15

Enough is Enough

Everyone slept late the next morning, as though deeply hung over from a raucous party at which people had swung from chandeliers and windows had been broken and entire lives had been altered. There was a shocking quiet in the house now, and no one knew quite what to do. Coffee was brewed; the baby was nursed. Everyone was all talked out, and they attempted a collective mildness, an enforced civility. With only a week left on the summer lease, they knew they would all be scattering soon.

The awkward quiet in the house was interrupted in the early afternoon by the ringing of the doorbell. Almost nobody ever rang that rusting bell. Now Adam answered the door and found a young Japanese man standing on the step; he was athletic and handsome and slight.

"I'm looking for Shawn," said the man. "He tell me to come by. I teach him to surf today."

"Shawn is gone," said Adam carefully, "and I don't think he's coming back."

"Excuse me," said Natalie, pushing forward from behind Adam. "You're the surfer we met on the beach that day, aren't you?"

"Yes, Mrs., I'm Kenji."

Natalie paused. "Would you do me a favor, Kenji?" She asked. "It will only take a few minutes."

"Okay," the surfer said. "You want to learn to surf too? All the ladies want to surf."

"No, no, nothing like that," she answered. "Please, come inside."

Adam followed, puzzled, as Natalie led the surfer up the stairs. She invited him into Sara's room and began rummaging through the top dresser drawer, while Adam and Kenji stood stiffly in the doorway. Then Natalie pulled out Sara's red leather notebook, which was filled with Japanese characters.

"This is my daughter's writing," she said slowly to Kenji. "I believe it was her work, her dissertation, or notes for it, anyway. She has died, and these are the things of hers that I have left. I would love to know what she was writing, to be able to read her words. She wrote so beautifully. Do you think you could translate them for me?"

"Well," said Kenji, "I guess perhaps. I am not very good at this, but I will try." He bowed once, lightly, then began to read in a cautious voice. "This say, 'December 10. It is a Saturday. I am lying here alone after Sloan has gone home.'"

"This must be a journal," Natalie interrupted. "Sloan was that man she was seeing for a while, the forestry person. Please go on."

"So then it say this," said Kenji, 'Of course we . . .'" He paused here, blushing. "Well," he said, "it say something not very polite."

"It's all right," said Natalie. "You can tell me. I won't be shocked."

"'. . . we . . . *fucked*,'" he continued, painfully. "But now I am feeling alone. It's almost as though my mother, she has not prepared me for being grown up. I cannot . . ." He paused, squinting over the writing. "I cannot figure out a way to live my life. My mother was always with me, wanting to know everything. And, of course, I always told her. It was our deal, our . . . pact. Now I want to be on my own, but something makes me still need to call her and tell her intimate things. I wish she would let me live my life. I love her, but sometimes I want her to leave me the hell alone. I mean, enough is enough.'"

Kenji looked up into Natalie's startled face, and then he said softly, "Mrs., I cannot read any more. Please do not ask me."

LATER, FOR lack of anything else to do, Adam forlornly walked to a nearby vegetable stand to buy some ears of corn, and he was standing with his hands buried in cornsilk, when he saw a familiar pink and owlish face on the other side of the bin. He stared for a moment, and the man seemed to stare right back. Who was he? Adam was reminded of a kind uncle, now dead, who had always showed an interest in Adam's schoolwork. The man was looking through the ears of corn too, and in silence the two of them worked, like quilters at a bee. Most of the corn was imperfect— the season was virtually over, and what remained mostly had tiny, baby-teeth kernels. "It's not great," said the man.

"No," said Adam. "It's too late." Then, with a start, he realized who he was talking to: *Neil Simon*. He gasped lightly, then said, "Mr. Simon, I'm Adam Langer."

Neil Simon registered no surprise, but merely peeled back the silk on an ear of corn and examined it closer. "I know who you are," he said calmly. "You're the gay version of me, isn't that what they said in the paper?"

"Yes!" said Adam, thrilled. "That's exactly what they said." He paused, suddenly horrified. "Oh, I hope you didn't mind too much," he added. "I mean, it's hardly true or anything."

"I think I can take it," said Neil Simon. "So, how's your work going? You writing something new?"

"Well," said Adam, "You probably just meant that in a perfunctory way, but the real answer is that I'm trying to write another comedy, but I've had something happen in my life this summer, a tragedy, and the two don't seem to go very well together."

"You've had a tragedy in your life," said Neil Simon. "I'm sorry. No doubt there will be more. But what's tragedy got to do with it? My wife died; what do you think, I suddenly turned into Sophocles?"

"Aristophanes, maybe," said Adam softly.

"So who did you lose, if I may ask?"

"A friend," said Adam.

"AIDS?" Neil Simon asked, shaking his head in sympathy.

"No," said Adam, and he remembered that "friend" had become the vague, catchall word that gay people used to describe people they lived with, slept with, exchanged rings with, grew old with. It was difficult to exactly describe who someone was in relation to yourself. If Adam had had a serious lover who had died, he would still say "friend." Sara had been his friend too, but now, given that he was a gay man, the word carried improbable weight. Gay men and straight women made for amazing, complicated couplings. They both felt slightly out of the loop, out of the epicenter of the world. They could form their own small band, they could talk about men, they could hold hands as innocently as Hansel and Gretel. Eventually it would cease to be enough; they would want different things that one could not give the other, and they would have to find other people who could give them those things.

But Sara and Adam hadn't reached that point by the time she was killed. She was his friend; they were not a couple, but he had loved her. They had insulated themselves from the outside, but didn't all friends do that? It was true that his world could use

more light, more politics, a wider aperture. And certainly, if
Adam were to find a man he could love, then his world would
begin to widen. He realized how much he wanted this expansion,
was suddenly impatient for it. He would never have had that with
Shawn, even if they had stayed together. Before Sara's death,
Adam had been in no hurry for change. He and Sara had hung
out endlessly in her small, overheated apartment, and he had
loved it when she laughed at something he had said or written.
Now, staring into the face of Neil Simon, Adam was determined
to find some way to make his new play funny, if he possibly could.

THEY WERE ALL home when Mrs. Hope Moyles unexpectedly
arrived that evening. She pulled her clanking Chevrolet into the
driveway, let herself into the house, and stood in the living room.
She wore a wrinkled housedress and slippers; she had driven the
entire way here from Virginia with big pink slippers on her feet.
Peter walked into the room, saw the landlady, and almost
jumped. "Oh, Mrs. Moyles, you surprised me! What are you
doing here? I mean, it's nice to see you and everything, but don't
we have another week left?"

The others came into the room then too. "What's happening?"
Adam said when he saw her.

Mrs. Moyles took a look at them and said in a sharp voice, "I
heard you trashed the place." But as she looked around she
appeared bewildered. In fact, the house was surprisingly much
cleaner than she had left it. All the dirt in corners and dust bun-
nies under the beds, all the sand in crevices and dampness on surfaces, all the gumminess that had been a part of the Moyles home
for many, many years, was clearly, oddly, gone. The place had
been sponged, mopped, vacuumed into submission. She couldn't
have known that a grieving mother had put all her energy into
cleaning; anyway, she didn't want to know. Mrs. Moyles seemed
confused. She had come here on a mission, had driven for hours to

do this, and she couldn't stop now. "I want all of you out by tonight," she said without much conviction. "This is a decent house I run. I don't want any trouble. I'd appreciate it if you'd all pack up and leave by nightfall."

"What are you *talking* about?" said Maddy. "What have we done?"

"What haven't you done?" spat Mrs. Moyles. "Just tell me that."

"But we have another week," said Adam. "This is insane."

"I don't care," said Mrs. Moyles. "I've heard things about you people. I have my sources. I don't care what you say, I want you out."

Her voice was threatening and effective. They thought of the helicopter prints that had been left on the lawn; was that what had done it? They went upstairs and huddled in Natalie's room to discuss what they should do. "Frankly," said Peter, "I guess I'm ready to leave."

They all looked at one another. "Me too," said Adam in a quiet voice.

And then they looked at Natalie.

"Yes," she said. "It's not the worst idea."

They hadn't exactly realized this until this very moment of expulsion, but suddenly the thought of being away from here a week early, gone from this ugly mustard-colored house once and for all, seemed a good idea. "So this is it," said Adam. "We're out of here?" It was a question, but not really. They took a look around the confines of what used to be Sara's room. The bed was small, the ceiling low. Being in this room, thought Adam, was like visiting the childhood home you haven't lived in for many, many years, and which your parents sold long ago. But still you possess a stubborn trace of nostalgia, and so you force your way into the house. The current owners accommodate you as you lumber up the stairs to see all the places that used to be yours, and which now are irrevocably someone else's. Suddenly, Adam wanted to be away from Sara's room, from the house that this group of friends had lived in together. He understood that as soon as he left the house, he probably wouldn't have his sleepwalking episodes anymore. He wouldn't wake up at night to look for Sara.

The irrational landlady waited downstairs. She wanted them out, and although she didn't know it, they were glad to be expelled. They had no rage or resistance, only a mild relief that after all that had happened this summer, they would finally be going home.

They separated to pack their things. Peter set to work taking apart the Portacrib. The life of his fragile little family was entirely portable and manageable, he thought, as the bed the baby had slept in all month was folded up and zipped into something resembling a golf bag. Across the room, Maddy packed up too, leaving behind *The Upbeat Baby* in a drawer for some future tenant.

In Sara's room, Natalie tossed Sara's belongings into a suitcase. In her haste, the items lost their special meaning; she didn't treat them reverently, but lobbed them into the bag without ceremony. In went the beach hat, the bathing suit, the Japanese notebook, and assorted books and papers. When she was all packed, she convened with Peter, Maddy, and Adam in the upstairs hallway, all of them holding luggage and standing as stunned as tourists getting off a transatlantic flight.

"What exactly is it we're supposed to have done again?" Peter asked.

"I don't know," said Maddy. "Terrible things, I guess. Orgies; freebasing crack cocaine; human sacrifices."

Sara had been the first sacrifice of the summer, the first ever in their relatively short and uneventful lives. They all knew they would not come back to the house anymore. Next summer they would be living elsewhere, and apart. They thought of Sara across a table, Sara explaining how to make perfect sushi, Sara rolling seaweed as carefully as she used to roll a joint in college. If she had lived, would they still be staying in this house next summer, and the summer after that? Would time stop for them, the way people often wished it would? Her clothes and her cassette player and her books were all packed, and her mother was carrying them out of the house for good.

They took turns embracing Natalie, as in a receiving line, and they made plans to speak to her very soon. They would all meet in the city to help clear out Sara's apartment, and Peter would bring his truck. Even Peter hugged Natalie how, and she felt a small, leftover pulse of feeling toward him, and then it was gone. "I will miss all of you kids," Natalie said in a voice that was pointedly parental. "I want to thank you for letting me stay. It's meant a lot to me; I can't tell you how much."

"What will you do now?" Maddy asked. "This fall, I mean. Will you just go back to your job at the travel agency? Will you be all right on your own?"

"Oh, maybe I'll take a trip," said Natalie. "I can get myself a dirt-cheap fare to Japan." They nodded knowingly, imagining her among the rush-hour crowds in Tokyo, this intense, pretty Westerner, searching for what her daughter had once searched for, and had eventually found.

They said a round of intense and endless good-byes. Standing on the front porch in a small circle, Natalie looked at the others. "*Owakare ni narimasu,*" she said, with a decent accent in her pronunciation, and the words meant: *This is the parting.* It was a formal phrase she had learned on the Berlitz tape, used only in farewells of real importance. They hugged lightly, formally, then separated. Peter, Maddy, Adam, and Duncan would be riding home in the truck, and Natalie would be taking her car.

As they drove away from the house for good, they left Mrs. Moyles to glare at them from the front window, indicting them for infractions both imaginary and real. The lawn still bore vague helicopter prints, but everything else was intact. The house was amazingly clean, as clean as it had ever been, although despite

Natalie's efforts, a tiny cluster of mushrooms was shooting up from an ungrouted spot between the bathroom tiles. The outside world always managed to find its blind way in. You kept yourself clean, safe, organized, but eventually there it was, the disorder of the natural world, finding its way inside your home. A young woman could die; people were routinely stolen from earth, as though by UFOs. Ascending in the Normandy helicopter the other day, Natalie had felt as though she was leaving the earth for good, rising up and getting a last glimpse before the details spun away and left her vision, which was perhaps the way you felt at the end of your life. Everything grew smaller, experiences more remote, left in fragments: the taste of a particularly good dinner eaten a long time ago; a favorite novel; the pale blue comforter used on winter nights. There had been men, her husband and others, and she remembered them, the gratification of their weight on her. But they had not registered in exactly the way that other experiences had. Her daughter had left a deeper mark; daughters did.

Sitting beside Natalie and watching *The Wizard of Oz* so many years ago, Sara had buried her head under her mother's arm during the frightening moment when the witch wrote "SURRENDER DOROTHY" in the sky. But now the idea of surrender did not seem so terrible. Natalie thought of a young girl wandering through a strange land among trees that spoke and reached out their knobby arms to touch and warn her. Perhaps it was better to surrender, to collapse into the inevitable. That was what a mother wanted for her children; life was frightening, but if you gave in you could somehow be pushed through it all, and perhaps it would not be so painful. You wanted to think of a wide and easy path for your children. Of course it always led to death; it had to, even when you saw them for the first time in all their wet and slick and misshapen-headedness at birth. You were always saying good-bye, starting then, when an anonymous nurse took the baby away to be cleaned, drops put in her eyes, the white, protective curds of birth sponged from her body. You wanted the baby not to struggle, not to shriek; if she did, it made it so much harder for you to let her go. If she went quietly, let herself be wheeled down the hall as passive as a room-service dinner, then maybe you could rest.

Now Natalie drove and drove, the sparse landscape of the country slowly turning to city. Trees appeared less frequently, their branches starting to thin out and lose their green. There were signs advertising cigarettes and Goya canned pineapple and Jockey shorts; there were buildings being erected, highways under repair. Traffic blossomed. She imagined herself in Japan, wandering lost, searching for the places Sara had studied. Suddenly she was embarrassed at this image. She would not go to Japan this winter; she would go somewhere new, perhaps with her best friend, Carol, or even with Melville Wolf. She would go to Cancún, or maybe St. Bart's. She would go someplace her daughter had never been.